**ISLINGTON** 5/16

Please return this item on or before the last date stamped below or you may be liable to overdue charges. To renew an item call the number below, or access the online catalogue at www.islington.gov.uk/libraries. You will need your library membership number and PIN number.

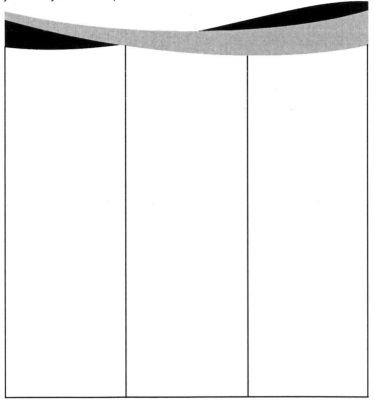

Islington Libraries

020 7527 6900   **www.islington.gov.uk/libraries**

D0784593

Published by Inspired Quill: July 2015

First Edition

Sugar and Snails © 2015 by Anne Goodwin
Contact the author through her website:
http://annegoodwin.weebly.com

Chief Editor: Sara-Jayne Slack
Cover Design: Vince Haig

Find Anne on Twitter via @Annecdotist and use #SugarandSnails to tell us what you think!
Typeset in Adobe Garamond Pro

Paperback ISBN: 978-1-908600-47-9
eBook ISBN: 978-1-908600-48-6
Print Edition

Printed in the United Kingdom
1 2 3 4 5 6 7 8 9 10

Inspired Quill Publishing, UK
Business Reg. No. 7592847
http://www.inspired-quill.com

Praise for *Sugar and Snails*

I loved this book. Sugar and Snails is beautifully written and a truly impressive debut by Anne Goodwin. It reminded me a little of Claire Messud's The Woman Upstairs. The character of Di, at first frustrating, grows more endearing as you begin to understand her. Her friend Venus and lover Simon are well-drawn; there as foils to Di's story. A beautiful and gripping read.

– Fleur Smithwick,
author of *How to make a Friend*

Sugar and Snails is a brave and bold emotional roller-coaster of a read. Anne Goodwin's prose is at once sensitive, invigorating and inspired. I was hooked from the start and in bits by the end. Very much to be recommended.

– Rebecca Root,
actor and voice teacher

An absorbing, clever and heartening debut novel.

– Alison Moore,
author of Booker-shortlisted *The Lighthouse*

A very moving portrayal of how paralysing the shame of one's identity can lead to lifelong isolation and secrecy. A gripping, compelling and moving read.

– Dr. Victoria Holt,
Consultant Psychiatrist

A probing debut novel and, like its protagonist, not what it first seems.

– Gavin Weston,
author of *Harmattan*

Vivid and visceral, Anne Goodwin's debut novel provides an astute and fascinating portrait of a protagonist struggling with unusual demons.

– Victoria Best,
blogger, *Shiny New Books*

Dedication

For the Coast-to-Coasters and old school friends,
September/October 2008

Chapter 1

HALFWAY DOWN THE stairs, I sink to my haunches and hug my dressing gown across my breasts.

Below me in the hallway, Simon reaches up towards the row of coat hooks. His hand hovers above the collar of his black fleece and then falls, combing the sleeve as his arm flops to his side. "This is ridiculous, Di. We should at least talk about it."

Can't he see this has gone beyond talking? "It's late. You've got a long day tomorrow."

"Come to Cairo, then. Whatever's bothering you, I promise, I can help."

"We've been through all that."

"Yeah, and you've served up one feeble excuse after another. Don't you trust me, Di?"

Staunch as sculpted granite, Simon exudes reliability from every pore. Over the past five months, I've imagined him sharing my duvet, my toaster, my council tax bill. On good days, I persuaded myself I could summon up enough maternal sentiment to play mother to his kids. After tonight, I can't envisage a casual catch-up over coffee.

Yet Simon rattles on, as if hope were a virtue: "Come to

Cairo, Di. Come for a long weekend if that's all you can spare."

If I could explain, if I could open my mouth to speak, even, he would come to me. He would spring up the stairs and cradle me in his arms. If I could cry, perhaps, as other women can, and let my weakness make him strong. But tears don't come naturally to me: I haven't cried for thirty years.

———

I'M SANDWICHED BETWEEN my parents in the back seat of a taxi, crawling along the Corniche with the Nile to our left. I'm fifteen years old and this is my first and only foray out of Europe.

We've wound down the windows but there's not even the promise of a breeze. The driver hits the horn with the heel of his hand. Every time he does it my mother flinches and he hits the horn almost as much as he curses other drivers, which is practically all the time.

My father fans his face with a tourist map of Cairo. "It's not too late to change your mind," he tells me. "We won't think any less of you if you do."

My mother breaks off from rummaging through her patent-leather handbag. "Honestly, Leonard, you certainly choose your moments."

I try not to squirm on the tacky plastic seat. I've heard the quiver in my mother's voice often enough, but I've never heard her call my father by his Christian name.

Our driver waves his fist and growls in throaty Arabic as he pulls past a camel cart weighed down with builder's rubble. My eyes prickle, but I save my tears for later; crying is my mother's prerogative after all.

———————

THE FRONT DOOR slams. I rise stiffly and stumble down the remaining stairs. Dragging my fingertips along the dado rail, I reach the kitchen and flick the light switch on the wall. I note the lustre of the sunshine-yellow cupboards and the chill of the tiles on my bare feet, but from a distance, as if I'm researching a stranger's home.

I pull out drawers and rummage through the contents. I select my best knives and rank them by length along the worktop, the way a toddler might arrange her toys: breadknife; chef's knife; carving knife; the whole gamut of blades, right down to the fruit and veg knife with the yellow handle, still smeared with dried threads of pumpkin from our supposed romantic meal. Pushing back my sleeve, I test each one against my forearm. None of them up to the job.

I fumble in the cupboard under the stairs for my torch and beam it around until it highlights an old shoebox stuffed with tools. The Stanley knife is a work of art in its simplicity, with its green plastic casing and satisfying heft in my hand. The blade seems sharp enough but it's freckled with dirt-coloured paint. Taking a crossed-tip screwdriver, I unleash the blade and turn it over. The triangle of pristine steel peeping out from the sheath gives me an artisan's sense of accomplishment.

My ears are abuzz with white noise as I push back the sleeve of my dressing gown to the crook of my arm. Flexing my wrist, the blood vessels reveal themselves below the surface like waterways on a map. The pads of my fingers trace a raised blue-green vein, from the middle of my forearm, through crossings of taut white scar tissue to the base of my thumb where it branches out with arteries and purple capillaries in a sanguineous river delta.

I locate a patch of clear skin amongst the tangle of old scars and apply the blade. At first there's nothing more than a puckering at either side. As with sex, I'm sorely out of practice. I press harder, digging the tip of the knife so deep that by rights it should reach bone. Still nothing. Pressing harder still, a tiny red bauble bubbles at the tip of the blade.

Maintaining an even pressure, I scrape the knife along my arm. The bauble clones itself over and over, beads on a rosary that multiply and merge into a glistening red band. Dropping the knife, I bring my arm to my mouth: the vibrant colour, the taste of hot coins, the pain as sharp as vinegar spearing the fug of nothingness with the promise of peace. When Simon left, I was drowning. Now I'm floating on a sea of calm.

In the kitchen, I bind a folded tea towel round my forearm, gripping one end in my teeth to brace the knot. Secure as a swaddled baby, I mount the stairs to bed.

SOMEWHERE BETWEEN SLEEP and memory, regret sneaks in. The jab-jab-jab of guilt, the rumbling shame. Part dream, part reminiscence, I look down on my ten-year-old self sprawled on the bathroom floor. Blue pyjama bottoms draped across the rim of the bath, blood pooling between my legs onto the chessboard lino. My mother screaming *What have you done? What have you done?*

Now it's my arm that's screaming. My mind wants to

dive into oblivion but my arm is pulsing me awake. Patting the pain beneath the bedclothes leaves my fingers sticky. The digital alarm shows three-seventeen.

Switching on the bedside light, I steel myself to push back the duvet. The tea towel looks like it's been boiled with beetroot; not only the towel, but the sheet, the duvet cover, my torso from my breasts to my pubic hair are smeared with blood. *Oh, Simon, if only I could show you what your leaving means.*

My mind on automatic, I shake a pillow from its case and wrap the cloth around my arm, the fabric blotting steadily from salmon pink to crimson. The night chill slaps my bare skin as I shuffle along the landing to the bathroom, fingers pressed on the gash. I fill the basin and, tossing the makeshift bandage in the bathtub, submerge my arm. The pain makes my eyes sting as the water flushes pink.

Out of the water, the wound dribbles blood the moment I release the pressure. The sides cleave apart like the crevice in a cartoon earthquake, picking out layers of skin like bands of rock in cross-section. It's going to take some expert needlework to heal the rift.

AT FIRST, THE A&E department seems like every other: the same weary people on the same jaded chairs. The same hiccupping lighting and ragged magazines. The tang of antiseptic that triggers the urge to pack away my feelings someplace the medics can't get to, safe from their condescension and contempt. Yet tonight there's an extra element that, until I pause to analyse it, makes no sense.

Compassion. It greets me in the soothing voice of the

triage nurse who takes my details at reception. I shrug it off as due to youth and an unfinished apprenticeship in cynicism, until it pops up a second time in his grey-haired colleague, who lays a gentle hand on my shoulder as she ushers me through the swing doors to a couch in a curtained cubicle, apologising for the wait. It lurks again in the form of the bleary-eyed doctor, a petite woman sporting a turquoise sari beneath her white coat, who won't move an inch without explaining what she's doing. It's as if they're too gullible to register they're dealing with a self-inflicted wound.

The nurse helps the doctor ease her hand into a latex glove. She rests my arm on a pillow and peels back the sodden cloths. Under the glare of the angle-poise lamp it looks like I've been attacked by a madwoman.

"We could arrange for you to talk to someone about this." The stick-on bindi between the doctor's eyebrows brings to mind that first bauble of blood. "Entirely up to you, Diana, but it might help."

I smile noncommittally as she shoots anaesthetic into my arm. The doctor is so well intentioned it would be churlish to argue, but NHS bureaucracy would surely save me from that indignity: all those letters shuttling back and forth to help me scramble onto the bottom rung of a lengthy waiting list. Simon would be back from Cairo before my appointment came through.

"It's a lady called Pammy," says the doctor. "She's very sympathetic and discreet."

"Tammy," says the nurse, handing her colleague what looks like a pair of slim-line pliers. "Tammy Turnbull, the liaison nurse."

The doctor eases black thread through my skin with the pliers, double wrapping it around the tip to form a loop. "Comes on duty at eight, doesn't she?"

The nurse passes her a pair of scissors to finish off the stitch. "Seven-thirty. Even less of a wait."

"You want me to see this liaison nurse here? This morning?"

The nurse strokes my knee. "Try and relax for Doctor if you can, Diana. Won't be much longer."

WHEN I WAS thirteen, my mother took me to Lourdes. "Don't let on what we've come for," she whispered as we boarded the coach.

So many people, so many queues, ever anxious of joining the wrong one. Lining up for breakfast in the hotel. Lining up again at the stalls near the grotto to buy holy water and souvenirs. Joining up with pilgrims and penitents of every nationality to process by candlelight through the night-time streets. Waiting to be dipped head-to-toe in the water, one queue for the able-bodied and another for the cripples.

"What have we come for?" I said.

"A miracle of course," said my mother. "Why else would I bring you?"

WITH MY LEFT arm in a high sling, I prepare to tackle the vending machine one-handed. Feeding it some coins and punching a few buttons, the machine responds with some serious whirring and gurgling. I'm still undecided as to whether I'm passing the time till Tammy Turnbull comes on duty, or I fancy a synthetic coffee before making my escape.

The drink almost scalds my fingers as I extract the styrofoam cup from the machine and take it to a seat in the far corner of the room. I could walk to the university in ten minutes, be at my desk before my colleagues are out of bed. Another five minutes would take me down to the Haymarket, three stops on the Metro to be home with the milk float. Put the bedclothes in the washing machine and mop the blood from the bathroom tiles.

What would I say to a liaison nurse? What possible use could she be?

I picture an earnest woman positioning her chair at a nonthreatening ninety degrees. *What made you do it, Diana? Let's start with that.*

I feel foolish even thinking about it. I take a sip of bitter coffee and leave her to guess. She may be a figment of my imagination but, if she wants to know my secrets, she's going to have to put in some spadework.

Boyfriend trouble, is that it?

I'm amazed I've enough blood in my system to blush, but I do. I'm forty-five years old for chrissake. Even my first-year students wouldn't be so gauche.

Simon is off to Cairo for six months and he wants you to go out and visit. Lucky you!

Doesn't feel so lucky from where I'm sitting.

You don't want to go?

Of course not.

Sun-streaked hair parted down the middle, flower-power clothes: my imaginary liaison nurse bears a striking resemblance to the social worker they foisted upon me after Cairo. Yet Ms Thompson wouldn't need to ask why I can't go back.

You can't tell Simon the real reason but, if you don't, he'll think you don't care. You're caught between two stools, scared of losing him if you don't go …

And losing myself if I do.

The phantom Tammy Turnbull-Thompson looks pensive. Her bangles clatter as she pushes her hair back from her face. *I must admit, it's a tricky one, but if we put both our minds to it, perhaps we can find a way …*

I COME TO with a jolt. My arm is throbbing and there's a coffee-tinged damp patch down the front of my jumper.

A middle-aged woman looms before me. "Diana Dodsworth? I'm sorry to startle you, but I believe you wanted to see me. I'm Tammy Turnbull. The liaison nurse?"

In her sombre skirt suit and tamed hair, she looks nothing like Ms Thompson. Her eyes brim with well-meaning confidence as she offers me her hand. She reminds me of those Home Counties girls at boarding school, raised on gymkhanas and tennis lessons and tea on the terrace at half past four. They were always very jolly and willing to have a go, but real life with all its pain and contradictions would've sent them careering into a tailspin.

How could I be so naive as to imagine anyone could even begin to understand? *If we both put our minds to it!* What an ass to let my guard down and leave myself so open. Like a dance-floor buffed to a silky sheen, hope is riddled with risk for the unwary: let yourself go and, sooner or later, you're bound to come a cropper.

Chapter 2

I FIRST MET Simon five months earlier, 17th April 2004 to be precise, the date clear in my mind because it was Venus's forty-fifth birthday.

It was the Saturday after Easter. She phoned at breakfast to thank me for the card. "You're still on for tonight?"

"Of course. Half past six at Pizza Hut."

"Slight change to the programme," said Venus.

I looked down at my plate, butter congealing on the cooling toast. I'd been an integral part of Venus's birthday celebrations since she turned nineteen, except when she'd been doing post-doctoral research at Harvard, and the time Paul whisked her off for a romantic weekend before Josh was born. I didn't relish the word *change*. "Oh?"

"No need to get so het up, you goose," said Venus. "I just fancied something without the kids hogging the limelight."

The warbling in the background shaped itself into Ellie singing *Happy Birthday*. "Won't they feel left out?"

"Not so long as they get to blow out the candles on my cake. And we can go to Pizza Hut any time."

I plucked a mouldy grape from the withering bunch in

the fruit bowl and set it down on the edge of my plate. "So what's the plan? Is Giles's daughter going to babysit?"

"Nothing so outlandish," said Venus. "A little supper party *chez nous*. A few close friends: Giles and Fiona, Mohammed and Mumtaz, and you."

My gaze drifted from the unwashed pots by the sink to the heap of dirty laundry on the floor below it, to the stack of marking on the table before me. I'd been planning to pick up something cheap and cheerful for Venus from Acorn Road when I went to do my grocery shopping. But if she were having a dinner party with official guests I'd have to battle the hordes on Northumberland Street for a proper present. "Sounds lovely. What time do you want me?"

"Half-seven for eight. Bring your toothbrush and stay overnight if you can bear to leave that bally cat for once."

I glanced towards the back door, half-expecting Marmaduke to come clattering through the cat flap to take a bow. "I'll think about it."

"Make sure you do," said Venus. "I hate you cycling across the Town Moor in the dark." Her voice tailed off into *Just a minute, Munchkin, Mummy's on the phone,* before a final: "Got to love you and leave you already. See you tonight … and Di, make sure you wear something nice."

MY SHOPPING TRIP kicked off well. Too well. Within twenty minutes I'd ferreted out an Italian-leather handbag edged with gold filigree: the perfect partner for the pair of knee-high boots Venus seemed particularly fond of. Only while taking out my credit card did it strike me that my confidence stemmed from the fact she'd been toting the exact same bag around since Christmas. Waiting at the till in Waterstones with a chunky celebrity memoir, I suddenly realised I'd had it in mind because Venus despised its author with such passion. After that, I flitted about, picking things up and putting them down again, dashing back to the shop from which I'd fled only minutes before. *Just choose, you goose! It's hardly quantum physics.* Venus would be content with whatever I gave her, the way she accepted a bunch of dandelions from Ellie or a cheap box of chocolates from Josh, delighted in the giver if not the gift. Yet I couldn't kill the fear I'd disappoint her, or the snip of hope I'd surprise her with the perfect gift.

Couldn't kill my fear of the other guests' disapproval. If I bought the apricot cardigan, would Fiona think I should've gone for the duck-egg blue? If I plumped for the fifty-quid designer vase from Fenwick's, might Mumtaz see a tacky affair picked up in the Grainger Market for under a tenner?

When I found myself in Bainbridge's basement reaching for a pack of chequered tea towels with a trembling hand, I had to concede defeat. Decision-making wasn't my forte; I'd exhausted my capacities in that regard the year I turned fifteen.

Flopping into a vacant seat on the Metro, squeezed in alongside an obese woman with a howling child, I longed to spend the evening curled up on the sofa with Marmaduke, nursing a gin and tonic and watching rubbish on TV. Bolt the front door and not speak to anyone till Monday. I wouldn't, of course. I'd as soon turn down an invitation from Venus as I'd fail to show up for a scheduled lecture or neglect to feed my cat. Venus might be frustrating at times, but our lives had been intertwined since we'd met as fresh-faced undergraduates and I wouldn't be me without her.

THAT EVENING, SNAKING my bike through the wooden gate, I saw Paul standing in the bay window, a fluted glass in his hand. I waved, but he was facing into the lounge, intent on the other guests.

I veered away from the porticoed front door and followed the path round to the back. Parking the cycle against their battered shed, I knocked on the kitchen door and, without waiting for an answer, stepped inside, blinking at the light. I hadn't felt hungry, but the smell of sizzling meat had me salivating like Pavlov's dogs.

Venus crouched at the cooker, a khaki apron and giant oven-mitts clashing in both style and hue with her taffeta dress. Behind her, at the far end of the room, Ellie and Josh sat at the pine table, bedtime-scrubbed and angelic-looking in their Magpie football-strip pyjamas. The little girl noticed me first: "Di, Di, I've got a wobbly tooth."

Venus turned and, shedding her gloves and apron, grabbed me in a mother-bear hug to plant a kiss on my cold cheek. Her dangling earrings brushed my neck and I caught the familiar scent of sandalwood.

Ellie jiggled in her seat. "Look, Di, look!" Pushed from behind with her tongue, her front tooth swung towards the horizontal.

"Well, isn't that something?"

Josh dipped a ginger snap in his milk. "She's trying to force it out herself, when everybody knows the Tooth Fairy won't come unless it drops out natural."

"Is that right?"

Venus clapped her hands. "Hurry-scurry, you two, Di's here, so you can finish off your milk and scoot upstairs to bed."

"Can I have a story?" Ellie asked.

"Only if you promise to go straight to sleep afterwards and let Mummy see to her guests."

"Can I have the one where you rode to school on a camel?"

Josh groaned: "For the zillionth time!"

"We'll see." Venus dipped into the fridge for a bottle of wine.

I shrugged off my Gore-Tex jacket and hung it by its hood on a hook at the back of the door. I took a lavender envelope from the pocket. Before I could hand it to Venus, Ellie had launched herself out of her chair and snatched it from my hand.

"Manners!" snapped Venus, but she smiled indulgently as her daughter ripped open the envelope.

Ellie frowned at the contents. "Another card? But you already sent one."

I followed her gaze to the line of birthday cards on the waxed pine dresser. Mine stood slap in the middle: a pair of dolphins springing from the ocean in one synchronised movement, showering glitter across the surface with their tails.

Venus thrust a glass of fizz into my hand. "Ah, but this is a special kind of card."

Ellie looked unconvinced.

"I thought, you know, with a gift card you could get

whatever you wanted."

"Absolutely." Venus's words were as sparkly as the wine, but I sensed a stiffness about her as she leant forward to kiss me once more. "That's marvellous! Thank you so much!"

Perhaps even the tea towels would've been more welcome. Could I redeem myself by complimenting her earrings? They were unusually pretty, with their double helix of metallic blue. But the more I studied them, the less sure I felt. Were they a special birthday gift from Paul, or something she'd been wearing every day for years?

Ellie abandoned the gift card beside the fruit bowl on the dresser. "Di, Di, which pwincess does my mummy look like?"

Venus wore an electric-blue sleeveless dress with an all-round collar. Pinched at the waist with a knee-length flared skirt, on anyone else it would have seemed old-fashioned. Her thick dark hair, which ordinarily hung in a loose cataract to her shoulders, was pinned up above her face and neck, not in any ordered manner, but in dribs and drabs, as if she were determined to have the best of both worlds. Her high-heeled sparkly mules might've been nicked from Ellie's dressing-up box, but princesses could get away with anything.

Venus put an arm around her daughter. "All right, Munchkins. Why don't we go up and do your teeth and let Di join the party? You don't mind introducing yourself, do you, Di?"

"I'm supposed to introduce myself to Giles and Mohammed?"

Venus merely curved her cinnamon-painted lips into a

smile, and switched her attention to herding the children up
to bed.

WEAR SOMETHING NICE, Venus had said that morning and,
back home, checking my outfit in the wardrobe mirror, with
Marmaduke supervising from the bed, the rosebud-
patterned blouse, with its pin-tucks on the bodice and ruffle
at the wrists, had seemed so dressy – so girly – I'd toned it
down with a pair of stonewashed jeans. Now, as the other
guests welcomed me into the lounge, I realised I'd
underestimated the formality of the occasion. Giles, dressed
as always in chain-store sweatshirt and chinos, didn't worry
me. Nor did Mohammed, albeit more dashing in a black
shirt and trousers with a slim white tie and two-tone shoes.
Yet their wives set a higher standard: Fiona, despite the
northern chill, in a floor-length backless shimmering grey
gown and Mumtaz in white silk evening trousers and glittery
sleeveless top.

I'd barely recovered my composure when Paul led me
towards a man in a suit and crisp pink shirt. "Let me
introduce you to Simon!"

Smiling, the man rose from his seat on the buckskin
sofa. "Pleased to meet you, Di." His handshake made ripples
in my wineglass. "I've heard a lot about you."

"Nothing bad, I hope."

"Nothing you wouldn't want your students to know,"
said Giles.

"Take no notice, Di." Fiona dragged her husband away
into a huddle with Mohammed and Mumtaz.

A clutter of packages and torn wrapping paper lay on

the coffee table and, among them, a matchbox-size carton stuffed with cotton wool. I'd missed my cue with Venus's earrings. I resolved to do better with Simon. "How do you know Venus?"

"I don't, actually, unless you count being in the same conga line at Giles's wedding."

"So you've gate-crashed her birthday party?"

"Not exactly. I came with Giles and Fiona. I think I've been invited to make up the numbers."

"I can't see Venus being hung up on numbers."

"Then she must be the first mathematician who isn't."

I scanned the room for a partner for Simon, but there was no sign of a surrendered wife addicted to bad jokes and ironing. I was still trying to summon up a suitable riposte when the door opened and Venus sashayed across the room. "Mega apologies, Simon, but may I borrow Di a moment? Di, would you do me a humongous favour? Ellie wants you to read her a story."

"Me?" It seemed a long time since the little girl had sat on my lap, correcting my pronunciation of Rapunzel and Rumpelstiltskin.

"Would you mind? It needn't be a long one – five minutes and we could all be sitting down to supper."

"Of course." Somehow I felt more confident about revisiting my inner Cinderella than making small talk with Simon.

I COULD HEAR the tinkly music as I mounted the stairs, Ellie's little-girl voice bouncing above it, colliding intermittently with the tune. Passing her brother's door with the Lord of the Rings poster peeling away at the corners, I stepped into her room. Ellie stood at a pinewood desk, tapping out a rhythm on a purple CD player with a sparkly fairy wand. My voice was hardly better than hers as I joined in the refrain: "*Today's the day the teddy bears have their picnic!*"

Ellie beamed. "Di, did you go to the teddy bears' picnic with my mummy?"

I laughed: "Come on, get yourself into bed and I'll read you your story."

Ellie snapped off the music and jumped into bed. I surveyed her bookshelves while she arranged the teddies and dolls around her. "Which one would you like?"

"I don't need one of those stories." Ellie danced a furry orange rabbit across the duvet. "I don't need a made-up story."

"What do you mean?" I pulled out a book with a ragged spine. The cover showed a boy and girl snuggled up under a weeping willow. "All stories are made up."

Ellie pushed her tongue against her loose tooth. "I need a real story. About when you were a little girl."

"When I was a little girl?"

"When you were a little girl going on adventures with my mummy." Ellie shuffled herself and the ginger-haired rabbit towards the wall to make space for me on the bed. "Once upon a time, there was a little girl called Venus, and another little girl called Diana …"

I hovered by the bookcase. "I'm sorry, Ellie, I didn't meet your mummy until we were eighteen." We might have been geriatrics as far as a seven-year-old was concerned. Ellie bit her lip, as if I'd told her Father Christmas didn't exist. Or the Tooth Fairy. "How about *Babes in the Wood*? Or should we get your mummy to come up and tell you about riding to school on a camel?"

Ellie sniffed: "It's all right, Di. You can tell me about when you were a little girl going on adventures with another friend."

"You expect an old lady like me to remember her childhood? It's practically ancient history."

"You're not as old as Granny, and she's got millions of stories about when she was a little girl."

I skimmed my fingers along the ranks of day-glo coloured hardbacks. I could've insisted it was *Babes in the Wood* or nothing, but I didn't want to let her down.

"Please, Di? Once upon a time there was a little girl called Diana …"

As she spoke, a girl burst into life in my mind, bounding down the street in a green seersucker dress with puffed sleeves and smocking on the bodice, curly red hair flopping against her shoulders as she hopped through the looping skipping rope. A scene from Bessemer Terrace almost forty years before: Geraldine Finch, the girl who ruled my childhood.

Ellie wobbled her tooth with her tongue as she patted the space on the bed beside her.

My thigh nudged her elbow as I took my seat. "Once upon a time, there was a little girl called Geraldine …"

Ellie giggled. "Gelatine?"

"*Gerald*ine. She was my best friend when I was your age."

"Like my mummy's your best friend now?"

"Kind of."

"So …" Ellie wriggled closer. Her hair smelled of lemonade. "Once upon a time there was a little girl called Geraldine, and another little girl called Diana."

I hesitated, but only momentarily. "Geraldine and Diana went everywhere together."

Ellie pushed her warm hand into mine. "Did they go to school together? And the park and Brownies?"

"They spent as much time together as they could." Surely even *I* could fashion enough drama from my scraps of childhood memories to entertain her. "Although their parents tried to keep them apart."

"That's not fair."

I squeezed her hand: "Now, the two friends loved dressing up in their finery." In my mind's eye, Geraldine dragged the dressing-up box out from the cupboard under the stairs. I could almost smell the musty skirts and dresses, but I didn't yet know where to send my two characters to parade in their glad rags.

I glanced at the bookshelves. Geraldine hadn't been much of a reader, but she loved performing. I'd find the stories and together we'd act them out. *Snow White, Babes in the Wood* and, later, Lamb's *Tales from Shakespeare.* Purely for our own entertainment; we had an implicit understanding to ensure our antics wouldn't get back to my dad. "But as I said, their parents didn't like them hanging around together. They threatened to keep them locked up in their bedrooms unless they promised never to meet again."

Giggling, Ellie kicked at the duvet. "That's cruel!"

"Diana couldn't bear to be parted from Geraldine so, one day, she concocted a plan. She'd read in an encyclopaedia about a magic potion ..." I paused, breathless, as if I'd been cycling up a particularly steep hill. I was a child again, with total faith in the power of wanting. Believing in the magic that made dreams come true.

"Magic?"

Or the fairy-tale ending that would carry a little girl to sleep. "A magic potion that could mimic death. And Diana thought, if she drank it, and her parents were convinced she was dead, they'd feel really sorry for how they'd neglected her. They'd wail over her coffin saying, *If only by some miracle our child would be resurrected, we'd give her everything she'd ever wanted. We'd let her eat chocolate for every meal and play with Geraldine from dawn to dusk.*"

"Di, Di, my tooth's really *really* wobbly now ..."

"Shh, Sweetheart, and listen to the story!"

"But Di ..."

"The idea was that, while they were weeping and gnashing their teeth, the drug would wear off and Diana would leap from the coffin to find Geraldine waiting for her in the graveyard. And the two of them would run away to live happily ..."

An insistent digging at my ribs. Looking down at the little girl in the bed, I was startled to see her hair was not red, but black, her skin not freckled cream but deep caramel.

"Look, Di, look!" Inches from my nose, Ellie held out her baby tooth between thumb and forefinger. "I said it would come out tonight."

I FOUND VENUS in the kitchen peeling cling-film from a ceramic bowl. I snatched a pimento-stuffed olive and popped it in my mouth: "The tooth's out and safely under her pillow."

"Marvellous! Remind me to swap it for a pound coin later. Did she settle all right?"

"Fine." But something still bugged me: "You said tonight would be just close friends."

"I couldn't invite Giles and Mohammed without their wives."

"And Simon? He told me he's here to make up the numbers."

Venus arranged some pitta bread in a rattan basket. "Don't you like him?"

"That's hardly the point. I don't appreciate being treated as a spare part."

"Oh, you goose! You think I'm matchmaking?"

"I wouldn't put it past you."

Venus smiled. "I abandoned that as a lost cause yonks ago. The poor chap's wife's just left him. He and Giles have been friends since the year dot. Giles practically begged me to ask him along. Go and talk to him – he won't bite!"

THE MEAL HAD a Lebanese theme: spicy dips for starters, followed by rice-stuffed squashes and a delicately perfumed lamb stew. Simon asked if that was where Venus was from.

"Where isn't she from?" said Paul. "Thirteen countries, wasn't it, before you came here at eighteen?"

"She spent her first three years in Beirut," I said, "which makes her almost Lebanese."

"Although she was born in Cairo," said Paul.

"You can't really count Bhutan as one of the thirteen," I said. "She was at school in Switzerland all the time her parents were stationed there."

"Hark at you two," said Fiona. "I can see you on Mastermind. Specialist subject – the places Venus lived in as a child."

Simon, seated on my right, leaned in closer: "Cairo – I've been dreaming of seeing the pyramids since I was six."

"That's way too long to harbour a dream." Still smarting from Fiona's teasing, my words sounded more judgemental than sympathetic.

"We were hoping to go for our twentieth wedding anniversary next Christmas. Don't suppose I'll ever get there now."

I could almost hear the violins. Men became so gutless once a woman let go of their hands. "There's nothing to stop you going on your own."

"It wouldn't be the same, would it? It's supposed to be romantic."

"Romantic?" Slicing into a slow-cooked zucchini, my irritation seemed to render it as hard as a calabash. I tried to catch Venus's eye but she was closed off in a tête-à-tête with Mohammed. If she'd invited the extra man to keep me company she might have picked someone less wimpish. Yet, on reflection, the smoothly-ironed shirt suggested there might be more to him: either Simon sent his shirts to the laundry – unlikely on a lecturer's salary – or he possessed some life skills independent of his former wife. I decided to give him another chance: "I suppose so, especially at dawn with the sun coming up in the background."

"I don't know about that," said Simon. "According to my guidebook, the site isn't open till eight."

"Isn't it?" For the second time that evening, I was buffeted by childhood memories. A world away from Bessemer Terrace and Geraldine Finch, these were warm and abrasive, blowing a sheen of dust over all the familiar landmarks, fierce enough to knock me off my feet. "It's thirty years since I was there. It's probably changed."

"Thirty years? You must've been only a tot."

I smelled the spices, felt the sun scorch my face. Mesmerised by the cadence of the ancient language, the fascination of a culture so different to my own. "I'd just turned fifteen."

"School trip? Or did you have a peripatetic childhood like Venus?"

I took a slug of Prosecco. "Not at all. Cairo was only my second time abroad. And I was travelling independently; my school didn't do that kind of trip."

Simon put down his knife and fork. "You went to Egypt on your own at fifteen? What were your parents thinking?"

"Of course I didn't go all that way alone. My parents took me to Cairo. Although I did go to Giza on my own for the day."

"On an excursion?"

"No, I caught the local bus."

"I wouldn't want my daughter roaming around a strange city alone."

I didn't need to justify my trip to a man who was only invited to make up the numbers, but I felt the tug of something I needed to justify to myself. "Kids were more independent back then."

"Didn't your parents want to share it with you? The pyramids at Giza – one of the Seven Wonders of the World."

Ms Thompson had said to put it behind me. But this was one memory I'd been determined to keep. A picture-postcard image of the sphinx sheathed in pink light. I couldn't let Simon import storm clouds into the scenario. "My father was tied up at the bank. And my mother, unfortunately, was sick a good deal of the time. But I enjoyed exploring by myself."

Simon nodded. "Needs must, eh? Sounds a bit like my childhood. My folks had a corner shop. Open all hours. Not much time left for me."

"No, it wasn't like that! Not at all!" It had been a magical time, those few weeks in Cairo, basking in my parents' attention. I mustn't give the impression I'd been deprived. "Did your guidebook tell you about the market?"

"The Khan el Khalili?"

"It was like something out of the Arabian nights. Lanterns suspended from the ceiling. Stall after stall sky-high with silk and copper and gold. Perfume, spices, clothes, and cooking pots. Embroidered shoes with curled-up toes and enough reproduction funerary goods to stock the British Museum."

"They say it's got rather touristy. You have to watch their prices."

What a wet blanket! "You have to watch, obviously, same as you would anywhere. But once you figure how to play it, you can have a whale of a time. Especially if there are two of you working together."

"I'm glad you didn't have to go everywhere on your own," said Simon.

"Me and my dad. We had this scam going."

Simon raised his eyebrows.

My cheeks tingled. Was it the memory or the wine? "Perhaps it was a scheme. Or a double act."

"Tell me about it," said Simon. "Whatever it's called."

"You know how you have to bargain for everything?"

"I'd be rubbish at that," said Simon.

"We were perfectly coordinated – like Ryan and Tatum O'Neal in *Paper Moon*. I'd pick out a papyrus painting, say, or a brooch in the shape of a scarab and he'd be: *You can't have that! It's way too expensive!* He'd storm off and I'd follow, droopy shouldered and looking down sulkily at my shoes. Nine times out of ten the stallholder would call us back and offer it to us cheaper."

"Sounds like you enjoyed it."

"Enjoyed doesn't begin to describe it. It was like our minds were in perfect harmony and, so long as we stuck together, we could get away with anything. We got all our souvenirs at knockdown prices."

"Including," quipped Venus, "the galabeyah she was wearing when we first met."

Simon looked quizzical but, before he could enquire further, Giles cut in: "Dads and their teenage daughters, eh?"

I'd forgotten, for a moment, we weren't alone. Now the others' comments seemed intrusive, shockingly inappropriate, as if they were spearing food from my plate. I cast about for the memory I'd chanced upon with Simon: the scent of incense, the rhythmic voices, the rare intimacy with my dad. It was hopeless, like trying to climb back inside a dream. "We made a good team," I mumbled.

"How could you not?" said Fiona. "It's a mutual admiration society at that age."

What did she know? What I had in Cairo was unique; it couldn't be whittled down to the tired old cliché of Freud's Electra syndrome.

As the conversation drifted on to the highs and lows of parenthood, I felt relieved, for once, to have nothing to contribute beyond the occasional academic abstraction better kept to myself. At such moments, the only thing required of the childless was that we should avoid nodding off, keep smiling and, perhaps, pour ourselves another glass of wine.

Yet as I extended my arm, Simon stretched across me and snatched the bottle, gleaming with condensation, from its bucket of ice. My glass frothed as he poured.

"Thanks." I looked down at my plate, streaked with lamb sauce and a few glistening grains of rice. Simon, I assumed, would be intent on the current conversation, waiting for a suitable gap to chime in with some anecdote about his own offspring. Some well-rehearsed vignette to illustrate the amusing quirkiness of children in general, highlighted by the spectacular talents of his own. Yet when I looked up, his gaze was directed not down the table towards the three couples, but at me.

He spoke as if emerging from his own dream: "If I ever

make it to the Khan el Khalili, I hope I'll find a guide who can match your enthusiasm for the place."

WHEN FIONA AND Mumtaz rose to clear the table, Venus took the opportunity to pick up on some unfinished university business with their husbands. She was incensed by a recent decision by the mathematics department admissions panel.

"What's the problem?" said Giles. "The kid got top marks in all his papers at A-level. He'll sail through his degree."

"University isn't only about the academic side," said Mohammed. "Socially, he'll struggle."

I was considering lending a hand with clearing up, while silently fuming at the men for leaving it to the women, when Venus drew me in: "What do you think, Di? Would a fifteen-year-old be too immature for university, even if he *is* a mathematical genius?"

It's an old cliché about psychologists: people either dismiss your scrupulous research as common sense, or demand a pat analysis of a complex issue aeons away from your own area of expertise. That's if they don't confuse you with a gypsy fortune-teller and ask if you can read their minds. Before I could compose my reply, Fiona rushed in, fluffed up with self-importance, to say Ellie was crying. Venus pushed back her chair, but Paul pre-empted her. "You're the birthday girl." He drained his glass and dumped his napkin on the table.

Freed of parental responsibility, Venus launched into a somewhat slurred synopsis of my PhD thesis. "How can an adolescent decide his future? In fact, fifteen-year-olds are appalling decision-makers, the absolute worst. Di proved it already. The evidence is there in her book in black and white." Having helped recruit my research participants, Venus, when it suited her, considered herself as much an authority on the work as I was. "They should give him a couple more years to make up his mind."

"I don't think you can extrapolate from my lab test to the kid's entire university career."

"She's just modest." Venus winked at Simon. "You should read her book."

"I'd like to," said Simon.

I didn't dare look at him. I guessed he was just being polite. "Too bad it's out of print." I stood up. "Come on, Venus. Let's get dessert."

WE WERE SCRAPING the dregs of cream and custard from our bowls when Paul rejoined us. "Where does that child get her ideas from?"

Venus spooned a generous helping of trifle into the last glass bowl and passed it over the table to her husband. "A nightmare?"

"She dreamt she was buried alive and couldn't get out of the coffin."

Fiona rubbed her bare arms as if imagining herself deep underground. "Poor lamb."

Across the wilting tulips, the guttering candles, and the full length of the spattered linen cloth, Venus shot me a look. "What story did you read her, Di? Jack the Ripper?"

"She asked for a story about my childhood."

Fiona sniggered: "What were you, a teenage vampire?"

Giles made a cross with his forefingers. "Anyone got any garlic?"

"I just told her about a game I played with a friend." I thought children liked being scared: wasn't that the Grimm brothers' whole *raison d'être*? Besides, Ellie hadn't seemed scared; she'd egged me on until the very end when her tooth proved more enticing.

"I remember the time I buried my brother in the sand," said Mohammed. "He screamed blue murder till I dug him out."

"Scarred him for life," said Mumtaz. Her eyes were sparkling as much as her high-necked sleeveless top, but I couldn't tell if it was from horror or amusement.

"Being covered in sand isn't half as traumatic as being trapped in a coffin," said Fiona.

"Di didn't say her game involved a coffin," said Mohammed.

"It may not even have been the story that did it," said Paul. "Anything could've set her off."

"Anyway, she's okay now, that's the main thing," said Venus, finally breaking into a smile.

I tried to return it, but Venus still wouldn't meet my gaze. Somehow it didn't feel as if the fault lay in something I'd *done*, but the whole essence of my being. I seemed about to be reprieved, when Fiona pitched in once more: "We still haven't been told what your game was."

"You know," said Simon, "I take it as a matter of principle to tell my kids the grizzliest tales about my childhood. I consider it one of the main parental responsibilities."

A hush descended on the table. Giles removed his rimless glasses and polished them on his napkin. Mohammed rubbed a hand across his shaven skull. Mumtaz dabbed at some breadcrumbs on the tablecloth. Fiona settled the straps of her gown around her shoulders and glanced from Venus to Paul and back again.

"Kids these days," said Paul, "they've got it all on a plate. Does no harm for them to know we never had half the luxuries they take for granted."

"And most of the world still hasn't," said Venus.

"Central heating ..."

"Computers in their bedrooms ..."

"Camera phones ..."

"Ey bay gum," said Giles, "when I were a lad   "

Finally, I found my voice again: "I'll say one thing, Giles, that Yorkshire accent would give anyone nightmares."

PAUL SERVED COFFEE and brandies and, for those with a tiny pocket of unfilled space in their stomachs, mini baklavas oozing syrup. At some point, we repositioned ourselves in the lounge. Venus gave Fiona her recipe for the spiced lamb and Mohammed discussed cricket with Paul. I sat quietly nursing my empty cup, cheeks aching with the effort of looking as if I were enjoying myself, wondering how soon I could take my leave.

Underneath, my mind reeled. Poor little Ellie, dreaming herself sealed up in a coffin with only a furry orange rabbit and a liberated tooth for company. The guilt burned in my throat, but I still couldn't understand how my story had engendered such a reaction. It wasn't logical for something that had given two children hours of pleasure to traumatise another little girl a generation later. As with an experiment that yields unexpected results, I juggled the variables in my head, trying to isolate the source of the trouble. Perhaps I'd told it badly, introducing a macabre slant I hadn't intended; perhaps, at seven, Ellie was too young to understand. Perhaps, like tug-of-war and hopscotch, those games from the Sixties would be unfathomable to any twenty-first-century child. Or perhaps it had more to do with me and Geraldine, the kind of kids we were, importing our peculiar pathologies into our play. The excitement of ransacking the dressing-up box, the jumble-sale smell of old clothes. Watching our reflections in the wardrobe mirror as we morphed into the star-crossed lovers: a purple bolero and a feathered hat for Romeo, a balding velvet dress and necklace of rosary beads for Juliet. With only the Lamb to go by, we had to improvise the words, but what we lost in poetry we made up for in passion.

Romeo oh Romeo, let us marry and live together happily ever after!

Oh my sweet Juliet, how can this be when our parents forbid it?

But I would rather die than live without my Romeo!

And I could not bear to live without my Juliet!

Listen, my love, I have a plan. You must try to be brave. There is a chemist who has promised me a secret potion to make it look like I am dead. He has warned me the medicine tastes revolting, a thousand times nastier than worm medicine, but I will drink it happily because it is the key to a lifetime by your side.

It was only a game after all, yet where I saw curiosity and creativity, and friendship against the odds, would others find signs of disturbance? I couldn't ask, couldn't possibly raise the topic again, not even with Venus in private, lest the answer be a resounding yes. Besides, a psychologist should know better than anyone what was normal. The only person I could possibly have discussed it with was Geraldine herself, but we'd hacked off all connection when Ms Thompson whisked me away to boarding school at fifteen. The whole episode was enough to give *me* a nightmare, and I had nobody to reassure me it was only a dream.

WHEN AN UNATTACHED man offers a single woman a lift home from a party, there is often a subtext. Yet I was oblivious, thinking only of reaching the solace of my own bed a little sooner, while avoiding an argument with Venus about my cycling home in the dark. She seemed particularly keen on the arrangement: "Marvellous! Saves you getting het up about leaving that bally cat alone overnight."

"How is that crazy *billah*?" said Mohammed. "Or is it a *billih*, I always forget?"

It was a worn-out joke, but spanking new to Fiona. "Billy, billa," she chanted. "What's all that about?"

Giles giggled. With his podgy face and floppy corn-coloured fringe, it made him look about ten-years old.

"I got her from the cat and dog shelter," I said, wearily. "I'd christened her Marmaduke before I realised she wasn't a tom."

Fiona laid a hand on my sleeve: "Di, darling, didn't

anyone ever explain to you the difference between boys and girls?"

I hid my clenched teeth with a smile.

THE INSIDE OF Simon's car smelled of synthetic pine, emanating from the cut-out cardboard tree dangling from the rear-view mirror. As it was an estate, we'd had no problem getting the bike in the back, but he had to shift heaps of CD cases and crisp packets, and even the odd child's sock, to make room for me in the passenger seat.

Three miles of small talk before I could collapse into bed. I hoped he wouldn't ask anything else about Cairo. I'd only mentioned my trip to the pyramids to show I wasn't the kind of woman who needs a man to make up the numbers. I hadn't intended to get so carried away.

Simon edged the car onto the roundabout. "I've been wondering about putting in for a sabbatical next semester."

I couldn't tell if he was thinking aloud or waiting for me to guide him through some pop-psychology problem-solving pro forma. "A sabbatical?" I sounded like a parody of a nondirective counsellor.

"I haven't taken one for years and I'd love to get away after all the drama of the divorce. On the other hand, the kids need stability. They need me nearby even if we're not living together."

It always came down to the children. I hadn't given them a thought when we'd bonded over the Khan el Khalili, or when he'd swept aside my responsibility for Ellie's nightmare. It was as if we'd tuned in to the same obscure radio frequency and, if we stayed on that wavelength, we'd inch closer, leaving no room for anyone else in between. But Simon's children were interferences on the airwaves, drowning our connection with an ear-splitting hiss. I didn't miss having flesh and blood children to care for. I loved Josh and Ellie despite the fact part of me still reeled from how, in her mid-thirties, Venus had suddenly discovered a sentimental streak. Yet, as I got older, I was painfully conscious of how my childlessness set me apart from my peers. As if a child were an extra limb that had become the norm, making those with a mere two arms and two legs the freaks. Still, I knew the ropes. "How old are they?" I asked, with feigned interest.

"Harriet's nine and Oscar's twelve."

At nine, all I'd wanted was to hang about with Geraldine. By twelve, I'd had one botched attempt at self-surgery and my mother was praying for a miracle at Lourdes. If *my* dad had gone abroad for a few months, it wouldn't have made much difference. "It's not for ever," I said.

Simon pulled up at the lights on Grandstand Road. "But maybe long enough to get my book finished. I've been working on it since before Harriet was born."

I watched the light dip from red to green. "Sounds like reason enough to take a break. I don't know about your department, but they keep piling on the teaching commitments in psychology. It's a wonder we have time for any of our own research."

He eased the car forward. "I don't imagine you're the type to be browbeaten by management. I bet you've dipped into the travel budget over the years. Where's best to go?"

It wouldn't do to admit I hadn't been abroad since

Cairo, that I felt intimidated by our new departmental head. I was enjoying Simon's picture of me with all my insecurities airbrushed out. I laughed. "You make it sound like a holiday. You must know better than I do where's right for your own research."

"Touché. Maybe I simply don't know whether it's a holiday or a sabbatical I need."

CARS LINED THE street down both sides. When I pointed out my red front door I expected Simon to stop in the middle of the road and let me hop out. Instead he reversed into a space a few doors along and switched off the engine. Was I supposed to invite him in and, if I did, would he assume there was more on offer than coffee? Did he even want more-than-coffee? Did he think *I* did? Or was there no deeper meaning to his parking the car than a wish to avoid blocking the road while we got my bike out of the back?

We hovered on the pavement, the bike between us, the front wheel nudging the doorstep. I wished I could read his mind, but I was so exhausted I couldn't even read my own. "It was lovely to meet you," I said, feebly. "And thanks ever so much for the lift."

A streak of marmalade fur shot out from under next-door's car and wove between our legs. Simon bent down to tickle the cat under her chin. "So this is Madame Marmaduke?"

"The very same." We watched, in silence, as she spurned Simon in favour of scraping her claws down the door. "She'll ruin the paintwork."

"Better let her in then," said Simon.

With a juggling of keys and wheels and feet, it was a matter of seconds before Marmaduke and I were on one side of the door, along with the bike, and Simon was on the other. My relief was as instantaneous as the flick of the light switch.

Outside, the engine rumbled, brayed and then groaned away into the distance. A stab of anxiety had me patting my pockets to check I hadn't left my purse in his car. But it wasn't my cash and cards I was missing. Simon had driven off without even attempting to kiss me.

Chapter 3

M Y EARLIEST MEMORY: my mother clattering dishes in the kitchen while I'm upstairs clambering onto a stool to reach the wooden hangers in my sister's wardrobe. It must have been a weekday: my dad's at work and Patricia's at school and Trevor hasn't yet been born, although my mother's fat with him already. I'm about three and too young to notice.

I tilt the clothes hanger and Patricia's tutu drops to the floor. I jump down from the stool and pick it up, hold it against my body by the shoelace-slim straps. My heart thunders against my ribcage. It's a magical garment, vest and skirt and knickers all of a piece, but more: the pelt of a swan disguised as a little girl's dress.

I step out of my shorts and push through the leg holes with my socked feet. I hitch up the top and thread my arms under the shoulder straps. I wriggle till it moulds itself to my frame, the satin bodice chill against my chest.

I point my toes, the netted fabric scraping my thighs like a cat's tongue. There's a draught up my back; I twist and turn but I can't reach the zip, and I'm not sure my fingers could manage it anyway. Downstairs, I can hear my mother singing along with the wireless, but I daren't go and ask for help. She'll give me a walloping if she finds me like this.

A rhythm ripples through my bones without reference to my mother's crooning. I hop and jump and jiggle my limbs to its beat. If I raise my arms above my head, the bodice stays in place despite the gaping zip. So I prance, I pirouette and twirl with my hands in the air. I flow like a fish, like a bird, like Hail-Mary-full-of-grace. Head, hands, heart guided by the music written in my veins.

WAKING ON THE morning after Venus's party, stretching my arms above my head and pointing my toes into the corners of the bed as the bells of St George's tumbled in the distance, I felt as free as that twirling toddler in the oversized tutu. Revelling in the full four-foot-six of bed width, and the whole house beyond it. Alone, but not lonely. An entire day ahead of me to spend exactly as I wished. Answerable to no one but myself.

Spring sunshine filled the window, lending the curtains a ruddy glow. Turning my head, however, I became conscious of a pulsing at my temples; the result, no doubt, of a glass or six too many of sparkling wine. Before I knew it, the light was too bright, the bells too loud, the memories thick with shame.

I drew up my knees, folded in on myself, fingering the network of old scars on my arm. I was back at Venus's dinner table, analysing everything I'd said and done through the prism of Fiona's critical gaze. I didn't know why I'd told Ellie a story that did neither of us any favours. Why I'd showed off to Simon about what was, at bottom, nothing more than a glorified shopping trip. And why, if I had no intention of inviting him in, I'd let him drive me home.

I shoved aside the duvet and grabbed my dressing gown from the hook on the door. No point wasting my Sunday agonising. A hot shower and a couple of aspirin would have me back on form. Breakfast, a cafetiere of strong coffee, and a stroll through Jesmond Dene. I'd put it behind me, exactly as Ms Thompson had advised me all those years before. Pack it away and my feelings with it; lock it up and throw away the key. The whole damn lot of it: Cairo; Fiona; Simon Jenkins. But I couldn't shrug off the memory of Geraldine Finch.

———————

AS THE FINCHES lived only a few doors from us on Bessemer Terrace, I must have known Geraldine before I started school. But I have no recollection of her out in the street with the other kids. Back in the Sixties, with little traffic to threaten us, and enough older ones to keep an eye on the tots, we'd make the street our playground from the moment we munched our cornflakes till it was time to brush our teeth for bed. As soon as we could walk unaided, we were absorbed into the local gang, running and jumping, hopping and skipping, laughing and screaming between the chip shop at the top of the street and the dairy at the bottom. Our mothers would put us out the door in the mornings like they might put out the cat, depositing us on the doorstep and directing us towards the rabble with, if need be, a tap on the behind. The tarmac would become a racecourse, cricket pitch, or battlefield; coats became hurdles, goalposts, tanks; the pavement a chalky art gallery, hopscotch grid or both. We swarmed from one end of the street to the other, flowing like water from one game to the next. Apart from the leaders, giants of ten and eleven who were almost grown-ups as far as the little ones were concerned, we had no need to distinguish one child from another when we moved with the herd. Dark or fair, fat or thin, boy or girl greyed out in a blissful merger of body and soul

It was only at school, assigned a specific seat and expected to stick with it hour after hour, day after day, that the differences between us began to matter. Later, kids would be bullied on account of a pair of national health glasses, an odd haircut, or a name that rhymed with willy; shame we brought from home and could do little about. But school imposed its own distinctions, a sham personalisation designed, it seemed, to cut off other options and keep us in place.

This is your classroom, said a beaming Miss Bamford, but when I thought I might like to sample the classroom down the corridor where my sister's paintings adorned the walls, I was hauled back and made to stand in the corner. *This is your chair*, but when I wanted to sit on a seat that was bathed in light from the high window, I was slapped on both hands with a ruler. *This is your coat peg with a lovely picture of a panda above it*, and lovely it was, but so were the sailing boat, the gingerbread man, the scarecrow and the thirty other images arranged around the cloakroom, each one out of bounds.

I could hardly contain my disappointment. So many

times I'd stood with my mother, my hands clutching the bars of the rusting gate, gazing across the yard at the slate-grey schoolhouse, longing for the day I could take my place inside. Twin stone staircases led to a heavy wooden door, the numbers 1873 embossed above it, as grand as the entrance to a castle. At school I'd learn to read, and never have to go without a story. I'd glide up those steps like a fairy-tale princess, entering one day by the left side, the next by the right.

All my hopes that school would widen my horizons caved in on me. I didn't understand that the letters above the stairs spelt out BOYS on one side and GIRLS on the other. That my mother would laugh, then plead, then slap me hard on the legs and carry me up like a sack of coal when I tried to go up the wrong one.

"Look at Geraldine," said Miss Bamford. "See how good she is, getting on with her work."

Through my tears, I studied the little girl on the seat beside me. Hunched over the hinged double-desk, she copied strings of noughts and crosses from the blackboard with a fat wax crayon. I recognized her carroty hair and freckled nose from the day before, although we hadn't spoken. I was in awe of how at ease she seemed, as if she'd been at school forever.

She saw me eyeing her furry white cardigan. "It's rabbit wool," she whispered, as Miss Bamford turned her back on the class to chalk some more shapes on the board. "If it gets up a baby's nose they could suffocate."

I thought of my baby brother. If he were to die, would I still have to go to school?

Geraldine held out her arm. "You can stroke it if you like."

I had to stay at school, or I'd never learn to read. Perhaps Geraldine, who seemed to understand the rules, could help me.

"Go on," she said. "It's lovely and soft. Like a kitten."

I wiped my eyes with the back of my hand and reached out towards her. As I did, she jerked her hand away under the desk and nipped me on my thigh. I yelped.

Spinning round, Miss Bamford glared. "I will not tolerate this behaviour in the classroom. Go and stand in the corner!"

Geraldine watched me go, angelic in her angora cardigan, a beatific smile on her face.

THE SUN THAT had been too bright that morning was sulking behind the clouds by the time I got to Jesmond Dene, but I was glad to be out in the open. The trees were putting out new leaves and daffodils, albeit tinged with brown at the edges, nodded their heads on banks of lush grass. I walked briskly, thinking I might follow the Ouseburn through to Heaton Park and back again, the exercise sending endorphins pumping through my brain.

As I approached the ruined mill by the waterfall, the park seemed busier. Among the couples arm in arm, the dog walkers and young families with three-wheeled strollers, I was conscious of being a woman alone. Determined not to be intimidated, I held my head high and met the gaze of those coming towards me with a smile.

A young couple hovered by the waterfall, the man toying with his camera. They seemed to be waiting for a family to move off the bridge so they could take their romantic photograph uncontaminated by strangers. I looked up, sharing their irritation with the family who seemed oblivious to their needs. The father had his back to us as he held on to his daughter, a girl not much older than Ellie leaning over the low parapet towards the water.

Recognition rippled through me. I couldn't be sure from that angle, but it looked very much like Simon, and the girl was the age for – what was her name – Harriet. Where else would a divorcee take his children on a Sunday afternoon? A stroll through the Dene finished off with tea and cake in the café opposite the petting zoo.

Along with the young couple, I stood awkwardly, waiting for some movement on the bridge. If it *were* Simon, I wondered how I should approach him, or whether I should approach him at all.

I hadn't considered his son initially, but now I spotted a boy, face riddled with acne, engaged in some fancy thumb-work on his phone. But this lad had a good three years on Oscar: a friend of the family, a cousin, perhaps.

A woman leant towards the teenager, her words muffled by the gushing water. I stepped back towards the shelter of a rhododendron bush. The woman was blonde, around my age or a bit younger and decidedly more glamorous. The ex-wife, perhaps? My head began to pound.

I was about to shuffle off when the father hoisted the girl up from the wall and into his arms. They spun round, mouths gaping with laughter, and another shiver passed through me.

I'd been right to think I knew him, but what had possessed me to mistake Garth Bradshaw, my head of department, for the man who'd driven me home the night before? Beyond their solid build, they hardly resembled each other. While Garth was almost a decade younger, Simon was by far the better looking.

I marched on, keeping my head down and avoiding eye contact with the mass of people coming my way. The river, heavy with recent rain, smelled of blocked drains. A child on a scooter all but barged into my legs and, when the mother smiled an apology, I kept my face a blank, barely holding back a snarl. When I heard the screech of the peacock from the petting zoo, I longed to scream in chorus.

What was wrong with me, so obsessed with Simon I'd hallucinated him onto the improbable figure of Garth Bradshaw? I'd drawn a line under such fantasising when I'd closed my front door on him the night before. I didn't need a man in my life; I was perfectly content on my own.

TRAMPING HOME THROUGH the residential streets, with no pressure now to feign enjoyment, I thought of my dad. When my mother was doling out the pennies for Patricia and Trevor and me to put into the offertory collection, he would be preparing for his own Sunday ritual, wrapping corned-beef sandwiches in a waxed bread-bag and filling his flask with tea. Kneeling beside my mother in the cold church, palms pressed together in prayer, I would picture him shouldering his haversack, sucking on his pipe as he waited at the end of the street for the bus. I'd imagine him climbing aboard, handing the conductor his fare, but after that the image blurred. I knew he went hiking, but I could no more connect with what that might mean than I could unscramble the Latin words of the litany.

He'd promised that one day he'd take me with him. When I was big enough to keep pace with his strides. Each week I'd pray for him to remember his promise, but not to fulfil it quite yet. I wanted to be ready when he called me, to be sure I wouldn't let him down.

My father wasn't like other dads. Lots of dads didn't go to church, but they went to the pub instead and came rolling down the terrace at half past two, red-faced and smiling, with a bottle of fizzy pop in each hand. Geraldine's dad managed to fit in both mass *and* the pub on a Sunday morning if he wasn't doing overtime, and would lurch from one lamppost to the next singing *The Rose of Tralee*.

My dad was different. If I'd asked my mother, she might have said it was because we were more respectable than the Finches. While we lived in the same kind of house with three small bedrooms upstairs, we had plenty of space for the five of us, but Geraldine and her siblings were three to a room. My dad, although he worked at the pit like everyone else, had an airy office above ground and the only way he got his hands dirty was from counting out the half-crowns and worn ten-shilling notes that he stuffed into small brown envelopes on pay day.

I never asked my sister why my dad was different, but she told me, in that matter-of-fact way she had about her. *Daddy doesn't like children*, she said and, for a while, it seemed a good enough explanation for why he kept his distance. It didn't bother Patricia and it didn't matter to me until I approached my teens and, by then, I'd forgotten she'd ever said it.

Chapter 4

FOR THE NEXT few days, I was on edge. Whenever I heard the jingle of my mobile, or the landline at home, I expected Simon to be on the other end, apologising for begging my number from Giles. At work, when the icon flashed in the corner of my computer screen to announce a new arrival in my inbox, I was convinced he'd looked me up on the university intranet. Walking through campus to buy a sandwich for lunch, I scanned the passing faces for his smile.

Even as I searched for Simon, I hated the effect it had on me; as if some weird cult had colonised my mind. I hadn't been looking for a partner, so why should I care that Simon made no contact? I replayed Venus's supper party in my head, the way I'd comb through a research paper before despatching it to a journal for review. Simon must have liked me. Why else would he have refilled my glass and been so keen to drive me home?

Yet the evidence was unequivocal; the chemistry I'd sensed simply due to his aftershave and the sparkling wine. Once I'd shrugged off my disappointment, it was a relief to feel normal again and to focus my energies on my work, where they belonged. There were amendments to sort out on a paper for the *Journal of Adolescence*, a stream of students knocking on my door to check out some aspect of theory before the exams, and a PhD student failing to meet her deadlines. And my first ever appraisal with the new department head.

That afternoon when I tapped on the door, it swung open as if Garth had been hovering behind it since a minute to three. His moon-like face shone like an over-eager undergraduate's as he ushered me to a seat. Such a contrast to the laid-back attitude of Max Neasden, our previous head. Garth had replaced Max's old wingbacks with some futuristic contraptions of leather and aluminium, with elegant undulating backs that challenged anyone with a normal skeleton to sit straight. As he booted his laptop, I wondered if the intimidating chairs were deliberate. Our baby-faced professor hadn't leap-frogged his way up the academic hierarchy on rosy-cheeked enthusiasm alone.

I maintained a fixed grin as Garth scrutinised my student-satisfaction averages on the screen. The edges of my paper copies were crinkled with sweat. Professor Neasden would've spent the whole meeting celebrating the pending publication of *Belonging and Unbelonging Among Adolescent Street Groups*, yet Professor Bradshaw, high priest of targets, league tables and budget spreadsheets, cared only about squeezing me for more. He'd already got me to agree to sign up for the new staff development workshops on *Equality and Diversity* and *Pastoral Care*, when he returned to my CV. "I can't see any overseas conferences here. Is there anything to prevent you going abroad? Some caring responsibilities perhaps?"

"I have a very pampered cat."

Garth raised one eyebrow. "Your cat certainly helps keep the travel budget under control. But seriously, you're holding yourself back if you restrict yourself to Britain. I'm surprised Professor Neasden didn't pick you up on it."

My cheeks ached, but the thought of Max Neasden picking me up on anything almost evoked a genuine smile.

"Let's set it as an objective! Put the cat in a cattery and give a paper at the APA next year."

He tapped away on his laptop, but I wasn't defeated. Submitting an abstract was easy; not even Garth could make the conference committee accept it.

After a few more prompts to work harder, he brought down the lid of his computer. "I've really found that useful, Di. I know the staff are cynical about these reviews but, for me, they're great for getting to know people."

"It takes ages to settle into a new job." Not that I knew anything about that, but it seemed the right thing to say.

"And your PhD. Adolescent decision-making. You weren't tempted to persevere with that line of research?"

I'd relaxed my cheek-muscles prematurely. "I did get a book published." Now out of print.

Garth wiggled up his seat. "Fascinating area – what got you into it?"

I pictured my twenty-one-year-old self, in a scoop-necked peasant blouse and flowery cotton maxi-skirt, knocking on the door of an office one floor up. A third-year module in abnormal psychology had thrown up some fascinating questions about the psychotic mind. When I should've been cramming for my finals, I delved instead into obscure papers on loosening of associations, knights-move thinking and selective attention. I was excited by the prospect of bringing the irrational under experimental control.

I'd gone first to the clinicals, but they'd passed me on to the developmentals. "Colin – Dr Carmichael, my supervisor – thought there were parallels between the cognitive processes in schizophrenia and adolescence."

Garth ran his hand across his buzz cut. "He thought adolescents were psychotic?"

"Not quite. But they made similar processing errors."

His gaze darted to a photo amid the timetables and flyers for public lectures on the pin-board beside his desk. I remembered the little girl leaning over the stone parapet towards the waterfall and the pimply boy absorbed in his phone. "No wonder they're so chaotic. Pity they can't take advice from those with more life experience."

"It's all down to information overload. They get overwhelmed. Should I? Shouldn't I?" I moved my cupped hands up and down like a balance-scale. "It's not that they're not bright enough, not rational enough. They can't bear the feelings that come with the uncertainty. Their own ambivalence terrifies them. They've got so many other changes going on they can't tolerate not knowing their own minds."

"So it's one day they're vegetarian, the next they're on the Atkins diet?" Garth no longer judged me from on high, but as a fellow psychological enthusiast.

"Colin and I developed a laboratory task to test it out.

We showed our subjects two opaque jars: each containing a hundred balls. One jar held ninety black balls and ten white. The second was the other way round. We took balls at random from one of the jars and presented them one at a time. Subjects had to guess whether the jar contained predominantly black balls or mostly white. There was no limit to how many balls they could ask to see before making their choice. You'd need to see a minimum of eleven balls before you could be sure, but some subjects would hazard a guess after only a couple."

"Adolescents jumped in too early? Before they had a fair chance of getting it right?"

"We tested them at different ages. Fifteen-year-olds were the least patient. And guessed incorrectly more often than their ten-year-old siblings."

Garth's gaze flicked to the family photo on the pin-board. "Amazing!" He shook his head. "So why didn't you stick with it? Results that striking don't come along every day."

"Well, I did the book." It had good reviews, too, not that they were worth much now.

"You could've had enough for a dozen books."

Was he playing with me, the way Marmaduke would tease a mouse, tossing it back and forth between her paws, or did he really not know? Garth would've started his degree shortly after the Colin Carmichael scandal erupted. He must have heard of the psychologist accused of fiddling his results. "I put in a few grant applications but they didn't get anywhere. Colin had taken early retirement so I was on my own. Back then, my work didn't link up with anything else.

We didn't know what we know now about adolescent brains."

"You were ahead of your time."

I scanned Garth's boyish face for the hint of a smirk, but he was serious. If he genuinely didn't know, perhaps it would be prudent to leave it that way. I worked my shoulders up the chair-back like a child trying to grow. Colin Carmichael had led me towards a seam of research which resonated with something deep inside me. Yet before I could properly explore it, he'd closed it down. No one had accused *me* of faking my research – Colin's alleged transgression had occurred before I'd teamed up with him – but I'd been tainted. When my results looked almost too good to be true and all my publications bore the name of a discredited psychologist, I wasn't going to win any awards for promising newcomer. If Professor Neasden hadn't kept me on, my career would've been over before it had begun.

"Why not present it at the APA?" said Garth. "There'd be tons of interest now."

I stuffed my papers into a manila wallet file. "It's too long ago. I'm into other stuff these days." Max had thought it best for me to start afresh and distance myself – and the department – from anything involving Colin Carmichael.

"But nothing inspires you as much as this did."

I shuffled to the edge of the leather seat, my file clasped to my chest. Not much longer and I'd be out of his office and I could forget about this baloney until next year's appraisal.

Garth raked his crew cut with his fingers. "Actually, I've got an idea. There's one of the second years still not fixed up with a project for next year. Bright girl, extremely enthusiastic and hard working, but she's been through a rough patch this past semester. Missed a lot of lectures and got some catching up to do. Megan Richardson, do you know her?"

"The girl with the red duffel coat who never says anything in seminars?"

Garth flinched as if I'd criticised one of his own kids. Good thing I hadn't mentioned her peculiar asymmetrical fringe. "I suppose she is a little shy," he conceded, "but she's great on a one-to-one. Really insightful. She's one of my personal tutees."

Max Neasden had never had personal tutees. He considered it divisive.

"I'd been hoping to set her up with something special to help her get back on her feet," said Garth. "Your decision-making research would be ideal. And it might just fire you up to take an interest in it again."

I rose to my feet. The only thing firing me up right then was exiting the office without lumbering myself with any more impossible tasks. "Send her along and we'll have a chat about it."

"I'll do that," said Garth. "She's planning to be around for most of the summer so there's plenty of time to work up a really meaty proposal."

My hand rested on the doorknob before it struck me: "She's had a rough time, you say. Anything I should know about?"

"Confidentiality, Dr Dodsworth. I'm sure Megan will tell you whatever she thinks you need to know."

BACK BETWEEN THE breeze-block walls of my office on the second floor, I flung the manila folder on the desk. I'd wanted the stimulation of work to distract me from my childish fantasies about Simon, but not in this way. Two full days twiddling my thumbs as part of the university corporate training initiative might be just about tolerable. Pretending to submit a paper for a conference in America would be no worse than a lot of other mindless admin. But mentoring the talented but fragile protégée of my boss while revisiting my own adolescent ambitions could be a personal and professional challenge too far.

I edged past the shabby so-called easy chairs to the low bookcase. Easing my bike out of the way, I snatched two grey hardbacks, *Adolescent Ambivalence by Dodsworth and Carmichael* dancing down the spines. I remembered my pride at first holding them in my hands, convinced they signalled the start of a brilliant career. Yet, twenty years on, I was stuck in the same department, still a junior lecturer, while testosterone-fuelled young men clambered past me to grab the position of Chair. Garth must have thought me a terrible cliché, sacrificing my career for my cat.

Looked at dispassionately, I hadn't *chosen* Colin Carmichael. Like a princess in some happy-ever-after fairy tale, I'd accepted the first supervisor who had offered me his hand. I'd been as impulsive as the fifteen-year-olds in my research, jumping to a decision without weighing up the evidence. I'd been painfully naive in my early twenties; still convinced of my rosy future. The biggest decision of my life already taken, all I had to do was frolic along the yellow brick road.

I slid the slim volumes back onto the shelf, unopened. My knees creaked as I rose to my feet. I didn't need to look inside my book to remind myself of its conclusion. I'd carried out my research meticulously – no inventing subjects or shifting decimal points for me – but now I wondered if I'd always had an inkling of what the results would show. Perhaps, even as an overly optimistic twenty-one-year-old, I'd been sceptical about the way I'd made my choice at fifteen.

———————

A FEW WEEKS after my return from Cairo, the headmaster summoned me to his office. When I realised my parents were present, my greatest concern was that they'd see I'd hitched up my skirt a good few inches since leaving the house at ten past eight. But I knew they wouldn't bring in a social worker for that. Ms Thompson was there to ask me if I'd like to go away to boarding school.

I looked from Ms Thompson to my mother. Clearly, they each wanted something, and they wanted different things. I looked to my father, to the headmaster; I looked down to my spanking new platform shoes.

It never occurred to me to ask for more time, to have Ms Thompson show me a few more balls so I'd know for sure which jar contained the promise of a happy and successful life. I chose. I chose freely. But I was fifteen, and the fifteen-year-old brain isn't equipped to make a life-transforming decision.

Boarding school was to be the gateway to a glittering future. The academic rigour to get me into a good university. A bunch of ready-made friends, with midnight feasts in the dorm. A retreat in which to nurture my femininity. A chance to draw a line under my first fifteen years.

Ms Thompson hadn't mentioned that, once I left, I couldn't go back. Of course, I could turn up with my suitcase and knock on the front door, but a public-school girl couldn't slot back in to the working class community I'd come from. I gave up my family when I chose Dorothea Beale.

DRAGGING MYSELF BACK to the present, I riffled through a heap of papers on my desk to find the essays on adolescent identity formation I'd taken home the weekend of Venus's party. I'd marked them the following Monday and given back all but two at the tutorial the next day.

Sure enough, one of the remaining essays bore the name Megan Richardson. Squinting against the fancy font, I turned over the title page to skim through the introduction.

Adolescence is a period of tremendous turbulence. The human organism undergoes a profound physiological revolution mirrored by an enormous psychological transformation, which may leave them literally not knowing who they are from one moment to the next. Daunted by the challenges of adulthood, especially the search for sexual intimacy and a fulfilling occupation, yet cast adrift from their childhood certainties, they experience a discontinuity between how others see them and how they want to be. This state of role confusion can be sufficiently explosive to induce psychosis. Psychologists should not be surprised therefore that adolescents can be grumpy and withdrawn.

I couldn't resist a smile at that sudden switch from academic language to the vernacular. Megan's essay wasn't bad, not bad at all. Flicking through to the end, I saw I'd assigned her a high 2:1. Prior to my meeting with Garth, the passion of the language had impressed me, yet now I questioned her capacity for scientific objectivity. For Megan's sake, as well as my own, I was wary of taking responsibility for a student who understood adolescent turbulence a little too well.

Chapter 5

O NE WEEK LATER, while I waited at the interlibrary loans desk, someone tapped me on the shoulder. The librarian couldn't find the books I'd ordered, and when I turned towards the source of the interruption, my face would have betrayed my irritation.

Yet Simon had enthusiasm enough for two: "I thought it was you! How are you?"

"Not bad." The assistant had finally located my books misfiled on the bottom shelf. "How's yourself?"

"Okay. Yeah, not bad in the circumstances."

"That's good." We hovered like a couple of teenagers, his initial exuberance apparently expired, while the librarian stamped my books. Simon's hair was a little shorter than when I last saw him, adding a beguiling touch of innocence to his manly good looks. A primrose-coloured button-down collar peeped out from under a black fleece jacket. I had to hold myself back from unzipping it to see how well the rest of the shirt was ironed.

Simon tilted his head towards the stack of hardbacks cradled in his arms, his library card sandwiched between two fingers. "Better get these through the scanner."

I imagined the credits rolling, two figures receding into the distance, one heading into the sunrise, the other to sunset. Then I clocked the titles of his books: *Coptic Art and Archaeology. A Practical Guide to the Islamic Monuments of Cairo. The Cult of the Immortal: Mummies and the Ancient Way of Death.* "Dr Jenkins, do I detect an Egyptian theme to your reading?"

Simon went pink. I felt the blood rush to my cheeks in sympathy. "Don't laugh," he said, "but I thought I might wangle a way of doing my sabbatical in Cairo. Kill two birds with one stone. Like you said, it's time to stop dreaming and get out there."

Did I say that? I'd never considered myself as Ms Motivator. "What's your angle? Won't you need to focus down a bit?"

Simon jiggled his books in his arms. "I know it's rather broad at the moment, but I thought, if I read around the area, something would come to me."

He'd have to be a lot more rigorous if he had Garth Bradshaw scrutinising his application. "Well, good luck with it."

"Look, why don't I pick your brains over lunch? You can help me think it through."

Two weeks before I'd have thought my dreams were coming true. Now I felt slightly nauseous at the thought of Cairo. "I doubt I'd be much use, to be honest."

"Sure," said Simon, "if you're busy ..."

Gosh, he's easily deflected. Up to me, then; decision time, which jar do I choose? I made a show of checking my watch. "I'm expecting a student at two-fifteen."

"That's bags of time," said Simon. "I know this lovely old-fashioned Italian behind St Mary's Place. They do a decent cheapo business lunch. And they're quick."

"Why not?" After all, Mediterranean food was supposed to be healthy.

SMALL AND STEAMY, the restaurant was decked out with red gingham tablecloths and dusty wine bottles in baskets as candleholders that made us both giggle. "As if the millennium had never happened," said Simon. The service was brisk and cheery and the portions generous. Even on iced water, I felt a little tipsy.

"So what can you tell me about Tutankhamen?" asked Simon.

I swallowed a forkful of lasagne, inwardly smarting that the only man who had shown any interest in me in the last twenty years was most intrigued by the part of my life I wasn't at liberty to discuss. "You can see his sarcophagus and his funerary goods in the Egyptian Museum near Tahrir Square ..." I mustn't let the memories derail me as they had at Venus's party, nor would I do myself any favours to give Simon a lecture, and a rather poor one at that. Then I remembered Geraldine. "When I was a kid we used to play at being Egyptian mummies. We'd wrap a few bandages around our arms and legs and lie down in an old tin bath we found in the allotments ..." Fiona's voice whispered in my head: *What were you, Di, a teenage vampire?* Yet Simon was grinning. "We'd fill the empty space with toy soldiers and dolls to act as servants and scraps of food filched from our mothers' pantries ..."

"All the stuff you'd need for the afterlife." Simon didn't look as if my stories would give him nightmares.

"Dolls' tables and chairs, too, and anything we didn't have in three dimensions, we'd draw a picture of and shove that in instead."

"What did you do when you'd got all the stuff in there?"

"You know, I can't remember. Maybe we just lay amongst it all with our arms crossed until we got bored or our mothers called us in for tea."

"Sounds like an interesting childhood."

I thought of the Chinese proverb: *May you live in interesting times!* I bit my lip. "You don't think it was morbid?"

"It was just a game, surely? Like little boys running around pointing guns at each other going *Bang bang! You're dead!*"

I glanced at the water jug, slices of lemon floating on top amongst the eroded chunks of ice, as light as my head felt. Whatever it was that Simon had done to me, I knew I wanted more.

———

MY CHILDHOOD GAMES with Geraldine were no doubt rooted in our Catholic culture. We were fed and clothed with its morbid symbolism: the body and blood of Christ, the fetish of the crucifix, the story of Christ's death and resurrection re-enacted every Sunday at mass. My mother had an image of the Sacred Heart hung above the mantelpiece in the front parlour: a bearded Jesus, one hand pointing up to heaven, the other peeling back the cloth from his chest to reveal his pumping heart. It had fascinated and appalled me, this mystical marriage of glory and self-immolation. So we were already on the way to romanticising death the day our play was interrupted for a funeral cortege processing down the street.

I was still quite young, more identified with the amorphous mass of kids streaming the street than with school. I remember the shock when, half the terrace still in shadow and our hands and faces not yet layered with grime, our mothers called us back inside. One by one they stood in their floral pinnies on their front doorsteps and called our names until all the children were indoors, having our faces rubbed with a wet flannel for the second time that day.

When we were put out again, it was not to merge with the crowd, but to line up in family groups on the pavement alongside our parlour windows. While we'd been indoors the sky had clouded over and a chill quiet settled over the street. I may have imagined it, but even the pit was silent, as if it were the end of the world. I started to ask my mother but she slapped me on the legs and told me to shut up until the procession had passed by.

We had processions at church, but they were just people; now I could hear the clip-clop of horses' hooves. Soon our mothers' threats weren't needed to keep us in order, we all stared open-mouthed as a grim-faced man walked slowly down the line of cat's eyes. He wore a long black coat more suited to winter, and held a top hat fast against his chest. Behind him came two white horses with plaited manes pulling a shiny black coach edged with gold like something from a fairy tale. My mother hissed at us to lower our eyes as the carriage went past, but I caught a glimpse of the flowers massed against the glass. I vowed that when I grew up I'd be the one sit up top, urging on the horses with a gentle flick of the whip.

People followed behind it, parading in twos and threes, like in our church processions, except that their clothes were dark and sombre and nobody was singing. When they'd all gone by and we could finally use our voices again, I asked my sister: "Was that the Queen?"

She punched me so hard on the shoulder the ache kept me company all day. "Don't you know anything? It was a little boy who died."

I gazed down the street towards the dairy, hoping to catch a glimpse of the coffin, but it was too late. Instead, bunched up among her red-haired sisters was Geraldine, my desk-mate at school. I squirmed to find myself caught in the arc of her gaze, until I realised she was smiling, as if we shared a secret no one else could reach.

Chapter 6

THROUGH THE FROSTED glass of the fire door, I saw a petite figure, clad in red, slouching against the breeze-block wall outside my office. As the heavy door thudded behind me, I chased all thoughts of death cults and lunch dates from my mind. "It's Megan, isn't it? Sorry to keep you waiting." I offered her my hand.

The girl unplugged herself from her earphones, leaving them to dangle around her shoulders. "No probs, Dr Dodsworth."

Her hand in mine was as light as a child's. I wondered if the rough patch Garth had referred to might be an eating disorder. I let go and swung my backpack around to fumble in the front pocket for my keys.

"Sorry I couldn't make the tutorial the other week," said Megan, shuffling behind me into the office. Below her red duffel coat she wore black leggings with flat suede ankle boots that made her waddle like a penguin.

I dumped my backpack on the desk and picked up her essay. "You missed out on a lively discussion." I handed her the papers and lowered myself onto the less frayed of the supposed easy chairs and gestured to Megan take the other.

"It would've been helpful if you'd let us know you weren't able to attend."

Checking the mark I'd scrawled on the final page of her assignment, Megan looked relieved. "I know, sorry, I really wanted to come but it was, like, straight after a really heavy session with my counsellor, and I was, like, totally numb for the rest of the day."

I felt awkward, unsure if this were an invitation to enquire further about Megan's rough patch. It must have been serious if she were seeing a counsellor. "Right, well, have a look at my comments and get back to me with anything you don't understand. Okay?"

"Thanks, Dr Dodsworth." Megan folded the paper and slipped it into the canvas shopping bag by the side of her chair.

I steepled my hands. "So, about your final year project ..." I noticed she hadn't removed her coat. Was it shyness or was she feeling the cold? With the radiator on, I was almost sweating, although that could have been the excitement of lunch at Luigi's. Anorexics, I noted, struggled to keep warm.

The girl delved into her bag and placed a library copy of *Adolescent Ambivalence* on the coffee table. "That two-jars method was well cool."

The book, protected by a sheath of clear plastic, was otherwise identical to the twin hardbacks on my shelves. It felt strange having someone else bring a piece of me into the room, as if she'd unearthed a forgotten photograph from my youth. "Well, thank you, Megan," I mumbled. "And you'd be interested in doing something similar? Replicating one of the early experiments, perhaps?"

Megan shuffled her pixie boots. "I thought I might extend it, kind of. Test out whether people might be more likely to jump to conclusions when they had another difficult decision to make."

"Oh?" Garth was right, the girl *did* have initiative, although that peculiar sloping fringe made it hard to take her seriously. "What kind of other difficult decision did you have in mind?"

"Choosing a university?"

"That might work." The outcomes hardly mattered at undergraduate level, it was more a matter of learning about the process. "A within-subjects design, comparing the same students' test performance before and after they've made their choice?"

"I was thinking a correlational study. Seeing if those with the most complex choice performed worse."

"And how did you think you would measure complexity?"

Megan bit her lip. "That's the problem. I don't know."

"Well, that's no reason to give up at this stage. It's an excellent idea, Megan, and if it's something you're particularly interested in, it won't feel such a hard grind."

"You mean I can go for it, Dr Dodsworth?"

"Let's take things a step at a time, Megan. Go off and do a literature search and come back and see me when you've come up with something more concrete."

———

GERALDINE'S WHITE ANGORA cardigan was a cut above

what most of us wore for school. It was a cut above any of her other clothes, which were mostly hand-me-downs from her sisters. It was the kind of thing a little girl might wear for church on Easter Sunday or, draped across her shoulders, over a frilly dress for a party.

On Tuesday mornings, Miss Bamford marched us in a crocodile down to the school hall. Static hissed around the room as she tuned in to Music and Movement on the Bakelite radio. We didn't need P.E. kit: we stripped off blouses and skirts, shirts and shorts, socks and shoes, and pranced about in our vests and knickers.

Along with learning to read and my fascination with Geraldine, the gym class made school bearable. Holding Geraldine's hand on the way there. Skipping barefoot across the polished floor or waving my arms in the air like a tree. A whole half-hour free from inhibitions, I was almost as buoyant as that day I'd dared to dress up in my sister's ballet tutu at home.

I savoured every minute of it, and Geraldine and I were among the last to return to the benches at the side of the hall where we stowed our clothes. But this particular day, when the music came to an end, I was at one side of the room and Geraldine the other. Two steps away, on top of a tangled heap, was her furry white cardigan. I couldn't resist.

Miss Bamford would surely be pleased I'd got dressed so quickly and, if I were going to wear Geraldine's cardigan, why not her skirt and blouse as well? If it weren't for the fact that my hair was a pale brown instead of that fiery red, I could be her.

Geraldine found me, fumbling with the buckle that

secured her tartan kilt. I braced myself for a slap or a nip, but she giggled as she scooped up my clothes. I imagined going home to her house at half past three, scrabbling with her five sisters for a place at the table for our cream crackers and milk. I imagined playing with her dolls and her dad swinging me into the air when he came home from the pub with bottles of pop.

Our classmates broke off from fretting with buttons, laces and zips to watch us. I crossed my arms loosely, caressing myself from my shoulders to the ribbed cuffs of the rabbit-fur sleeves. The tartan kilt flared out as I did a twirl. One little girl began to applaud, until she saw the expression on Miss Bamford's face.

Miss Bamford screamed our names. When she drew breath, it was like the space between the thunder and the lightning. "Put your own clothes back on this instant! You're impossible, the pair of you!"

We kept our eyes on the polished floor as we rearranged ourselves in the clothes our mothers had put out for us that morning. But Geraldine had recognised a need in me and, perhaps, a need in herself to feed it. Although only I was made to stand in the corner on our return to the classroom, our childhoods were entwined from then on.

FLAKES OF GREEN paint came off in my hand as I pushed my bike through Venus's garden gate the Sunday after my meeting with Megan. I followed the sound of high-pitched laughter down the side of the house to the back garden. The kids were in their black and white football strips, kicking a ball across the worn grass. Leaning the bike against the pebble-dashed wall, the ball bounced against my leg. Ellie giggled. I saw Venus wave from the kitchen window and mouthed okay as I right-footed the ball back to Josh. Instead of passing it on to his sister, he bounced the ball in the air with his foot. Once. Twice. Three times.

"Keepy-uppy. When did you learn to do that?"

On the fourth go, he kicked too hard and the ball rolled away into the flowerbed. "Ages ago." Josh retrieved the football from among the wounded tulips and let it drop onto the top of his foot. "Guess how many I did yesterday!"

I watched as he flexed his foot and tossed the ball up again. Four times before he lost his balance and the ball was back in the border. "Ooh, I don't know. Six?"

"Six? Even Ellie could do six. Even *you* could do six."

"How many then?"

"You have to guess," said Ellie.

I adopted a posture of perplexed concentration. "Twelve?"

"Twelve?" Josh had given up foot-juggling the better to concentrate on teasing me. "Loads more than that."

"Let me think. Sixty-nine?"

Ellie ran around in a circle, whooping with laughter. "Even my daddy can't do sixty-nine keepy-uppies."

"So how many?"

Josh smiled. "Nineteen."

I widened my eyes. Shook my head. Looked incredulous. "You're having me on!"

Josh rocked on the balls of his feet. "No kidding."

"Well, I'm impressed."

"How many can you do, Di?" said Ellie.

"I don't know."

"My mummy can't do any," she said.

"How many can you do, Ellie?"

Josh bounced the ball with his hand. "She can't do any either. Only me and dad. Keepy-uppy's for boys."

"I'm sure she'll be able to manage when she's bigger."

"Mum's really big and she can't do them," said Josh.

"It's too hard for ladies," said Ellie, "and girls."

What little confidence I'd had in relating to children had drained away with Ellie's nightmare, but, knowing how overheated Venus could get at the marketing of different toys for boys and girls, I couldn't let this one go. "Your mummy can't be good at everything," I mumbled. "I'm sure there are lots of other ladies who are really good at keepy-uppy."

"I don't know any," said Josh.

"I don't know any, neither," Ellie chimed in.

"There isn't a lady in the whole world who can do nineteen keepy-uppies," said Josh.

Ellie squeezed her hand into mine. "It doesn't matter, does it, if girls can't do things?"

As we turned towards the house, I felt something thump against my calves. I spun round. Josh grinned.

I let go of Ellie's hand and nuzzled my foot under the ball. I flexed my toes and flicked the ball into the air. It landed solidly in the angle between my foot and ankle. I jerked and the ball rose higher before dropping onto the top of my foot. I flexed my muscles again, sent the ball into the air before rolling off towards the headless daffodil stems.

Ellie clapped her hands. "Two times. That's more than mummy."

Josh retrieved the ball. "But still not very good."

I snatched the ball from his hands. "That was just the warm-up."

I dropped the football onto my left foot and bounced it into the air. Once. Twice. Three times. Finding my rhythm. Seven. Eight. Nine. Total concentration. Total coordination of eye and mind and limbs. Thirteen. Fourteen. Tossing the ball across to my right foot. Back to my left. No longer bothering to count. A little extra effort had me bouncing it up on my thighs.

"Wow!"

The ball hitting the turf brought me back to the real world. Sweat trickled down my back as I grabbed the ball and tossed it to Josh.

"Not bad for a lady," he said.

Venus and Paul stood on the patio, arms round each other's waists. "Not bad?" said Venus. "She was absolutely fantabulous."

Ellie tugged on my arm. "Will you teach me?"

"Of course she will," said Venus. "But not just now. Lunch is ready."

WE ATE IN the dining room. The arrangement wasn't as formal as the last time I'd sat there, and I was too buoyed up with football acrobatics to fret about unbalancing the sexes. We clustered around one end, Paul serving at the head, and Ellie cosying up next to me. The little girl called across the table to her mother: "Mummy, where is it we're going on holidays?"

"Minorca," said Venus. "And don't ask me how many sleeps, Munchkin. It's too many for me to count already!"

Ellie put her hand to her mouth, shielding her lips, if not her voice, from me. "Mummy, can Di come with us to Minorca?"

"Why don't you ask her, Munchkin? I'd love her to join us."

I spiked a carrot with my fork. Beside me, Ellie did likewise. "Di, Di, will you come to Minorca on holidays with us?"

My face wasn't up to smiling at Ellie while glowering at her mother. "That's very kind, Ellie, but I don't tend to go abroad."

"Is Minorca abroad?"

"Of course it is, Dimwit," said Josh. "Why do you think they talk in Spanish?"

"Oh yes," said Ellie. "You have to say *bwonnas notches* and *silver plate*."

"*Silver plate*'s French, Numbskull," said Josh.

I speared a sprout, unusually grateful for the squabbling.

Ellie speared one of hers. She caught me watching and smiled, proud, as if the celebrity had acknowledged the convener of her fan club. "Di, why don't you go abroad? Is it cause you don't like talking in French and Spanish?"

I laughed. "Maybe."

"In fact," said Venus, "Di's scared of flying."

Ellie looked set to tender her resignation from my fan club. "Scared of flying! Why?"

Paul shook his head. "Stop pestering the poor woman!"

Ellie dropped her knife to place her hot hand on mine. "I'd look after you, Di, if you came with us. I'd sit next to you and hold your hand."

"Thanks, Ellie, that's really sweet of you, but not this year."

Ellie smiled. She had a double gap between her front teeth now. "Next year? When I'm eight?"

"Hey, Josh," said Paul, "what did you think of Di with that football? Do you reckon she's up to Wayne Rooney's standards?"

Ellie cut in before her brother could answer. "Did you do football at school, Di? Did you do football when you was my age?"

I hacked a piece of chicken away from the bone. "I suppose so."

"You didn't do football at school, did you, Mummy?" said Josh.

"Di was lucky," said Paul. "At my school the girls were kept indoors, sewing pincushions when the boys were out in the yard playing football."

Ellie turned to me, her whole body fizzing with mischief. *Tell me a story about when you were a little girl!* "Did you do keepy-uppy with Gelatine?"

"Geraldine, you mean."

Ellie giggled. "Mummy, I thought Di's friend was called Gelatine."

"Gelatine is what jelly's made out of," scoffed Josh.

"I know," said Ellie.

"Who's this Geraldine?" said Venus.

"Just a friend I had when I was a kid."

"Her best friend," said Ellie. "They wanted to live together always."

Venus still looked put out. "I'm surprised you haven't mentioned her before."

"She was in the story," said Ellie.

"I see – she's a little girl in a story." Venus shot a glance at her husband.

Beyond the patio doors, the black and white football sat in a pool of sunshine in the centre of the muddy lawn. I couldn't remember whether I'd ever played football with Geraldine. But the day her twin cousins taught me keepy-uppy was clear in my mind.

———————

ONCE WE PROGRESSED to secondary school, Geraldine found herself a new set of friends. Confused at first, I'd seek them out at break time, but they turned their backs and pretended not to hear when I spoke. After a while, I accepted it, and grew accustomed to going around on my own.

I was far too big by then to lose myself in the mass of kids streaming by hops, skips, and jumps from one end of Bessemer Terrace to the other. On Saturdays I read myself dizzy in the library and on Sundays, after mass, I did the same upstairs in my room. Nobody bothered me in general: my father watching *Grandstand*, or off hiking; my sister at her Saturday job or cavorting with her friends. My brother would be lording it over the gang of feral kids; my mother content within the confines of housework, shopping and her magazines. But that Saturday she wanted something more.

It was late October, one of those mild autumn days that fool you into thinking winter is still far away. My mother had been acting strange for days: cheerful and energised, but prickly with it, like a balloon stretched so tight it's sure to pop. That Saturday she was up early, force-feeding Patricia eggs and bacon before she scuttled off to work. Saturday was usually porridge, but she produced a cooked breakfast for the rest of us too, whether we wanted it or not. "Beautiful day," she said, "why don't the four of us go off somewhere nice for a picnic?"

I dipped a corner of crisp fried bread into the yoke of my egg. Families in books went somewhere nice for picnics, not us.

"I'm meeting my friends," said Trevor.

"I'm going to relax with the paper," said Dad. "Then I might watch the wrestling on the box."

"I was going to the library," I said.

"You don't want to be cooped up indoors on a day like this," said Mum.

"I work my socks off all week," said Dad. "Surely you don't begrudge me a quiet morning with the paper."

A whole catalogue of excuses were assembling in my head. But my mother looked crumpled. "Let's you and me go to the park," I said. "Have a go on the pitch and putt."

I HADN'T BEEN to the park since the summer holidays, when Geraldine and I had a craze for crazy golf. But two months on, I didn't want to be seen bashing a ball through a fairy-tale castle. It was embarrassing enough to be there with my mother without playing a game meant for kids.

Mum tried to take my hand as we wandered past the bandstand and the infant play-area. I rendered my rebuff less brutal by delving into my pocket for my money. "My treat."

I left her on a bench with her face tilted towards the watery sun and joined the queue at the pavilion. At the counter, an old chap in a battered straw hat counted out his deposit in ha'pennies. Behind him, a couple of youths with thick ginger hair hanging loose to their shoulders were mimicking his every move. I recognised them immediately: Geraldine's cousins, Paddy and Pete, were prefects at my new school. They were as tall as men and as princely as pop stars, each with a fuzz of reddish hair above their upper lips. I longed for them to acknowledge me as much as I dreaded bearing the brunt of their derision.

Yet when the twins took their clubs and putters and turned away from the window, they looked straight past me and marched off to the green. Being ignored was better than being laughed at for coming out to play with my mother. I leant into the window: "One and a half, please, for pitch and putt."

I shoved the ball into my pocket, along with the score-sheet and the stubby pencil, and shouldered the clubs. Back where my mother had been soaking up the sun, she was bent double. My stomach knotted until I saw that she'd succumbed to nothing more than a fit of the giggles. "Them hippies," she said when she was finally able to speak. "Till they turned around and I clocked their moustaches, I was convinced they were girls."

I WOULD'VE PREFERRED to hold back, but Mum was keen

to follow the twins onto the green. I'd got quite skilled at crazy golf over the summer, but pitch and putt took me right back to being a novice. My mother was no better and seemed to find it one huge joke.

I grew convinced all the other players were laughing as, once again, we marched off to retrieve the ball from the long grass fringing the green. I was mortified when the twins asked if we'd like a bit of help. My only consolation was that they didn't seem to recognize me.

Mum went quite peculiar when the boys joined us, shrinking into herself like Geraldine playing Juliet. While I immediately understood Pete's instructions to stand at right angles to where I wanted the ball to go, my mother needed him to position himself directly behind her, up close with his hands on hers, and practically swing the putter back and forth for her, before she cottoned on. Yet somewhere between the eighth and ninth hole, embarrassment gave way to pleasure. The twins laughed, not at us, but with us and, when I got a hole in three and then a hole in two, they led me in a zany jig, yodelling and hooting around the green. After returning the clubs to the pavilion, Paddy asked if we fancied a game of footie.

Mum fluttered her eyelashes. "I'm sure you don't want an old woman tagging along."

The twins peered theatricality over their shoulders. "Can't see any old woman here."

Running across to the football pitch, Paddy and Pete dribbling the ball between them, my mother lagged behind. When I looked back, she was bent over as if she had a stitch.

I glanced across at the twins, the ball careering back and

forth between their feet and their heads. I knew where I'd rather be, but I wasn't used to putting my own needs before hers. "You don't look so good."

She waved me off. "Just a bit wheezy. I'll be right as a cart once I've had a sit down."

As I ran back, Paddy kicked the ball my way. "Bravo!" he cried, as I stopped it smartly with my foot and passed it back.

We stood in a tight triangle, moving the ball between us. Pete caught it in the angle between his foot and his shin. He flicked his foot and bounced the ball into the air and down to his foot. Again and again, up and down, without the ball ever once touching the ground.

When he finally dropped the ball, Paddy took over, catching it on his foot, his thigh, his chest. It was beautiful.

When my turn came I was tense and overeager. I caught the ball once in my ankle and lost it again. But the boys coached me, advising me how to angle my body, when to ease the tension and when to crank it up. Soon I was managing five in a row. The twins seemed as proud of my performance as I was. Then, as suddenly as it had started, my audience drifted away.

I let the ball roll onto the grass as first Pete, then Paddy, raced across the field to the bench where I'd left my mother. She was slumped forward, a man in a porkpie hat holding her hand. My throat dry as cardboard, I jogged after the twins. The man called out to the boys: "Run to the phone box and call an ambulance! This lady's having a heart attack."

VENUS STACKED UP the plates. I collected the serving bowls and followed her into the kitchen, where I tipped the leftover sprouts and carrots in with the roast potatoes and stretched clingfilm over the bowl. Neither of us spoke, the only sound the clatter of cutlery and crockery, and the humming of the fridge.

Venus slipped the last plate into the dishwasher. "I've been such an ass."

I gripped the edge of the worktop. Was this about my declining the holiday invitation or was she gearing up to reopen the inquest into Ellie's nightmare?

"I'm sorry, Di." Venus closed the dishwasher with a thud. "Of course you'd be furious when I tried to set you up with Simon. In fact, the signs were there from the day we met."

I almost preferred her being cross with me. At least I knew where I stood. "I haven't the foggiest what you're on about."

Venus turned on the tap above the sink with her elbow. "Of course I'm a tad disappointed you didn't come out and tell me already."

Sweaty palms and a sinking feeling in my stomach: symptoms of the fight-flight response reporting for duty. I counted five paces to the outside door. I could grab my bike and be home in under an hour.

"Come on, Di, it's nothing to be ashamed of." Venus plunged her hands under the gushing tap. "It's obvious you're gay."

The idea was so preposterous, I had to laugh. "What?"

"Homosexual. Lesbian. What do you want me to call it?"

Ever since I was tiny, I'd hated to be categorised. Long before being introduced to labelling theory, I'd understood the tyranny of if you're *this* you can't be *that*: "What on earth gave you that idea?"

Venus rubbed her hands on a chequered tea towel and flung it into the washing machine. "One, the passionate friendship with – what was her name? – Geraldine, never mentioned, even in passing. Two, the football. Three, the fact that you haven't been out with a man in nigh on twenty years …"

"Mu-um." We both jumped as Josh poked his head round the kitchen door. "We're waiting for dessert."

Icy mist wafted from the freezer as Venus reached inside for a tub of ice cream. "Take that. We'll be along in a minute." As soon as the boy moved out of sight, she edged closer to me. "In fact it's quite common for folk to repress their true sexuality. Of course, you're brought up to think there's only *one* way. If you don't fit the norm, it takes a humongous amount of courage to admit it. You could waste your entire life contorting yourself into a mould that's not for you. But, Di, isn't it time to admit that it's making you unhappy? I'm here for you, you must know that." She turned away, embarrassed perhaps by her rambling homily, and unloaded a stack of gaudy painted ceramic bowls from the pine dresser. "Of course, you'd feel awkward going into gay bars on your own, so I could come with you. In fact it'd be a pleasure, like being a student again."

"There's really no need. I'm seeing someone."

Venus wrapped her arms around me. I caught the smell of sandalwood as her shelf of a bosom cut into mine. When she stepped back, still holding on to my elbows with her manicured fingertips, her eyes were glistening. "That's marvellous! Who is she, Di? If you need me to be discreet, I won't even tell Paul."

"I told you, Venus, I'm not gay."

"You're seeing a man?" She looked perplexed, as if one of her equations refused to balance.

"It's no great mystery," I said. "I had lunch with Simon."

Venus gasped before treating me to a repeat of the *That's marvellous!* and massive bear-hug routine. "So when are you seeing him again?"

"I'm not sure. We didn't exactly arrange anything."

"You let him go without fixing up another date already?"

Two minutes earlier she was convinced I was gay. "He never asked." I wasn't sure our bargain business-lunch even qualified as a date.

"Of course the distinguished Dr Dodsworth hasn't a tongue in her own head!"

It was all very well for her. A married woman didn't have to worry about making a fool of herself if she invited a man in for coffee. "It's not easy, you know. Not at my age."

"You're such a goose! The world's swarming with people looking for love on the other side of forty. Nobody finds it easy. Not even Simon, especially if you don't offer him any encouragement."

"You think *I* should've asked *him*?"

"Let's not fret about what you should've done. But you can certainly ring him up and arrange something now."

"I don't have his number."

"Even you could manage to find him on the university intranet. Or would you prefer me to get his number from Giles?"

Chapter 7

B ETWEEN THE AGES of five and ten Geraldine and I were inseparable, despite my parents' disapproval and, to a lesser extent, hers. Of course we kissed. Romeo pecked Juliet on the lips and cheeks, accompanied by a slurping soundtrack. We mimicked what we'd seen in films or television, or embarrassing teenagers smooching by the bandstand in the park. It wasn't much to go on. Our parents never kissed us, or each other, as far as I could tell.

Later, as we grew away from role-play games of death and redemption, the mere thought would've sickened us. At senior school, Geraldine would rarely even condescend to look at me. But she was fickle; now and then she'd want something and, like a faithful puppy, I'd deliver it.

We were about thirteen when *Love Story* came to our local picture house. When Geraldine invited me to go with her, I didn't question why. We bought our popcorn and settled ourselves among the courting couples on the back row. The plot was borrowed from our old favourite, *Romeo and Juliet*: two young people forging a future together against the odds. The death angle, via the heroine's terminal illness, was so mawkish and manipulative even a rock would shed a tear. Yet I missed most of it, my view of the screen blocked by Geraldine's face mouth-to-mouth with mine.

Her technique had become more sophisticated since our dressing-up days. She pushed her tongue past my lips, past my teeth into the cave of my mouth. She pushed her hand between my shirt and the waistband of my jeans. I remember neither love nor lust but a desperation to please.

Were we so different to those boarding-school girls who wore their Sapphic crushes as a badge of honour? Thirty years on, would their best friend accuse *them* of being gay? We all crave acceptance, and we get it where we can.

AS MY PARENTS didn't drive, Ms Thompson's lime-green Citroen 2 CV took me to Dorothea Beale. I'd never met a *Ms* before and, each time I addressed her as Miss Thompson, she sucked her teeth sharply and drummed her jewelled fingers on the steering wheel.

We stopped off at a roadside café for tea and sandwiches. Ms Thompson left her crusts on the side of her plate. "Have you thought about what you'll say to the other girls? Why you're starting in the middle of term?"

I'd thought of nothing else. My family had been wiped out in a plane crash and I'd been granted a private education on the insurance money. I'd been struck down with polio and had to learn to walk again from scratch. There'd been a mix-up on the maternity ward fifteen years before and my real mother was an Arabian princess. "Not really. What should I say?"

"Best stick as close to the truth as possible. Without giving too much away."

It turned out Ms Thompson understood boarding-school culture as little as I did. I spent my first week wandering the draughty corridors in my ill-fitting uniform, rehearsing my response to a question nobody asked. Later, I discovered everyone assumed I'd arrived late because I'd been asked to leave another establishment for misbehaviour.

"No," I insisted. "I wasn't expelled. I got a scholarship from my local authority but I couldn't take it up till now because I've been sick."

The girls preferred their own explanation. If I'd understood how their minds worked, I'd have left it at that. But I didn't want a reputation as a rebel.

So I repeated my story until every girl in the school had heard it. Yet it wasn't the truth of my argument that convinced them, nor the force of its repetition, but the voice that conveyed it. My vowels were short when they should have been long and long when they should have been short. It was my accent, along with how I sat with my legs too wide apart and my total ignorance of the basics of lacrosse, that proved I'd come straight from a state school. The truth did not enhance my reputation. Even when I'd imbibed the rules well enough to captain the team to the finals of the inter-schools tournament, I was still *that scholarship girl*. Even when I'd reformed my elocution, they still loved to chant *Watch aht, Diana's abaht* if they thought I might be getting above my station.

But I was accustomed to isolation. When Ms Thompson came to check how things were going, I told her I was fine.

———

THAT SUNDAY, THE Skinner building was graveyard quiet as I wheeled my bike down the second-floor corridor, as if the place went into hibernation at weekends. In my office, I boiled the kettle and waited for the computer to go through its corporate login dance. Fortunately only one Simon Jenkins graced the staff list; no risk of propositioning the wrong bloke. With a steaming mug of green tea to calm my nerves, I hit the keyboard: *Dear Simon, Luigi's pasta was delicious, I wonder what his pizza is like! How are you fixed for a return visit? BW, Diana.*

Email was so much easier than a phone call; casual enough that, if Simon turned me down, I wouldn't have to avoid him around campus.

Energised by that small success, I decided to tackle my inbox. Megan had emailed at four o'clock that morning, requesting a follow-up meeting about her research. Four in the morning! Had she just got home from a party or had she been studying all night?

An ambulance screeched down the road outside. On an ordinary working day I'd hardly notice. But that Sunday afternoon, with the building in sleep mode, it made my stomach flip with memories of that day I learnt keepy-uppy while my mother was convinced she was dying of a heart attack.

———

I WAS FINE while we waited for the ambulance. I was fine while I sat inside as the vehicle howled through the streets.

Fine as I kicked my legs in the echoing waiting-room while, at the other side of the swing doors, they checked my mother out. So long as all the attention was on my mother, I could let my mind float off into tales of *Romeo and Juliet* and the boy king, Tutankhamen.

When the nurse came to tell me it wasn't a heart attack but they'd be keeping my mother a little longer for observation, I began to cry. The nurse fumbled with the fob watch pinned to the bib of her starched apron. "But she's all right, duck, honestly. It was no'but a panic attack. You can see her if you like before you get off home."

I shook my head. How could I see her? It was my fault she'd got in this state.

The nurse frowned. She had that what-can-I-do-with-you look my mother sometimes wore. "There's not much point you waiting here, duck. She'll be a couple of hours at least." She gazed around the waiting room, as if the man in the shabby gabardine with his arm in a sling might advise her what to do. "Is your dad at home? Could he come and get you?"

"We haven't got a car." I wiped my eyes on my sleeve and jiggled the coins in my pocket. "It's all right. I can get the bus."

"You're in no fit state to get on the bus on your own," said the nurse. "Come with me."

I didn't know why she'd suddenly decided to take care of me. Perhaps she was about to go off shift and would give me a lift herself. Ashamed of my earlier tears – after all, I'd be twelve next birthday – I wanted to look responsible. I slid off the grey plastic stacking chair and followed.

On the other side of the swing doors, a reception desk fronted a row of curtained cubicles. From a distance, they resembled the changing rooms down the side of the swimming baths, but I knew from experience they contained more than a wooden bench and a couple of coat hooks.

The nurse must have noticed me staring: "Sure you don't want to say hello to your mother?"

I dug my teeth into the soft flesh on the inside of my bottom lip. "No thanks."

"Suit yourself." The nurse curled her lip in a way that reminded me of the P.E. teacher at my new school. "Are you on the phone at home?"

We'd just got one, although only my sister seemed to have any use for it. I reeled off the number.

The nurse dragged the telephone across the desk towards her, slipped her finger into the dial. Even with the receiver pressed to her ear, I could hear it ringing on and on, like a baby crying.

I imagined my dad, sitting in his wingback chair by the fire, pipe in one hand, mug of tea in the other, the *Daily Mirror* on his lap. Cursing the infernal shrilling. "It's no problem," I said. "I know which bus to get."

A man in a pale green smock – a doctor, I guessed from the stethoscope dangling from his neck – snatched a buff file from the desk as he hurried past, turning momentarily to wink at my nurse. She pretended not to notice as she dropped the receiver and picked it up again, dialled the number once more.

A shift in her shoulders told me Dad had picked up. "Mr Dodsworth? It's Nurse Hetherington from the

Infirmary here. Now it's nothing to worry about, but your wife took a funny turn in the park and we brought her in for observation."

I didn't hear my dad's response, of course, although I heard Nurse Hetherington reassure him it was nothing serious. The reason she was ringing, she said, was that I'd been with my mother when she collapsed and was understandably shaken. Could he come and fetch me?

I shook my head, confused. She hadn't considered me as *understandably shaken* when I'd sat snivelling in the waiting room. And why was she asking Dad to come? I'd told her we didn't have a car.

Perhaps my father was explaining the same thing. But Nurse Hetherington didn't expect him to pick me up in our non-existent car. She expected him to get the bus to the hospital only to go straight back again with me. "I've got my bus fare," I said, but she wasn't listening. She pattered her fingertips on the desk as the conversation ratcheted up into an argument.

Her face had turned purple by the time she slammed down the phone. When she turned to me her smile was as wooden as a ventriloquist's dummy's. "Bad news, I'm afraid, duck. Your dad's too busy this afternoon to come for you. Shall I find you some magazines and a drink of pop and you can go home in the taxi with your mum when she's finished?"

I shook my head. My dad knew I was old enough to manage an eight-mile bus ride independently. Soon he'd find out my mother's collapse was entirely my fault. Yet Nurse Hetherington thought he should be all sloppy like

Geraldine's father. I hated her for that.

MOVING UP TO the comprehensive had been a dreadful shock. Only a few weeks in, I didn't know how I'd survive the next five years. Looked at dispassionately, as if preparing for confession, none of my problems were sufficient to account for my overriding sense of doom: Geraldine's abandonment; the unfamiliar uniform with the stripy tie and bulky blazer; the teachers' sarcasm; and the bell that howled through the full five storeys at thirty-five minute intervals all day long. Other kids settled smoothly into the rhythms of senior school; I remained the odd one out.

My mother had been taking her blue pills for as long as I could remember. I knew they were for her nerves, but I never wondered what that meant. Perhaps I considered it integral to being a mother, along with frizzy perms, suspender belts, and monthly obsessions with scrubbing the front doorstep.

She kept the bottle on the top shelf of the mirrored bathroom cabinet. I'd come across them whenever I was sent to fetch a corn plaster, or the tube of menthol throat-pastilles and tub of Vick's ointment for my father's rasping chest. They dwelt among bumper bottles of aspirin, the roll of sticking-plaster that smelt of zinc oxide, the round-ended scissors to cut it with, a tortoiseshell comb with snapped-off teeth that no one claimed ownership of, and my father's horsehair shaving brush dotted with flecks of white soap. From a young age, I'd climb onto the cork-topped stool to filch the doll-sized vial of green olive oil, to double up as a magic potion to let Juliet play dead. Or, a little older, to borrow my sister's luxury shampoo that my dad said was nothing but Fairy Liquid in a fancy bottle. The cupboard contents might be rearranged occasionally – the bag of pastel-coloured plastic curlers with the swimming-bath smell of setting lotion, the crepe bandage saved from unravelling by a rusting safety-pin, the scattering of rogue kirby-grips – but my mother's pills were a constant.

When I opened the bathroom cabinet that Saturday morning, a couple of weeks before my mother and I went to the pitch and putt, I had no particular goal in mind. I suppose I thought that if the pills could soothe my mother's nerves, they might help mine.

My mother, Patricia, and Trevor were all out that day, so it was my father who found me. From far away, I sensed him shouting in my ear, his tobacco-tinged panic and the slap of his hand against my cheek. I slept a while and then I was lifted, up and away. Even the ambulance ride felt peaceful, faces moving in and out of focus as if through mist. *Oh sweet Juliet*: all my problems about to be resolved.

Harsh lights, harsh words; I'd thought they were transporting me to Heaven but it must have been Hell. I wanted to sleep but they forced a foul brown liquid down my gullet, gripping my chin till I'd swallowed every drop. Then the vomiting, the sweats, the shakes, the stinging eyes. Another round and more vomiting until it seemed they wouldn't let me rest till I'd coughed up my very stomach, till my abdominal muscles caved in. In the middle of it all, my father's face appearing round the curtain, his frown, his turning away.

Afterwards, an acrid taste in my mouth and a dull cramp

in my belly as I lay, exhausted, waiting for Dad to take me home. He'd be put out to have missed the wrestling, to have to fork out for a taxi. Little wonder that, when he pushed back the wipe-clean curtain, I began to cry.

"Stop that!" he said. "It's done now. Let's hope you've learnt your lesson and we'll have na'more of this nonsense."

As I clambered down from the couch, my father kept his hands firmly in his pockets. He followed as I staggered towards the main desk. I couldn't count on his willingness to catch me if I fell.

Waiting at the desk in my socked feet, when the nurse handed my father a medicine bottle with the remains of my mother's blue pills, I saw what a fool I'd been. My father slipped it into his jacket pocket and hurried me towards the main doors.

Almost there, he changed his mind and darted into the Gents'. Standing alone with people flowing past me in and out, I felt unsteady, but I didn't dare follow.

I was relieved when he came back. "Don't breathe a word of this to your mother," he said. "She'll only get herself in a tizz."

As we climbed into the back of the taxi, I noticed the pocket of his jacket was completely flat. If he didn't want my mother to know about it, why had he got rid of her pills?

ELEVEN YEARS OLD and I'd already had two secret visits to Casualty: the first following an experiment with the breadknife I mustn't let my father find out about; the second when I'd swallowed my mother's pills. Having to hide this from my mother left me anxious and ashamed.

And guilty. How would she manage without her tablets?

For the first few days I observed her carefully, studied her demeanour as she went about her chores. When she seemed unaffected, cheerful even, I concluded my dad had fixed it; gone along to the doctor's for another prescription. True, I couldn't find a new bottle in the bathroom cabinet, but perhaps he'd persuaded her to keep them elsewhere. It was a relief not to have to worry about her going mental, whatever that might entail. I had enough of my own stuff to worry about; my visit to the hospital had altered nothing at school.

When we agreed on that trip to the park I knew my mother's cheerfulness had gone too far. Yet I didn't understand enough about what would make her pop to be able to prevent it happening.

As soon as the man in the porkpie hat mentioned a heart attack, I knew it would be my fault if my mother died. When Nurse Hetherington diluted the diagnosis to a panic attack, I felt even more to blame. Maybe I didn't quite know what the term *panic attack* meant, but it *had* to be about her pills. If I didn't confess what I'd done the guilt would dog me for ever; if I admitted I'd taken them, I'd be breaking the pact with my dad.

When she arrived home from the hospital, Dad, Trevor, and I were watching *The Generation Game* on TV. Patricia was upstairs getting ready to go out. Mum, still on edge, called for her to come straight down.

My sister walked in, smelling of bubble bath, wrapped in her dressing gown with cold cream smeared across her face. "Are you feeling better now?"

"I'll give you feeling better, young lady," said Mum.

"What the hell did you do with my pills?" Trevor laughed at something on the television, and she turned on him: "Was it you, took them?"

"Hold your sweat," said Dad. "Why don't you sit yourself down with a cup of tea?"

Mum hadn't even taken off her coat. "One of you three took my pills from the bathroom cabinet, and nobody's moving till I find out who it was." She grabbed Patricia by the wrist and yanked her forward. "Was this your idea? You're always on at me to come off them. And, like a fool, I took it as challenge, didn't I? Nearly ended up in the bloody loony bin!"

Acid burned in my stomach. Dad sat in his chair, stuffing his pipe with wispy tobacco. I'd hoped for some sign from him, but why should he bail me out? I was the one who'd swallowed her tranquillisers, not him.

"Well?" Mum was either about to punch someone or burst into tears.

"It was me," I said.

"You?" Like it was the ultimate betrayal. "Have you got straw between your tabs? I thought you were supposed to be the brainy one."

"Sorry."

"I'll give you *sorry*, you little devil! Running about that bloody football pitch, knowing your poor mother could hardly catch her breath!" She yanked me out of my seat and socked me one on the nose.

My father lit his pipe. My sister crept into the kitchen to put the kettle on. My mother began to unbutton her coat. I removed myself from the room and climbed the stairs to bed.

Chapter 8

"SO THAT'S THE both of us," said Simon. "Neither one thing nor the other."

"Pardon?"

Our second lunch at the Italian. He'd been talking about his childhood before the waiter came to whisk away our plates.

"Middle children. Caught in a perpetual no man's land."

"Oh. I never thought of it like that." Patricia and Trevor had always been more confident than me, but I'd put it down to their sparkling personalities, not birth order.

The waiter flourished the dessert menus. We'd taken to calling them all Luigi, even those who clearly weren't Italian, or male, although only between ourselves. We declined the zabaglione and tiramisu in favour of a couple of cappuccinos.

"For a psychologist, you're not terribly self-reflective."

"I didn't know I was meant to be. I was taught to be objective."

"Joke, Di!" Simon put up his hands, palms towards me, as if to hold back the torrent of my wrath. "I'm sorry, but I feel so relaxed with you, I forget you're not used to my sense of humour. Anyway, I'm glad you're not the type who rabbits on as if they're writing a thesis on the trauma of their sister scribbling all over the *Bunty* annual they got for Christmas."

I poured myself more water, although I was far from thirsty. How could I convince him I had the balance right between self-awareness and absorption? I tried to channel the ease with which I'd told him about the Khan el Khalili. "Okay, here's an interesting story about my childhood. The day I was born, my dad was a hundred miles away, helping lower his friend's coffin into his grave."

"Spooky," said Simon. "I wonder if that's where your Tutankhamen game came from."

I laughed at how easily I seemed to be piecing together in Simon's mind, all my awkward angles smoothed into a perfectly rounded whole. "I wonder." Simon needn't know that my dad didn't tell me about Wilf Pettigrew's funeral until long after my days of playing dead with Geraldine.

"I feel sorry for men of that generation," said Simon. "What they missed out on. Even if your dad hadn't been called away to a funeral, I doubt he'd have been allowed onto the labour ward. My dad was minding the shop when I was born. Just another day!"

His eyes glazed over as he tried to convey how moving it had been to witness the births of his own two children: the terror; the sense of redundancy; the sheer wonder of it all. I was pleased he felt no need to hold back. Yet I was even happier when Luigi brought the coffees and broke the spell.

Simon sprinkled brown sugar over the milky foam. He

let it melt, sink a little, before stirring it in. "How about dinner next time? I hear the view from the restaurant at the Baltic is rather special."

———————

IN RED DUFFEL and baggy suede boots, Megan lounged against the breeze-block wall opposite my office door. I hurried down the corridor and fumbled with the lock. "Sorry I'm a little late." Again.

Dreamily, Megan removed her earphones and looked me up and down. "Dr Dodsworth, you look awesome! Have you done something to your hair?"

I wasn't sure about courting the approval of a girl whose fringe made me seasick, not with my scalp still aching from where the hairdresser had tugged at the roots with a spiky brush. *Going somewhere special tonight?* I hoped the indignities I'd suffered at her hands would be worth it. I ushered Megan into the office: "So you've had some more ideas about your project?"

Megan scoped the room as if for the first time. Her eyes widened as she noticed my red bike, propped, as ever, against the bookcase. "That is so healthy! I keep meaning to bring my bike up but it's torture on the train."

We took our seats: "How's the literature search coming along?"

Megan rummaged in her sackcloth shopping bag and dumped a sheaf of papers on the table between us. It surprised me how much there was. Last time I'd played around on PsychLit I'd come up with a grand total of eight references to the two-jars method, and five of them were mine. "You *have* been working hard."

Megan skimmed through the pages. "Thing is, Dr Dodsworth, they're not all on decision-making."

As I swung my head, my sleek new haircut swung with it. "That's all right, Megan. It's always a good idea to read around your subject."

"That's what Professor Bradshaw said."

I smiled encouragingly, but Megan seemed to have dried up. With a head reeking like bubble-gum from the hairdresser's profligate attitude to hairspray, I struggled with my own sense of authority. "So would you like to tell me about what you've been reading?"

"I was kind of trying to find something that would link up with, like, where I was at myself, if you know what I mean."

I didn't, but I nodded all the same.

"Thing is, on the surface, my decision about which university was a real cinch. Like it wasn't about the course, the location or even the social life."

I sucked in my cheeks, stifling a yawn. If this was her rough patch, I'd better look sympathetic, although she couldn't be the first young woman who'd come to university to chase after a boyfriend. All adolescents considered their own tragedy unique and I assumed lost love had a better prognosis than anorexia.

"I came to Newcastle to see more of my dad."

I tried not to let my surprise show. *Dads and their teenage daughters*; shouldn't she have grown out of that by her age? "Well, thanks for sharing that with me, Megan."

The girl gripped me in a steely stare, the impact slightly

diminished by the fringe slanting across one grey eye. "Thing is, Dr Dodsworth, he's my, um, stepdad."

An avalanche proceeded down my gullet to my stomach. Megan's gushing earlier about my hair and my bike began to make sense: she needed me to be reliable, and not only in the academic sphere.

"My dad died when I was a baby and my stepdad moved in with us when I was three. He was absolutely great with me, brought me up like I was his own, and when he and Mum split up in my early teens, he kept in touch. Even when he moved up here, he'd have me and my brother for holidays."

When, at my appraisal, Garth had urged me to attend Pastoral Care training, I'd dismissed it as corporate bullshit. If I'd been less cavalier I might be equipped to support a student who needed to disclose an incestuous relationship with her stepfather.

"So when it came to apply for uni, it was a no-brainer. I'd come up here so I could spend more time with him."

I leant forward, close enough for the exchange of confidences, not so close as to intrude. "Megan, have you told anyone else about this?"

"What do you mean, Dr Dodsworth?"

The ice slid further down my intestines. "Only that you must have found it very stressful." I awarded myself full marks for an unbiased but encouraging response.

Megan frowned as if she thought it barely passed. Yet she pressed on: "What I didn't realise was the huge change process he'd be going through. Don't get me wrong, Dr Dodsworth, it's really cool that I've been around to support him with coming out and everything, but the thing is, like my counsellor says, that's not what university's supposed to be about."

"I see." The ice melted: I didn't need Pastoral Care for this. For one thing, her counsellor would carry the brunt of it – why did I forget her counsellor? – and for another, a parent or stepparent coming out as gay, disturbing as it must be to the child, was a whole lot more tolerable than their involvement in paedophilia. I almost didn't mind that Megan's decision to confide in me might stem from a mistaken assumption about my own sexuality.

"Sorry if I'm rambling, Dr Dodsworth. Thing is, what I'm trying to say is that I thought my decision was easy but it turned out to be real complicated."

"And you'd like to incorporate that into your research?"

"Do you think I could?"

Like Garth said, she'd had a tough time but she was keen and hard working. Her stepfather had fettered her with his own problems; I could help her spread her wings and fly. "You can certainly give it a try."

AFTER STRIPPING THE bed and fighting the duvet into a fresh pink cover, I stood at the wardrobe, rattling the wooden hangers back and forth. Would it matter that Simon had already seen the rosebud shirt at Venus's party? I held it up against my chest, studying my reflection in the mirror. I swung my shoulders back and forth, feeling the dizzy mixture of excitement and terror I more usually associated with presenting papers at national conferences. Tonight would be my fourth meal with Simon, but it remained a mystery to me whether he saw this as dating, or he simply preferred not to eat alone.

I caught a gentle tinkling sound as Marmaduke stole up and pressed herself against my ankles. I picked her up, buried my nose in silky fur that smelled of outdoors. I spun round; Marmaduke stretched her claws and hissed at her reflection in the mirror. *What's the matter, Puss? That lady's fur coat too flashy for you?*

As I let the cat go, my inner Venus began to nag at me: *Wear something nice! Make an effort for him!* I used to love dressing up with Geraldine, prancing about in flower-decked hats and sequinned skirts in lurid clashing colours. *When I grow up*, I said, *I'm going to wear a white dress with a different coloured satin sash for every day of the week.* My younger self would weep to see the drab sweaters and trousers that now comprised my middle-aged uniform.

Almost derailed by decisions again, I thought, as I grabbed a hanger and dashed to the bathroom. It was only a meal with a friend: not an audition for the rest of my life.

SIMON HAD BOOKED a table at the rooftop restaurant at the Baltic. I emerged from the lift to find him sitting with his drink on the squashy sofa in the reception area, looking out over the lamp-lit quayside through the floor-to-ceiling glass. Wearing a pale suit with a navy shirt which, with his jacket unbuttoned, I could see had been ironed with the dedication I'd come to relish, he sprang from his seat, seemingly delighted to exchange the view of the bridges ranked across the Tyne for one of me, spruced in my fawn-coloured A-line dress. He didn't kiss me but, as we sat down, his thigh brushed mine and stayed there, only a few thin layers of linen and nylon between our bare skin.

When the waiter led us through to the restaurant, Simon took my hand and squeezed it. From our table, the view extended right across the twinkling lights of the neoclassical skyline as far as the university. Simon joked that he could see the window of his office and challenged me to pick out mine. I was still puzzling when the waiter came to take our order.

"By the way," said Simon, once the wine had been poured and the menus taken away, "I've put in for that sabbatical."

"Cairo?"

"Yup. Don't ask me how I swung it. It's far too embarrassing."

"Think you'll get it?" I managed to make it sound like I wasn't bothered either way.

"Let's say I've seen stronger applications."

"When will you hear?"

Simon tugged at his shirt cuffs. "A month, maybe."

"Will you be disappointed if they turn you down?"

"I'm not sure. It's not really the best time, is it?"

Because of us? I stopped my mouth with an olive before I could make a fool of myself.

"The kids are just into their new routine, Wednesday teatime and every other weekend." Simon spoke some more about the complexities of dividing up the pots and pans and children. "I'm not boring you, am I?"

I speared another olive with a cocktail stick. "Not at all. It's where you're at right now, isn't it?"

The waiter brought our starters. My Thai fish cakes in a pomegranate reduction looked even better than I expected. We tucked in, exchanging appreciative noises.

"If I do go," said Simon, "I'm going to hold you to your promise."

I looked quizzically across the table as the chilli and sweet sauce alternately fired and soothed my taste buds.

"Don't say you've forgotten!"

What I had forgotten, when I plumped for the dress, was how awkward the flared sleeves were for dining. I had to hold my arms askew with my elbows in the air to prevent the scalloped edges dragging on my plate.

"The Khan el Khalili." Simon grinned. "You promised you'd show me the ropes."

"Did I?"

"If you didn't, you jolly well ought to have done. They'd eat me alive if I went alone."

"I wouldn't like you to get eaten but, I'm sorry, I can't help. I don't go abroad any more. My passport's expired."

"That's easily remedied."

Professor Bradshaw would probably think the same. I kept smiling.

Simon reached across the table and pushed my left sleeve away from my plate. "Careful!"

We both stared, not just at the smear of red sauce running along the edge of my sleeve, but at the patch of bare skin that had been revealed, and the scribble of short white scars crisscrossing my forearm.

"How did you do that?"

I tugged at my sleeve and pulled my arm under the

table. "Haven't you met my cat?"

Simon smiled but his voice was strained: "You might want to sponge your sleeve down in the bathroom. Otherwise you'll be left with a nasty stain."

I'D BEEN ALONE in the house when the postman came with the brown envelope from the Egyptian Embassy. About to turn fifteen, I was spending the long summer holiday keeping house while my mother visited Cairo with my sister.

My hands were sticky with dough when the knocker clattered against the door. I knew my mother would have a fit if she got to hear that I'd opened the door wearing a floral pinny, so I yanked it over my head and wiped my hands on the bib as I rushed down the passageway.

Summer's heat rose up from the pavement to hit me between the eyes as I opened the door. "Dad won the pools, has he?" The postman thrust a card with a picture of the pyramids into my hand. "Most of us have to make do with a fortnight in Skegness."

Avoiding his gaze, I turned over the card, skimming through Patricia's scrawl for something incriminating. "My sister's got an Egyptian friend."

The postman laughed lasciviously. I wondered if Egyptian friend might be slang for some version of intercourse. Words were always tripping me up in those days.

Winking, he hefted his bag onto his hip. "Not hot enough for her here, then?"

I blushed furiously; even my earlobes were tingling. I

thought of the racks of saucy postcards at Skegness, the cartoon women with breasts ballooning out of their bras. How I'd walk right past, pretending I hadn't seen them, taking huge strides to counteract the jittery feeling between my legs. I remembered Geraldine's tongue between my lips on the back row of the picture house and the awful mixture of anger and arousal and fear.

He was three doors down before I recovered myself. In my hand, streaked with scone mix, was not only the postcard from Cairo, but a brown envelope with a London postmark and the frank of the Consulate General of the Arab Republic of Egypt.

I PLACED THE packet on the mantelpiece, propped up against the bottle of holy water in the shape of the Virgin Mary we'd brought back from Lourdes. It was addressed to my father and, while I was tempted to steam it open to reassure myself about its contents, I resolved to hang on till he got home. Through the envelope, I could make out the shape of two passports. St Bernadette had failed to grant us a miracle the first time I'd gone abroad but, if my hunch was right about my parents' intentions, the caliphs and pharaohs might grant my wish.

I read my sister's postcard again, looking for a clue in her innocuous message. *Weather scorching hot.* Was the trail hotting up too? *Wish you were here!* Was that an invitation to join them? In the end, I had to force myself not to think about it, concentrating instead on perfecting the glaze on my scones and the ironed crease down the centre of my brother's jeans. I tuned in to Radio One and pranced about with a duster to Elton John and the Bay City Rollers.

A little after five, I set a couple of pans of water on the stove and took the transistor upstairs while I changed into my jeans. A melody started up, just a few simple chords strummed on the guitar that hit me in the solar plexus with such force, I doubled up on the bed in the foetus position. *Seasons in the Sun* was about a man saying farewell to his family and his childhood friend, the prospect of death freeing him up to confess how much he cared. It made me ache to be with Geraldine again, sitting on her front doorstep, brushing her thick red hair. But, by then, our friendship was firmly in the past.

THE FRONT DOOR slammed. I zipped up my fly and raced downstairs. Dad had settled into his wingback chair by the television and was stuffing the bowl of his pipe with shreds of brown tobacco. "Mash us a brew, duck, would you?" If he'd noticed the envelope on the mantelpiece, he wasn't letting on.

I was glad to be alone in the kitchen where my face couldn't betray my anticipation. I topped up the water in the saucepans and lit another ring for the kettle. While waiting for them to boil I studied the instructions on the carton of Vesta chicken supreme.

When I took him his mug of tea, Patricia's postcard had progressed farther along the mantelpiece, obscuring the figure three on the flat face of the clock. The brown envelope hadn't moved.

When the food was ready I arranged it on three plates in the kitchen, a dollop of fawn-coloured sauce ringed with fluffy white rice exactly as displayed on the carton, like a plumped-up anaemic poached egg. I could hear my brother chuntering in the next room so I guessed he'd seen what the postman had brought.

I set down the plates on the table. Trevor gave the meal a cursory glance and went back to thumbing through the black booklet with the lion and the unicorn emblazoned in gold on the cover. I knew it must be *my* passport he was handling when he stopped to snigger at the photograph near the front. But it wasn't enough to assuage his envy when he turned to the visa section. "It's not fair. I never go anywhere."

My father picked up his knife and fork, explaining that this was a special trip to aid my recovery.

Trevor threw the passport across the table. "Oh, I get it. If *I* threaten to top myself you'll take *me* to look at four-thousand-year-old dead bodies."

"Eat your tea before it gets cold," said my dad.

Trevor picked up his fork and began blending the stew into the rice. "Or do I have to go prancing down the street in high heels and get the shit beaten out of me?"

Dad raised his hand as if he might slap him across the head, thereby concluding all discussion. But I knew that if it were only my convalescence he had in mind, there'd be no need for Egyptian visas.

————

RETURNING TO THE restaurant table with the corner of my sleeve still damp and cold against my wrist, I was prepared to plough politely through the rest of the meal before splitting the bill and walking off into separate sunsets. Yet Simon seemed in no hurry to bring the evening to a close. He deliberated over the dessert menu as if it were the hustings for a parliamentary election, and even suggested following dessert with coffee and brandies. I had to conclude his priority was the food, until he suggested a stroll.

The Millennium Bridge spanned the river like a wide-open eye, blue light shadowing the arc of the upper lid. A chill breeze wafted up from the river. I buttoned my coat and turned up the collar. Simon wrapped his arm around my waist. "I've really enjoyed tonight."

I felt clumsy walking so close to someone, like twins joined at the hip. "Have you?"

He took a deep breath and his arm stiffened across my back. "Can I speak candidly?"

I shivered. "Of course."

Simon kept quiet until we'd almost crested the bridge. He stood me against the railings, half a width of water at either side. The Sage building dominated the left bank, plump and rounded as a reclining Buddha or a silvery grounded airship, the illuminated windows revealing concert-goers waiting at the bars. To our right, gangs of young women with bare legs raw below their miniskirts stuffed themselves into the neon-lit pubs and clubs below the sandstone law-courts. "I think I'm falling for you, Di." A drunken hoot came from the revellers on the quayside. Somehow they seemed more *compos mentis* than Simon.

"I need to take it gently, though. I can't risk hurtling headfirst into anything too serious right now."

"Of course. The divorce. Your children." *The sabbatical.*

"That's right." His fingers against my cheek made my face tingle. "It might be that I'm out of practice with all this, but I don't know how to read you. I can't tell whether you're stringing me along or you also need to pace yourself."

I shuffled to the side. An icy blast scudded up from the river. "Stringing you along?"

He clutched my arm, as if trying to read my scars through my coat. "A cat didn't do this. It's fine if you don't want to tell me but I need to be sure I can trust you."

This is where, in the films, the woman cries and the man comes on all manly and magics the awkwardness away. But my eyes were tinder dry. "It wasn't Marmaduke," I said. "I cut myself. Haven't done it for twenty years, but I'm entirely responsible for these scars."

"You don't have to tell me ..."

Why not? Sinking into a familiar numbness, I had nothing more to lose. "I had some bad experiences with men. With sex, actually. I let them do stuff I shouldn't have and then ..." I fumbled with my coat sleeve, trying to push it back, but the woollen fabric was too thick. "As if that wasn't bad enough, I had to hurt myself even more."

Simon dragged my right hand from my injured arm and brought it to his lips. "Di, Di, the last thing I want is to hurt you. Or to put you under so much pressure you end up harming yourself." He wrapped his arms around me and kissed me fully on the lips. The lights on the bridge morphed from highlighter blue to fluorescent green. I felt his erection through both our coats. "We'll go at your pace."

I wanted to believe him but I could hardly take it in. I laughed bitterly, remembering the clean sheets on my double bed. "Sex?"

"I can wait. Like courting couples in the old days."

"But it isn't the old days."

"Why don't we pretend it is?"

MY BOYFRIEND, I thought, as I scrubbed dried-on smears of rabbit stew from Marmaduke's bowl. *My boyfriend*, I thought, as hail machine-gunned my face and the wheels of my bicycle splattered my shoes with gutter sludge. *My boyfriend*, as the laptop in the downstairs lecture theatre of the Skinner building refused to recognise my memory stick. *My boyfriend.*

It was childish, but childishness was hardly a crime. I used to envy my sister popping round to her boyfriend's on Sunday afternoons, where they'd lounge on beanbags, listening to records while doing their homework. If I'd missed out on that stage of innocent intimacy, why shouldn't I grab it now?

I could have it all without betraying the rest of me: my friends; my work; my own private space. *My boyfriend* didn't snatch the time and energy I needed, didn't deplete my reserves. On the contrary, he stretched and magnified what I had already, so that each moment, however mundane, seemed twice as precious and twice as long. In giving myself to another I didn't lose myself.

This was the game I'd played with Geraldine, until life showed me it was false. Now, when I'd all but given up, I'd found a genuine Romeo.

Chapter 9

A T EXAM TIME, we had to use invigilators from a different department, but one of us would go along at the end when the papers were collected in. Walking into the sports hall as the students were putting down their pens, I could almost taste the heady mixture of relief and disappointment, the euphoria and plain exhaustion hanging in the air. At times like these, my own student days didn't seem so far behind. I made my way to the front desk as the second years stretched their arms and gazed dazedly around them, like afternoon cinema-goers blinking at the light.

Megan sat at the far end of the front row, her red duffel coat draped across the back of her chair. She bit her lip as the invigilator collected the pale-blue pad from her desk. I hoped she'd done all right.

She looked up and, as she spotted me, the pleasure seemed to ripple through her body. Embarrassed, I feigned not to notice, busying myself in straightening the piles of exam pads accumulating on the front desk. I wondered if I'd been overly enthusiastic the last time we met. It wouldn't do to let her get dependent.

When the papers were all in, I helped the porter secure

them in boxes for delivery to the department for marking. We worked in silence while, amid a scraping of chairs and a babble of voices and the raucous ringtones of their newly awakened mobile phones, the students fled the room. All but Megan. She waited, shuffling her feet in her baggy ankle boots that were surely unsuitable for summer even in the chilly North East, until the porter began to wheel the papers away. "I thought I should tell you, Dr Dodsworth …"

I shrugged on my backpack. "Not off to the union for a drink with the others, Megan?"

She hovered in front of me. "Thing is, I was doing the question on optical illusions …"

"No point worrying about the exam now, Megan. I'm sure you did your best." I hoped she wasn't going to ask if she could amend her paper. She wouldn't be the first student to remember the vital reference just as the invigilator called time.

"No, it's not that, Dr Dodsworth. I had this flash of inspiration about my research. You know the Necker cube?"

The Perception module couldn't have changed that much in twenty-five years. "I should hope so, Megan."

"Mostly we see the lower-left face as being in front, but the reverse perspective is equally logical."

I nodded.

"Thing is, I've been looking at my research question the wrong way round. I shouldn't be starting off from the perspective of my decision about which university, I should be studying the enormity of the decision my dad's making."

"Interesting, Megan." She really *was* dedicated, finding new insights even in the middle of an exam, but it was my job to help her keep the project in perspective. "Something to ponder when we next meet."

I'D ARRANGED TO meet Venus in the senior common room for lunch. I arrived first and, grabbing a tray, joined the queue at the hatch. I was ravenous, as if I'd been sitting the exam rather than facing the prospect of marking it, and wondered if I could justify a baked potato as well as the salad and a large portion of quiche. Intent on the rumbling of my stomach and wondering how to get Megan back on track, along with keeping an eye out for Venus, I wasn't paying particular attention to those standing in line before me. Yet I must have registered the frothy blonde at some level – the musky perfume overpowering the smell of food, the eyes and lips accentuated by heavy paintwork, the yards of peacock-coloured silk – because I was suddenly aware of how dowdy I must look with my mousey pageboy haircut, my no-coloured chinos and equally drab long-sleeved T-shirt. So far, Simon always seemed pleased to see me when he managed to squeeze me in around his Wednesday evenings and alternate weekends. Now I wondered if his commitment to his children might serve another function for him; likewise the moratorium on sex. As with the Necker cube, I'd failed to consider the alternative point of view. Did Simon relish the responsibilities that reduced his time with me? Did he not fancy me enough to want to get me into bed? He might consider me a stopgap to fill the empty space until his sabbatical; our relationship a dummy run before he launched himself into the post-divorce marriage market.

The glamour girl neared the front of the queue. Venus

wouldn't need persuading to take me shopping, to kit me out in some girly clothes. Yet I balked at the prospect; thirty-odd years had gone by since I'd last enjoyed dressing up. Whenever I tried I felt constrained, dishonest, both cheating and cheated. I didn't want to airbrush myself to gain a man's approval. I wanted Simon to accept me as I was.

The serving woman smoothed the front of her crimson tabard. "Now what can I get you, Dr Marlow?"

I held my breath for the blonde's answer. As if, by pursuing the same diet as this epitome of femininity, I could become Simon's ideal.

It might have been the sound of her voice that broke the spell, but I reckon I came to my senses a beat before. It was crazy to compare myself with this creature. I was who I was.

Dr Marlow leant in towards the counter. Her Adam's apple wobbled as she gave her order in a rich baritone: "I'll have a jacket potato with a slice of spinach quiche and a mixed salad, please."

"WE SHOULD DO this more often," said Venus. "Goodness knows what shenanigans we've missed out on sat at our desks with a cheese and coleslaw stottie."

She'd turned up in the common room as I ordered my quiche and salad, Giles and Mohammed in tow, shoulders spattered from a sudden downpour. I'd found a table by the floor-to-ceiling bow windows with an excellent view of the rain bouncing off the walkway down below, the staff and students leapfrogging between the puddles and improvising bags and books for umbrellas. It also afforded us an excellent view of Dr Marlow, tucking into a baked potato three tables away.

"I'm all for freedom of expression," said Giles, "but won't it be unsettling for his students?"

It was unsettling enough for me, yet I wasn't prepared to admit I'd felt upstaged by a transvestite. Now, in the light of the plate glass window, Dr Marlow looked more like a cartoon caricature than the classic male fantasy, as if an alien had taken a child's drawing as the blueprint for a woman. The bouncy blonde hair couldn't have been her own, and the ruby kiss-me lips and caked-on makeup were there to hide, and not enhance, her features. Beefy biceps tested the seams of her frilly blouse while her chest lacked the bosom for said blouse to plunge into, and no amount of sparkly rings or nail extensions could make the hands clutching the cutlery appear any daintier.

Venus tweaked her thick dark hair, returning some of the springiness knocked out of it by the rain. "They'll find it a hoot, obviously. Like dressing up for Rag Week already."

Venus and I used to don green fuzzy wigs and checked pyjamas and go sashaying down Northumberland Street, shaking a collecting tin in shoppers' faces. Compared to Dr Marlow, we'd been quite restrained. Still, it would be awful if she heard. "Keep your voice down!"

Venus laughed, like a whinnying pony: "You're so uptight! If he chooses to come to work dressed like a pantomime dame, he can't expect people not to comment."

"It would make an interesting project for one of your students," said Mohammed.

In the early days of our friendship, Venus used to love to ferret out the town's eccentrics, regaling me with tales of

Born-Again preachers and the man who picked up litter from the pavement only to set it down again a few yards along. She gifted me these characters the way Marmaduke would catch a mouse and let it loose in my bedroom, more a reflection of her character than mine. It was no use trying to explain that I wasn't interested in the extreme or the unusual; I wanted to know what made normal people tick. "Not one of mine."

Giles shivered. "You must admit, it's rather surreal. Why would a middle-aged man suddenly decide he wants to be a woman?"

"Might not be suddenly," said Mohammed. "Probably been building up to it for years."

"Should've made a better job of it therefore," said Venus.

"Shh!" I glanced across at Dr Marlow's table, but she seemed absorbed in crunching through the Waldorf salad.

"I speak my mind," said Venus. "Shame none of his friends thought to do likewise. Saved him making such an ass of himself. Don't pretend you're not even a tad curious."

I'd never been comfortable with teasing. It gave me a sense of wrong-footedness. Of taking the world too seriously, seeing darkness where others found light.

"Come on, Di," said Giles. "How would a psychologist explain it?"

I shrugged. "I'm not convinced it's a psychological issue."

"Balderdash," said Venus. "In fact, perverted sexuality is the absolute essence of psychology. Ask my friend Sigmund Freud."

"Freud's terribly passé," I said.

Mohammed looked across the table like an eager student in a tutorial. "Isn't it an example of cognitive dissonance? The tension between two conflicting ideals."

Giles nodded. "Hard to reconcile a woman's mind with a man's body."

Venus sat back and toyed with the frilly cuffs of her blouse. "Remind me of the defining difference between the male and female mind."

"How long have you got?" At last, like the unfortunates caught in the rain, I was nearing shelter.

"In fact, it's perfectly simple." Venus stroked the sleeve of Mohammed's fine-knit turquoise cardigan. "We women are genetically programmed to obsess over our appearance."

I thrust my fists deep into the pockets of my drab chinos, recalling the discomfort I'd felt earlier in the queue for food. Across the table, Giles's awkward shuffling mirrored mine. Mohammed fingered the knot of his narrow white tie. Even at Venus's wedding, I'd never seen Giles in anything but dull sweatshirts and casual trousers that did nothing to flatter his middle-aged paunch. Mohammed dressed like a preppy leisurewear model crossed with a groupie for a Ska band and had more style in his shirt collar than Giles and I had in our entire wardrobes. "I think you'll find it goes somewhat deeper than that."

"Maybe it's largely how we think," Venus continued. "The way, when a woman gets home from work, it never enters her head to crack open a beer and lounge on the sofa like a man does. The way she instinctively rolls up her sleeves and starts cooking supper while helping the kids with their homework and ironing her husband's shirt for the next day."

"And gossiping on the phone to her mother," said Giles. "If you get my drift."

"I thought you wanted an academic discussion." I watched, with some relief, as Dr Marlow got up and carried her tray to the trolley by the serving hatch.

"I do," said Venus, "but there's nothing to discuss. A woman's brain is identical to a man's, largely. Any difference between the sexes is down to socialisation."

"Then how can a man know he'd rather be a woman?" said Giles.

"That's what we're waiting for Di to tell us," said Venus.

"Does it matter?" said Mohammed. "He feels he's a woman, isn't it. Believes he is,"

"Obviously what *he* believes is largely a delusion."

I wished I were more up-to-date on the neuroscience. But I'd stumbled my way through axons and synapses as an undergraduate, and the knowledge base had moved on in the last twenty-five years. "They've shown that six-month old babies recognise their own gender."

Venus laughed. "You can train a parrot to say *Who's a pretty boy?* Of course, by six months a baby's been subjected to a humongous amount of stereotyping."

"How does it happen?" asked Mohammed. "Farida wouldn't touch girly stuff when she was little. Now it's all pink dresses and puffed sleeves."

I really should have had an answer, yet here I was, being out-psychologised by a bunch of mathematicians. I chased a chunk of red pepper across my plate with my fork while the others spoke of their experiences of the gender stereotyping of children.

"I'm glad I've seen you."

I looked up. Simon had arrived at exactly the right moment. We made a space for him to set down his tray. The warmth of his kiss made my toes tingle.

"Have you come to whisk her away for a romantic weekend in Paris?" asked Venus.

"Not quite," said Simon, "although, now you mention it, we could probably fit something in before I go away."

"You could go for her birthday," said Venus.

Simon had the look of a man who had learnt the hard way not to forget a lover's birthday. My face shunted between glaring at Venus for meddling and reassuring him I wasn't the type to get excited about the passing of another year. Both expressions provided a useful mask against my deeper feelings: Simon going away spelt the end of us.

"You got your sabbatical?" said Giles. "Jammy sod."

I forced a smile. "Congratulations!"

"When do you leave?" asked Giles.

"End of September. Less than four months to sublet my flat, press-gang my colleagues into baby-sitting my PhD students, and get the kids adjusted to the idea."

I shuffled my knife and fork on my empty plate. No mention of me in his plans.

"Which lucky institution are you going to grace with your presence?" said Venus.

"Didn't Di tell you? I'm off to the University of Cairo."

Venus raised one dark eyebrow. I turned towards the sheets of rain lashing the window.

"So you'll be clocking up the air-miles, Di," said Giles. "I assume Air Egypt's got a frequent-flier scheme?"

"I'm sure Harriet and Oscar will get a lot of benefit from it."

We could hear the rain in the quiet that followed. I knew from the heat of my face and the knot in my stomach I'd overreacted. And from the embarrassed expressions on the faces around the table. It was petty to be jealous of his children, shameful to let this show. But I couldn't unsay what I'd said.

Simon took my hand. "I hoped you'd come out and visit." His voice hardened. "I've said so often enough."

But that was when his sabbatical was safe in the world of make-believe. I pulled my hand away. "You seem to forget I have my own work commitments."

Now would've been the time for Venus to launch in with some pithy observation on the gender divide. Something about a man assuming a woman will prioritise his ambitions over her own. Yet she had become uncharacteristically quiet. Likewise Giles and Mohammed. The knot tightened.

"I'm sure you could manage to fit me into your schedule somewhere. You are allowed annual leave in the psychology department, aren't you? If you were really pushed for time you could squeeze it into a long weekend."

"What about Marmaduke?" They probably thought I was hilarious, the sad spinster concerned about her cat, but at least Marmaduke never judged me, never tried to push me beyond what I could bear.

Simon looked flustered. Part of me felt sorry for him,

yet even as I realised I was making a fool of myself, I was furious that he considered it so simple. I'd wanted the relationship to continue as long as it could, but perhaps it would be easier to end it right then instead of letting it limp on for the rest of the summer.

Venus clapped her hands, beaming like a nursery teacher. "Of course this is tremendous fun, but I would appreciate a teeny word with Simon about your birthday, Di. Would you do me a humongous favour and take Giles and Mohammed to get us some coffees?"

Shaking my head, I pushed back my chair. "Don't listen to her, Simon. I never do anything special on my birthday. If she suggests some elaborate festivities, remember, it's a definite no."

Chapter 10

I DIDN'T MIND Venus chasing the three of us away like children, but I refused to sit with Simon and the others blithely drinking coffee. It would have been like holding a wake for our relationship. I could do nothing about his going away.

I asked Mohammed to give my apologies, citing exam marking as the reason for my hasty retreat. He looked sceptical but fortunately chose not to challenge me.

My hair had plastered itself to my head and my feet squelched in my trainers when I reached the department, my heart thumping as the automatic doors concertinaed apart to welcome me in. A trail of soggy footprints followed me upstairs. I considered grabbing a yellow hazard sign from the cleaners' cupboard, except that the danger wasn't the wet floor, but me: a simmering rage that, most of the time, not even *I* registered.

I needed a door to slam behind me, but the one to my office had a top closer that eased it sedately into the frame. I needed hail pelting the window, but sun streamed through the glass, the deluge abated. I needed to kick my bike over, but the space between the bookshelf and easy chairs was so narrow, the saddle was caught by the chair back and all I got was an aching toe. I sank onto the seat, pushing my fingers under my soggy sleeve to caress the old scars on my forearm. *How can a man know he'd rather be a woman? How would you explain it, Di?*

My lack of passport would have made Simon's sabbatical difficult, but Cairo rendered it impossible. He thought he was inviting me to explore a bustling marketplace, to watch the morning sun cast a ruddy glow across the pyramids. He didn't know, and I couldn't tell him, that returning to Cairo would mean diving back into the maelstrom of emotions that had engulfed me all those years ago in Mr Abdullah's clinic.

In my head, Ms Thompson, my hippy-haired social worker: *Put it behind you, Diana, Sweetie!* I wished I could tell her how much I'd tried.

I SWITCHED MY phone to voicemail, deleted all Simon's texts and emails unread. The most efficient way to bring something to a close is to operate a total reinforcement embargo, but there's a good reason the behaviourists call it extinction.

Meanwhile, the students plodded through their exams, celebrated their results or drowned their sorrows, before drifting off to backpack round India or to search for a job to ease their overdrafts, or home to sponge off their parents. Except for Megan. I hardly recognised her when she knocked on my office door one morning in early July. Instead of the trademark red duffel coat and brown suede pixie boots, she wore a summer dress patterned with strawberries and wedge-heeled espadrilles. She brought to mind a photo of my mother when she was around that age half a century before. It made me feel both protective and in awe of her, as if she were a refugee from a generation where women studied nothing more complex than the *Bero Book of Home Baking*.

She spread out her skirt as she took her seat. "You probably heard, Dr Dodsworth, I passed all my exams."

"Yes, congratulations!"

The girl grinned. She seemed much freer without her heavy coat and boots. "But I've got some coursework to complete before I can go on to the third year in September. The essays won't be a problem but I've been talking to Professor Bradshaw about the labs I've missed. He said that if I, like, interviewed my dad that could count for one of them," Megan steepled her hands and sat back, waiting.

Max Neasden would never have let her get away with interviewing her father, but if Garth was willing to sanction it, that was his business. "So Professor Bradshaw's going to supervise you?"

Megan laughed. "No offence to the prof but you're the expert on decision-making!"

I could imagine him using those very words; it was a clever way of dumping extra work on me. This seemed a huge deviation from the methodological rigour of the two-jars procedure we'd originally discussed. "What about your project?"

"Thing is, Dr Dodsworth, like I explained, I wasn't as interested as I thought I was, and I'd never find enough people in my dad's position to do an experiment, so I thought, I'd do a different research project …"

"So you're giving up on the two-jars method?" The quiver in my voice surprised me. I must have been more invested in Megan breathing new life into my PhD than I'd realised.

Engulfed by my disappointment, I caught only the end of Megan's speech: "So Professor Bradshaw thought it best if you approved the questions beforehand, and sat in on the interview, to stop it degenerating into a father-daughter chat."

Dads and their adolescent daughters; fresh and eager in her bright summer dress, I couldn't turn her down. Although an inappropriate assignment, it would account for only a small percentage of her marks. So what if Garth expected me to supervise outside my main interests and expertise, I didn't have much else to occupy me over the summer.

It wasn't until Megan had left the room, and I'd sat down at the computer to delete another email from Simon, that I realised we'd both been so cautious, we hadn't yet named the exact nature of her dad's decision. But the emptiness she left me with had nothing to do with that. I was thinking about my own dad and how we'd never had a relationship in which I might question *his* decisions. I'd been too conscious of how much of a disappointment I was to him.

MY MOTHER HAD been nagging my dad for weeks to take me on one of his regular Sunday hikes. I'd just started at the comprehensive and was lonely without Geraldine, hanging around the house at weekends and getting under Mum's feet. My father, grumpy at first, complained I hadn't the right shoes for rambling and made no attempt to hide the fact that he laid the blame on my mother. But as the bus began to climb through rugged moorland, his mood lightened. "Look out for a pub on your right. The Robin Hood. That's our stop."

We got down from the bus and crossed the road, my dad jiggling his canvas haversack to sit more comfortably on his shoulders. He reached out to steady me as I clambered over the stile. The path cut through the dried-out bracken like a parting through hair. Swinging my arms, I marched behind my dad up the gentle slope towards the spinney.

He pointed out the ash and the spindly silver birch, its bark like alligator skin. I jumped when a squirrel scampered across the path and up a tree to safety. "Listen!" It was the tap tap tap of a woodpecker but, though we strained our eyes and necks to scan the treetops, it remained elusive. Somehow, it didn't matter; the shared not-seeing was enough.

I pressed further into the woods for a closer look at some bracken fungus clinging to the trunk of a dead tree like shelves made of scallops. I kicked at the sludge of fallen leaves with my wellies. At last I understood what drove him to come out here week after week: this was so much better than church. "Do you think we might find one of those bright red ones with spots on, like a toadstool in a story book?"

I thought he might call me a sissy, but he stroked his

chin. "I know the type you mean, pillar-box red with pale yellow spots, what are they called? Something foreign …"

"I should've brought my *I-Spy Fungi.*"

"Fly agaric, that's the name."

"How did you know that?"

My dad shrugged. "You pick up things."

We walked on. I was tempted to take his hand but I knew he wouldn't stand for that. "Do you know the story of *Romeo and Juliet*?"

"Load of rubbish," said my dad.

I swallowed hard. "What was your favourite book when you were my age?"

"I'd generally had enough of books by the time I'd done my schoolwork."

"Wasn't there anything? *Robinson Crusoe*? *The Swiss Family Robinson*?"

"Storybooks? Storybooks were for girls."

I caught a flash of orange through the trees ahead. I thought of Geraldine but the colour was too low down and too abundant to be another rambler's hair. "What about Biggles?" My brother liked Biggles, the gallant pilot who knew no fear.

"That's it, Biggles. One of them would've been my favourite."

I stopped short. "What's that?" The orange blur transformed itself into a procession of four-legged monsters descending through the thicket.

"I remembered the fly agaric but I'm no expert on cows."

"They've got horns. Like Vikings."

"They look like Highland cattle but, if they are, they're a long way from home." Seeing me faltering, my dad flipped from jovial uncle to the stern patriarch he was at home. "Come on! They'll not harm you. They're more scared of you than you are of them."

The cattle had assembled on the path, waiting. "I'm not going past them cows."

My dad grabbed me by the arm and dragged me forward. "Don't be such a softy."

With a deep lowing, reminiscent of the sound my grandad made when constipated, the orderly gathering broke apart. Cows galloped into the fields; others trooped back into the woods; the rest trotted up the path towards us. I escaped my father's grip and stumbled away to park myself behind a rock.

"Stop this nonsense! I said they wouldn't hurt you." He beckoned to me to join him.

Whimpering, I rose to my feet, caught between the wild beasts and my father's wrath.

The cattle had settled back into a steady walk, although one over-eager or sexually confused youngster was mounting one of her siblings. Ahead of the cattle, a woman in a green anorak ambled towards us.

"We can't sit here all day." Dad prodded me forward.

The woman drew level with us, smiling broadly. "Beautiful morning!"

My dad smiled back through gritted teeth. "Isn't it?"

A clunky walkie-talkie crackled from a belt around her waist. "Everything okay?" I noticed the National Park insignia embroidered on her anorak.

"We're fine, thanks."

The ranger cocked her head at the cattle. A few stragglers were still milling about on the footpath, like gossips outside church on a Sunday morning. She spoke directly to me: "They're quite intimidating with those horns, aren't they? I was petrified when I first came across them."

"But you walked right through."

"They're as soft as kittens," said the ranger. "More frightened of you than you are of them."

"That's what I said," said my dad.

"Why don't we walk past together?" said the ranger. "When you've done it once, you'll feel more confident for next time." She offered me her arm as if to lead me onto the dance-floor. "Shall we?"

Walking ahead of my father, the ranger told me about the national park. The cattle parted like the Dead Sea for the Israelites.

"See," said my dad, "nothing to it."

When both ranger and cows had departed, I did feel rather foolish and wondered how I'd recover my dad's good mood. If we heard another woodpecker or spotted a squirrel or stumbled across the shiny red dome of a fly agaric the day would not be completely ruined. I tried to remember what else he'd said we might see. "How far is it to the plague graves?"

My dad turned away as if I hadn't spoken. Checking the shoulder straps of his haversack, he strode off, and I had no choice but to follow. We marched for mile after mile, up hills and down again, through woodland and moorland, on mud and rocks and sheep-cropped grass. He didn't pause to help me over the stiles. He didn't reach into his haversack and offer me a sandwich or a drink of squash. He didn't ask if I wanted to rest and admire the view.

I was tired and hungry and, when I stopped to pull off my wellies and smooth out the wrinkles in my socks, I had blisters on both heels and one on my little toe, fiery cushions of pulsing pain. I considered them my penance for spoiling the outing. Perhaps this was why Geraldine preferred her other friends. I was a scaredy-cat.

I ran to catch up, my feet throbbing with every step. When I got to the top of the incline, there was no sign of my dad. There were other ramblers, but I was too ashamed to ask for help.

I hadn't any money for bus fare, and it would be too far to walk home before nightfall even if my feet were up to it. Would I die out here on the moors?

Through misty eyes, I scoped the terrain as far as the horizon in every direction. I stopped and looked again, and there was my dad, perched on a rock not a hundred yards from where I stood, drinking from the squat plastic cup of a thermos. He looked my way, but he didn't wave or beckon me across. I limped through the heather to join him, my ankles twisting on the uneven ground. The wind whistled around my ears when I sank onto the rock beside him. My dad said nothing, but he poured me some hot, sweet tea. We stayed there for the time it took me to eat two jam sandwiches, not speaking, and then he hoisted the haversack onto his shoulders and we marched back the way we had come.

Chapter 11

I WAS FOURTEEN when Patricia went to London to train as a nurse. I don't know who was copying who, but Geraldine's sister, Deirdre, happened to get a place at the Whittington at the same time.

Patricia phoned home every Sunday, but she rarely had occasion to speak to me. Yet I gained a sense of the riotous times to be had in the nurses' home from the stories Geraldine relayed to her wide-eyed friends in the school canteen, stories she took care to ensure I had ample opportunity to overhear.

One lunchtime, when I was toying with my mince and dumplings alone at a table set for four, Geraldine plonked down her tray opposite mine. I looked around for her cronies, but they were at the other side of the dining hall fluttering their eyelashes at Richard Mansfield. I'd just seen him get a hard-on at the serving hatch when the new dinner lady had offered him extra gravy, and was already feeling queasy.

Geraldine came straight to the point: "How do you fancy a weekend in London?"

I'd never been farther south than Derby, but I'd read

about the British Museum and the National Gallery in an encyclopaedia and I couldn't help getting a little excited at the thought of wandering through the halls with Geraldine. But it wouldn't be like that. "I don't."

"Don't you want to see your sister?"

"She'll be home for Christmas."

"Don't you want to see the changing of the guards at Buckingham Palace? Those sexy soldiers in their deerskin hats."

I thought again of Richard Mansfield, the abrupt and uncontrollable bulge in his crotch, and blushed. "Bearskin. And the answer's no."

Geraldine picked up her knife and fork and began to eat, dainty ladylike mouthfuls. "What happened to you? You used to be groovy. Up for adventure."

I shrugged. No-one at school was aware of my visits to the infirmary, and I was determined to keep it that way. "Anyway," I said, "why are you asking me? If you want to visit your sister, why not just go?"

"My dad won't let me go down there on my own."

Across the room, Richard Mansfield looked somewhat battered by the attentions of three chattering girls. "What about your *friends*? Don't tell me they've dropped you." I made it sound contemptuous, but if the girls had deserted her, Geraldine might have room again for me.

"Of course they haven't, dickhead. But *they* don't have anywhere to stay." Geraldine set down her knife and fork with a sigh. "Don't you see? They're only allowed one overnight guest at that nurses' home and, even then, it's a tight squeeze in your sleeping bag on the floor. You'd stay in

Patricia's room and I'd stay in Deirdre's, and then we'd all meet up to see the sights."

"How would we pay for it? London's awfully pricey."

Geraldine laughed: "You sound like your mother! Don't worry, I'm not planning on tea at the Ritz. Anyway, you must have a fair bit saved up from your paper round. And if you're short, I wouldn't mind helping you out. The pay's not bad stacking shelves at the Co-op."

Being a few months older, Geraldine had had a part-time job for some time. Hers was a proper grown-up job, even if she did have to fit it around school. I didn't know what to make of her offer to share her earnings with me. Clearly she had her heart set on this trip, but was she using me to get to London or was London the device to rekindle our friendship?

Tossing her russet curls, she turned towards the table with her three friends. "I heard Richard Mansfield's sister was applying to the Whittington, but what use is that to me? They don't let *boys* stay at the nurses' home." Geraldine leant in across the table. I could smell the institutional mince on her breath. "It would be a chance for us to glam up and try and pass for eighteen. Put on our glad rags and a bit of makeup. Like when we were kids, except this would be for real."

A wave of cramp passed through my belly. It would be like that trip to Lourdes: the outcome beyond my control. "You're forgetting one thing," I said. "My dad would never let me go down London with you."

"You're right," said Geraldine. "But if we could find a way, maybe make him think you were going with somebody else, would you do it?"

It would never work. It wasn't only a matter of convincing my parents; Patricia also had to sign up to the plan. "Sure."

My dad would flay me alive if he got an inkling of what we were plotting. But if it earned me one moment of Geraldine's approval, it was a risk I would willingly take.

———

OUTSIDE THE SKINNER building was a pair of raised flowerbeds where students huddled between lectures, fertilising the petunias with cigarette ash. With the students away, I hadn't expected to see anyone sitting there when the squeezebox doors released me into the sharp sunlight for a belated lunch break. I couldn't march past pretending not to have noticed the man perched on the redbrick wall, gazing nonchalantly out towards the small car park. As any student of perception will testify, it's the unexpected that grabs our attention.

Simon held up a brown paper carrier: "Lunch?"

"You've been camped here on the off-chance? How long have you been waiting?"

Simon pushed back the cuff of his crisp white shirt to check his watch. "An hour? An hour and a half?"

"What if I wasn't taking a lunch break? What if I wasn't even in today?"

"Well, I did send you an email, although I wasn't counting on you reading it."

"But how long were you going to wait? Haven't you got work to do?"

"Plenty. But I reckoned this was more important." Simon peered into the bag, sniffing at the contents. "Still, if I'd known you'd be so long I'd have brought an ice pack."

Try as I might, I couldn't help smiling. "You're impossible."

"I think you'll find, Dr Dodsworth, that *you* are the impossible one in this relationship." Simon jumped down from the wall. "Leazes Park? It's a great day for a picnic."

This relationship, he'd said. Was he especially generous or just desperate?

He didn't take my hand on the walk to the park. Nor did he demand an explanation for my failure to return his calls and texts and emails. He filled the space with neutral subjects: the welcome summer sunshine; Giles's pathetic attempts to toilet-train his daughter's new puppy.

We found a bench in dappled shade across the footpath from the lake. As soon as Simon unwrapped the sandwiches a group of mallards emerged from the shrubbery and began pecking at the worn grass.

We ate in silence, watching a boat thread along the fringe of the lake, sending ripples up the cobbled shoreline. One of the oars squeaked against the rowlock like a dodgy wheel on a supermarket trolley.

"I'm sorry this is so hard for you, Di."

"Oh, no, it's lovely."

"I think you know what I mean."

I swept imaginary crumbs from my lap. The ducks zoomed in, a scrum of bobbing tail-feathers and stabbing beaks.

"Tell me honestly. If you truly want to end the

relationship, I'll stop hounding you. But I've got to hear it from the horse's mouth."

I put down my half-eaten stottie on the seat beside me, my throat too tight to swallow another bite.

Simon waited. I could ignore his calls and emails. I could've got up and walked away. But I couldn't bring myself to lie.

"I'm so glad." When Simon pulled me close, he was shaking. We contorted our upper bodies around each other, arms entangled and the remains of our lunch on the bench between us until the squawking of the mallards spirited us apart.

The female led a troop of males across the asphalt footpath towards the water. Brown and dowdy, she moved in stark contrast to the males, splendidly coiffed with iridescent green shot with Bishop's purple. "I could never believe it when I was a kid," I said. "How, in the animal kingdom, it's the males that get to strut about in their finery."

Simon had kept hold of my hand. Now he pressed it to his lips. "Diana Dodsworth, you are amazing. Promise me you'll never change!"

The ducks launched themselves onto the lake. "What did I say?"

"I don't know. I just love the way you're you. Why do you think I've been sitting outside your department like a lovesick Romeo?" Simon squeezed my hand. "Sometimes I wish I'd never applied for that sabbatical."

It hit me how selfish I'd been. "Don't say that. Think of the pyramids. The Khan el Khalili. Think of finishing your book."

"All the people I'm going to miss."

"We'll still be here when you get back." Six months would whizz by if I held this moment in mind.

"I wish you could come out."

"If only."

"I've been racking my brains for what stops you. Is it the place? But you told me you were happy in Cairo. Is it me? Too much commitment too soon? But you could do your own thing. You wouldn't have to stay at my apartment if you didn't want to. It could be as close or casual as seeing each other here."

I looked at the ducks gliding across the water. I wished he would stop, but Simon was entitled to an explanation. I couldn't think of one that wouldn't blow us apart.

"Venus said you were scared of flying, is that it?"

"After a fashion."

"Well, let's do something about it! How about a weekend in Paris for your birthday? Something special before I leave *and* a chance to conquer your fear."

"It's really sweet of you, Simon, but I can't."

"I would like to do *something* for your birthday. If you'll let me."

"I told you before. I don't like a big fuss."

"Can I spend the day with you if I promise not to make a fuss?"

"Oh Simon!"

"Is that a yes or a no?"

The man was far better than I deserved. "There's nothing I'd like better."

"So we'll be doing the weekly shop with tinned tomato soup for dinner and toasting you with a cup of tea?"

"Something like that."

"But what would you really like to do? What would be a little bit special but not too much fuss?"

Nobody had ever taken this much trouble. Venus may have wanted to treat me in the past, but she had too many ideas of her own. For his sake, as much as mine, I wanted to come up with something. "What I really fancy, would be a day at the coast. A gentle stroll along the beach, a paddle in the shallows. Watching the birds. A pint at the pub. Fish and chips in the rain."

Simon gazed up at the cloudless sky. "Can't guarantee the rain, but I could manage the rest of it."

THINGS HAD PANNED out so much better than I could have imagined. Not only had he given me back *my boyfriend*, Simon had accepted that visiting him in Cairo was out of the question. He didn't demand an explanation; he trusted that my reasons were sound. To top it all, for the first time in years, I looked forward to my birthday.

Now I treasured his calls and texts, evidence he had me in mind. Our time together was precious and limited: Simon was busy with arrangements for going away and, as the school holidays approached, increasing commitments to his children. Confirmed of the strength of his feelings for me, I felt ashamed of my jealousy towards Harriet and Oscar.

I could have kicked myself for the time I'd squandered sulking. Yet if Simon could forgive me, I could surely forgive myself. Simon hadn't said he loved me; I'd probably have freaked out if he had. Yet I couldn't think of a better word for the bond between us. I'd been seeking it my whole life.

Basking in his warmth and generosity of spirit, I brimmed with goodwill, looking for ways of dispensing the surplus. I would coach Ellie in keepy-uppy. I would help Megan reconcile herself to her father's sexuality.

So when, a week or so later, I brought up my inbox to find an email from Megan with *draft interview schedule* in the subject line, I relished the opportunity to be of service. I made a cup of coffee and set the phone to voicemail so that I could give her effort my full attention.

I opened the attachment, skimmed the introductory paragraph on confidentiality and scrolled down to question one. *When you were a boy, did you like to dress up and play with dolls?* Oh Megan! Were you asleep during the lecture on stereotypes?

I took a deep breath. My role was not to judge but to nurture the necessary skills. On to question two. *When did you discover you were a woman trapped in a man's body?*

I sprang from my seat. Coffee lapped over the keyboard and my mug fell to the floor.

What had Garth been thinking? A student interviewing her father was contrary to everything we taught. I'd have to withdraw from the project. Tell the prof that in my professional opinion it required a complete rethink.

HIS SECRETARY INFORMED me Garth was away on annual leave. I asked for an appointment on the Monday he got back.

Val sniffed. "Are you sure it's urgent, Dr Dodsworth?

Professor Bradshaw will have a lot to catch up on that week."

I told her it was extremely urgent, then wondered, as I slammed down the phone, whether my haste would render him less sympathetic to my cause. Val had tried to warn me off: secretaries had a nose for organisational politics. What right had a junior lecturer to nobble the head of department immediately on his return from leave?

I printed off Megan's draft interview schedule and shoved it in my backpack, hoping I'd bump into someone around the department who'd help me sharpen up my argument before confronting Garth. Fat chance of that: with the boss away the place was like a cemetery.

IT WAS A Friday, with only the weekend between me and my meeting with Garth Bradshaw, when I came across Giles and Mohammed tucking in to fish and chips in the senior common room. They weren't exactly the supervisors I'd been looking for, but I was running out of options.

"*How can you be sure you're making the right decision? What happens if you change your mind? Why do you need to have such radical surgery when you could just go about dressed as a woman?*" Mohammed looked philosophical. "These are good questions, Di."

I took the papers from him. There were greasy fingerprints around the edges. "Maybe, but they're addressed to her father."

Giles's nose was sunburnt, flakes of skin peeling away around the nostrils. "I told you it would make a good project for one of your students. I'd love to be a fly on the wall."

"Well, I can't let it happen. The girl's emotionally involved."

"That's a bad thing?" asked Giles.

I stuffed the questionnaire back into my rucksack.

"You're right," said Mohammed. "It wouldn't be ethical to interview a colleague."

I followed his gaze to the counter where Dr Marlow was paying for a take-away sandwich. Venus hovered beside her, as if waiting to resume a conversation.

I shook my head. "You think *that's* my student's dad?"

"Must be," said Giles. "How many transsexuals can one university contain?"

Megan hadn't mentioned where her father worked. Yet if Dr Marlow *were* her proposed interviewee, I had the perfect get-out card. As Mohammed said, it would be unethical to pry into such a sensitive area with a colleague.

Dr Marlow left the common room and Venus strolled over, balancing a bowl of salad on a tray. "Susan was asking me where I got these earrings."

Of course, we all turned to look at the ornaments dangling from her earlobes, the metallic blue helix things I'd failed to compliment her on at her birthday dinner. A stab of anger took me back to that first time we'd seen Dr Marlow. "So the female impersonator has a name, has she?"

"Oh, Di," said Venus. "Like it or not, we've got to accept her as she is."

"You didn't seem to think so before."

Venus looked startled, as if she'd wiped her previous frivolity from her memory bank.

Giles scratched his peeling nose. "Di's supervising her daughter's project. Wants to analyse the process of coming to the decision."

"That's not her. Different surname." Yet I couldn't escape the fact that, while Megan had prattled on about *my dad*, she'd made it clear he was her stepdad.

"I hope it *is* the same one," said Venus. "Susan's been a tad concerned about her daughter. She could do with a sympathetic ear."

How had Venus swung so quickly from ridicule to confidante? Then I remembered how, when we were students, she sought out eccentrics the way others might chase the latest fashions. Even when she'd first collared me, that Sunday night in the halls of residence, it had been my quirkiness that had attracted her attention. "At least I wouldn't treat her like one of your maths puzzles."

Venus merely laughed and changed the subject: "By the bye, Di, has Simon made arrangements for your birthday already?" She turned to Giles and Mohammed: "The one year we're going to be around at the end of August and my best friend has a prior engagement."

I pictured a couple hand in hand on a quiet beach, castle ruins silhouetted against the sky. "I'm sure we could juggle things around so I could see you as well ..."

Venus touched my hand. "Oh, Di, you goose! Of course you don't want hangers on at this stage of your relationship. Especially not when he's about to go abroad."

———

ON MY FIRST Sunday night at university, I was en route

from the bathroom to my study-bedroom in the student halls, clutching a damp towel and my quilted wash-bag to my chest like a shield. My gaze levelled at my fluffy primrose slippers peeping out from under the hem of my stripy galabeyah as I shuffled along the corridor, I didn't notice the other girl until I'd almost bashed into her: tall, with a cascade of ebony hair and skin the colour of butterscotch.

I made to move on, but the girl blocked my path, looking down her long nose at me from beneath heavy eyebrows: "You do realise that's a man's galabeyah you're wearing?" Her voice was as haughty as the girls' at Dorothea Beale, with an exotic lilt that brought to mind the rhythms of Cairo.

No doubt I blushed. At boarding school I'd kept it hidden in my trunk. But university promised another chance and, besides, who was going to be able to tell the difference between a traditional Arab shift and an ordinary nightgown? Who, apart from this arrogant girl who was scrutinising me like I was an exhibit in the Egyptian Museum?

I glanced down at the loose cotton gown I'd picked out with my dad at the Khan el Khalili three years before. "That's what I like about it," I told the girl. "A dress that's meant for a man."

A wide smile softened her features. "Fair enough, although I prefer a dash of frill myself." It was only then that I recognised her floor-length lilac robe as another galabeyah, trimmed with lace around the neckline, with pearl buttons where mine fastened with bobbles of cord. "I'm Venus Najibullah, by the way. Come back to my room and I'll make you a coffee and you can tell me how an English girl came by such a thing already."

Chapter 12

GARTH'S SMILE BARED his teeth, tombstone white against his suntan: "And you have a problem with that, Di?"

I jiggled my shoulder blades against the leather chair back, trying and failing to find some purchase that would enable me to sit with my eyes on a level with his: "It's not very objective, is it, a student interviewing her father?"

"I'm sure you can signpost her to the limitations in the discussion section of the report."

"Of course, but it's not only that. I have reason to believe Megan's father is a member of staff."

"And?"

"We might come across each other outside the interview situation."

"You'd struggle to maintain the professional boundary?"

"No!" The more I opened my mouth, the more my confidence leached out of me. My credibility with it. I wiped my sweaty palms on my trousers. "You must admit, the situation is somewhat delicate. The nature of the decision she wants to investigate."

Garth laced his fingers as he sat back in his chair. He

knew that I knew he was busy, but he contrived to look as if he could sit and listen to my concerns all day. He even turned down the volume: "You have issues with transgender people, Dr Dodsworth?"

A rash of blood set my face aflame. "Of course not!"

Garth maintained his pose, despite the leather and aluminium contraption that seemed designed to prevent it. Cool, unhurried, content for me to find my own way into his trap. "How did you find the *Equality and Diversity* workshop?" He must have perfected the stance at some *How to Intimidate Your Staff without Falling Foul of the Bullying and Harassment Policy* training for smug young managers.

Ignoring the invitation to admit to unmet objectives, I summoned up the dregs of my fighting spirit: "I'm sorry, but in my professional judgement the project is unethical for all kinds of reasons. But the bottom line is that the single-case qualitative interview with an adult subject is outside my expertise."

"Come on, Di, let's keep a sense of perspective." Garth leant forward, only a beat away from giving me a friendly chuck on the arm. "Remember this is only a small second-year assignment, the equivalent of a single lab experiment, to enable a gifted student to proceed to the third year. It may be slightly outside your normal remit but, as we agreed in your appraisal, you've been getting a little rusty and need to spread your wings. Honestly, Di, I thought you'd jump at the chance." Now he looked genuinely baffled, disappointed even. "If you definitely think it's beyond your abilities, I'll take it off you, but I would expect any of my staff to be capable of tackling it with their eyes closed and one arm tied behind their backs." He glanced at his desk and the clock on the wall above it. "And now, Dr Dodsworth, if there's nothing else, I do have over a hundred emails to attend to before a meeting of the Scrutiny Subcommittee this afternoon."

I'd lost. Yet until I was evicted from the room I had to keep trying. "Couldn't she make up some data and write up a lab report based on that?"

Silence flooded the space between us, thick with accusation and shame. It struck me then, in the ache deep in my belly, that Garth knew about the charges against Colin Carmichael. Perhaps he'd known all along.

After what seemed like an age, he rose to his feet. Shakily, I followed. Garth didn't see me as an innocent, misguided in her choice of PhD supervisor. He saw me as potentially culpable, Colin's as yet unconvicted partner-in-crime. Someone to be watched closely. Someone who might be tempted to fiddle her results.

Garth held the door open: "I think it's best if we forget this conversation, don't you agree?"

EVER SINCE MISS Bamford in the reception class, all our teachers had been women. So when, in our final year of Juniors, we sat facing *Mr* Worrall, we were unsure what to make of him and his revolutionary ideas.

Mr Worrall was on a mission to introduce ten-year-olds to democracy. It began gently enough, with a vote to select the novel he would read to us in the half hour before home time. When that didn't result in all-out war, he outlined his plan to extend pupil participation to other areas. If a child could get ten signatures on a petition, the motion would be put to a ballot of the whole class, and Mr Worrall would abide by the outcome. Thus he switched to using coloured chalk on the blackboard. Brought forward morning break to ten o'clock. Moved it back to half-past, smiling the whole time.

We looked forward to school like we looked forward to Christmas. At break time, girls set aside their skipping ropes and boys their footballs to chat about what we might do with this strange new power. Geraldine and I were as enthralled as the rest. It couldn't last.

The final petition was different from the start. There was no crayonned border of fish or flowers. It didn't float like innocence from one desk to the next. This petition, crumpled and smudged, was passed furtively round the classroom. Children accepted it with lowered eyes, shielding it with their bodies, before daring to read. They might blanch or laugh or hide it in their desks but, in the end, they added their names to the list.

Yet whenever the petition seemed to be heading towards the double desk where Geraldine and I sat at the back of the class, it veered away. My classmates seemed not to see my outstretched arm and eager expression. They giggled, they squirmed, they nodded at Geraldine, and turned their backs on me.

The petition had been signed by almost everyone, when Mr Worrall swooped. "You. Can. Not. Have. A. Petition. Against. A. Person. Not only is it illogical but it's cruel and mean. Did you think you could eliminate one of your classmates? What are you? Nazis?"

Our artwork looked down from the wall in shame. Mr Worrall paced between our desks, cheeks puffed out like an inflated crisp packet, waving the sheet of foolscap above his head. He made me think of a plate in our classroom illustrated Bible, God disappointed with his creation and preparing to send the flood. Yet his gaze seemed to soften when it fell on me, and that was the most frightening thing of all.

I NEVER FOUND out how much Geraldine knew about the content of that petition and, if she did, whether she were complicit in its genesis or merely an unresponsive bystander.

I'd been gullible as a child; perhaps, as a middle-aged woman, I still was. I'd gone to Garth assuming that, once I outlined my argument, he'd be sympathetic to my point of view. *Of course, Di, you're quite right. I'm sorry I asked.* After my appraisal, I'd been ashamed I'd ever been suspicious of his management style. But this latest episode was blatant bullying.

I skimmed through the university grievance procedure on the intranet, only because I was so wound up after our conversation I couldn't bring myself to do anything else. It wasn't worth fighting; I had too much to lose and Professor Bradshaw knew it. I'd have to grit my teeth while a mixed-up student quizzed her equally mixed-up father about the most complex decision of his life, and then help her to shape the fiasco into a scientific report.

Nevertheless, I was determined not to let the incident sully my last few weeks with Simon. I'd have a relaxing summer; I'd give our relationship everything I had.

And yet I'd been a fool to trust Geraldine, a fool to trust Garth Bradshaw. Was I a fool to put my faith in Simon? He'd been so generous, right from that first day at Venus's party when he deflected the conversation from my reckless choice of bedtime story onto the cosseting of twenty-first-century youth. He'd shown remarkable patience with my insecurities, never making me feel like a freak. There'd been passion in his kisses but, after my confession on the Millennium Bridge, he'd never pushed for more. He'd shrugged off the scars on my arm, my childish cold-shouldering when his sabbatical was finally confirmed. I didn't deserve such kindness. Perhaps Simon was too good to be true.

GERALDINE FIZZED WITH excitement at the prospect of going up to secondary school. I was less sanguine. The boys boasted of gruesome initiation ceremonies, eagerly anticipating having their heads pushed down the toilet on the first day. It might have been a myth to scare the new kids, but how could I tell? Patricia, who'd been at the comprehensive three whole years, rarely spoke to me except to threaten me with a Chinese burn if I nabbed her bubble bath. Geraldine, more worldly than me, might have had the answer, but I didn't dare raise anything contentious after that petition.

It wasn't only the thought of the new school that drove me to my first experience of self-harm. Other rumours blew around the playground. If you were a girl, you were destined to get dreadful stomach cramps, severe enough to lead to bleeding between your legs and you'd have to go around with a mini-nappy in your knickers. If you were a boy, you were fated to get odd sensations in your cock, twitching and swelling till it forced its way out of your underpants. You'd start to dream of women's breasts and a liquid, thick like sour milk, would leave a smelly white patch on the sheets that told your mother you'd been thinking dirty. Boy or girl, the indignity was unavoidable, as sure as the school bus and black woollen blazers with an embroidered badge on the breast pocket.

The female way seemed marginally preferable. All that blood and pain could be a secret wound, like a saint's stigmata. I found where Patricia hid her Dr Whites in the airing cupboard and made my plan.

It was a Sunday afternoon. My dad was out hiking, Patricia doing her homework at her boyfriend's, Trevor playing at being guerrillas with his mates, and my mother downstairs watching an Ealing comedy with her feet up on the pouffé. I took the bread knife from the kitchen and crept upstairs. In the bathroom, I bolted the door and changed into clean pyjamas, the closest I had to a surgical gown. I tore open a fresh packet of Dr Whites and laid them beside the knife. I removed my pyjama bottoms and draped them over the side of the bath.

The ache matched all the rumours about period pain. The blood confirmed all reports about the mess. The blood kept flowing, no matter how many sanitary towels I used to mop it up.

Chapter 13

A UGUST. BLUE SKIES and sun as bright as in Cairo. Colleagues in shorts and sleeveless dresses joking that the work would be almost pleasant if it were always like this, freed from the tedium of tutorials and lectures.

Simon phoned from Manchester where he'd taken his kids to visit his parents. Would a boat ride to watch the seals at the Farne Islands be too special for my birthday? I told him I could cope, as long as he wasn't seasick.

They'd gone to some museum with a renowned collection of Egyptian sarcophagi. Oscar had been enthralled. "Kids are fascinated with death, aren't they? Maybe because they don't know enough about it."

"He'll have a whale of a time in Cairo," I said.

"Yeah." He sounded wistful.

"Hey," I said, "it's going to be okay. You're making the right decision."

"Well, my mum and dad don't think so. They think it's selfish to go gadding off when the kids still need me."

I remembered what he'd said about the corner shop, his parents leaving him to his own devices. I wondered if they were dumping their own guilt onto him, but didn't want to say so in case he thought I was psychologising. "You're the last person I'd call selfish. They'll be fine."

Simon sighed. "I don't know what's the matter with me. Nerves, I suppose; nerves and the fact that I always get a bit maudlin when I visit my parents. Anyway, not long now till your birthday. Excited?"

"I'm more excited about seeing you." I'd never dared be so open with him. But I was counting the days till I'd see him again. "I miss you."

"I'm glad to hear it. I miss you too."

I could almost feel my heart melting, and not only from the summer heat. It had never occurred to me, not properly, that Simon might need me as much as I needed him. For one brief moment, all the obstacles could be magicked away and I *would* accompany him to Cairo. We'd stroll hand in hand through the Egyptian Museum and, regardless of whether or not the complex was open at that time, watch the sun rise at Giza. I'd teach him to bargain in the Khan el Khalili and I wouldn't leave him until Cairo felt like a second home.

MY INTRODUCTION TO Cairo came through a friend of Patricia's at the nursing home at the Whittington. Suma was a final year student in the room next door. Recalling our childhood obsession with Tutankhamen, Geraldine and I were entranced by the notion of a twentieth-century Egyptian, proof that the line hadn't died out with the Pharaohs. With her ebony hair and regal bearing, her sharp nose and skin like a perpetual suntan, we both agreed she was the most glamorous creature we'd ever seen: Elizabeth Taylor plays Cleopatra.

Suma was kind, too. On the second morning when Geraldine was sleeping off her hangover and Patricia doing a shift on the wards, she invited me into her room to show me some photos from home. "You really live there? Right next door to the pyramids?"

"Not quite next door. I take a bus from near my house only."

"It must be beautiful."

"It is. Beautiful but also very dirty." She pronounced *also* as if the first syllable were *oh* instead of *all*. I tried to keep hold of the sound in my mind. "London is much cleaner." She took down a heavy tome from the shelf above her desk. "There's something here might surprise you." She flicked through the pages of dense text interspersed with black and white photographs, pausing now and then before moving on.

"Urgh, what was that?" I said.

"Only gangrene." Suma continued turning the pages. She stopped at 371. "Take it next door if you please. You can read it through at your leisure."

In a daze, I hefted the book back to Patricia's room. This was by far the weirdest thing I'd encountered all weekend. I lay on the bed, reading what it said, and reading it again.

I kept an eye on the time. I didn't want my sister to catch me reading a medical book. With half an hour of her shift still to go, I got up to return the book.

I don't know why I didn't think to knock. Maybe it was

because I felt so accepted in the nurses' home, I didn't see the need. But I regretted it when I realised Suma wasn't alone.

The two girls jumped apart the moment I pushed through the door. But not before I'd registered their lips clamped together, Geraldine's hand cradling Suma's neck.

"Oh, hi there," said Geraldine. "Do you want to grab something to eat before we go for the train?"

I WAS OVER at Venus's place in Fenham when Simon rang to say he couldn't see me on my birthday after all. I'd cycled over there on a whim after work, intending to fulfil my promise of teaching Ellie keepy-uppy. As it turned out, she'd moved on to other things since the end of the football season. The entire back lawn was capped by a trampoline, and Venus and I had to squeeze into the tiny patio by the back door while Ellie and Josh and a couple of their friends bounced and squealed nearby. The retro deckchairs, with a bolt of striped canvas hung over wooden frames, were nearly as challenging as Garth Bradshaw's office chairs although, with the early evening sun on my face and a glass of Pimms in my hand, I hardly cared.

When my phone began to chirrup in my bag it took a while to register above the screams of the children and my holiday frame of mind. I still wasn't fully accustomed to the ring of my mobile; until Simon came on the scene, I'd rarely bothered to switch it on.

When his name flashed on the screen, I got up and sauntered around to the side of the house, as much to avoid exposing my inner lovebird to Venus as to escape the noise. The path was in shadow and, after the sparkling heat of the back garden, I shivered.

Simon brimmed with apologies. I think I managed to hold myself together enough not to add to his woes. "It's hardly your fault Caroline's been whisked into hospital. Of course the kids have to take priority. It's not a problem, honestly. It's not as if we had anything booked."

"I can't believe the timing. It's almost as if she was doing it to spite me. *Listen up, Appendix, my ex has something special arranged this week, let's see if we can put the kibosh on it.*"

I laughed, although I couldn't quite tell if he'd intended the joke or the stress was making him paranoid. "You've got to focus on the kids right now. I'll see you when things are more settled."

"Thanks, Di. Hopefully it won't be too long. It's in and out with keyhole surgery."

Under my long-sleeved linen shirt, the scars on my forearm were itching to be scratched. The thought of surgery of any kind made me uneasy, regardless how miniscule the snip. We wound up the call and I stumbled back into the sunshine. I thought I'd managed to compose my face, if not my feelings, but when Venus saw me she sprang from her seat and hugged me. When she stepped back, her eyes were glistening: "Get that drink down you and you can tell Auntie Venus all about it. If that man has been misbehaving he'll have me to answer to."

WORK ALWAYS FELT more civilised over the summer, as if

the longer days and mild weather slowed the pace to a more human scale. A new email popping into my inbox, rather than seeming like another stalk of straw that would eventually snap the proverbial camel's spine, now served to punctuate the main business of the day almost as smoothly as a cup of coffee with colleagues. It took me back to the early days of networked desktop computers when a new message spelt, not intrusion, but connectedness.

The downside was that, unless the computer had been set up to send out an out-of-office reply, unwelcome approaches were difficult to ignore. With no more than four or five new messages a day, it was pointless to pretend the awkward one lay buried under layers of more urgent entreaties. So when I saw the name Dr Susan Marlow, shortly followed by Megan Richardson, I braced myself to read on.

How presumptuous of Dr Marlow to leave the subject line blank, but at least she'd taken the trouble to write it as a proper letter, instead of the awful text speak that had encroached upon email etiquette.

Dear Dr Dodsworth,

Thank you so much for your support of my daughter, Megan Richardson. You'll be aware she's had a confusing and stressful time this past year, but she's a bright girl and highly committed to the science of psychology. I'm very much hoping that the interview she has planned with me will significantly help progress her studies. She is very impressed with your seminal research into decision-making and grateful for your supervisory expertise. I'm very much looking forward to meeting you. I hope you're taking advantage of the fine weather!

With all best wishes,
Susan Marlow.

Megan, in a similar way, hoped I was enjoying the summer, but her message was more to the point. Did I want to make any amendments to the interview questions? When was I free to meet? Of the half-dozen dates suggested, the first was my birthday and the last in mid-September, the day after Simon would be leaving for Cairo.

I made myself a cup of soothing green tea and dashed off a reply to Megan saying the questions were fine and the final date on her list would be perfect.

I NEVER WOULD have expected to find myself, on the morning of my birthday, in a meeting room at Newcastle airport with Venus and sixteen strangers.

Once I'd explained about his ex-wife's appendectomy, Venus had decided against lynching Simon as revenge for his abandonment. After a suitable pause, filled by getting me another Pimms and the children glasses of juice and poster-paint coloured fairy-cakes, she began to speculate about how she might occupy the somewhat larger gap left by Simon. I had anticipated something along the lines of Pizza Hut with Josh and Ellie but, as usual, Venus's ambitions were on a grander scale than mine. "Marvellous. We'll have the whole day together. In fact I know precisely the thing. Mega surprise and absolutely my treat."

There'd been no point protesting that I didn't want to put her to the trouble of making alternative arrangements for the children. No point insisting I was happy to go back to the default position of spending my birthday as just another day. Besides, I didn't want to be the kind of woman who squeezes out her old friends as soon as there's a man in her life.

That's not to say I wasn't nervous. Just as I'd struggled to choose the right thing for her birthday, I wasn't confident that Venus's idea of a treat would fill me with glee. I imagined her whisking me away to some health spa in Northumberland where I'd have to pretend to be invigorated while some white-coated hag loaded my back with hot pebbles. I hadn't been reassured when, leaving her car outside my house, she marched me round to the Metro station and bought two tickets to the airport. "You do realise I don't have a passport?"

"Of course."

So there we were, enrolled on a Fear of Flying workshop: a morning of building up our coping strategies followed by a short ride in an aircraft. In Venus's mind, it would dismantle the barrier preventing my visiting Simon in Cairo. I felt such a fraud.

"In fact it's kindergarten psychology to you," she said, as we helped ourselves to refreshments on arrival. I'd been advised to go for the herbal tea instead of coffee, caffeine being too much of a stimulant. Venus, as my 'Motivation Buddy', could have whatever she chose but, in a grand gesture of solidarity, plumped enthusiastically for the camomile. "But being fluent in the theory doesn't mean you can put it into practice."

"You're quite right." Indeed, she might apply that analysis to every area of my life. But it wasn't the fact that Venus had paid good money to have me sit through a whole morning of first-year behavioural psychology that made me feel so uncomfortable. It was that, even before they'd propped us up with coping skills, I hadn't the slightest anxiety about boarding a plane.

They kicked off with a full half-hour of relaxation. The woman who talked us through the exercise had such a mellifluous voice she could have got a job as a continuity announcer on Radio Three. Although she denied it later, I'm convinced I heard Venus snore.

I teased her about it afterwards, but the sound, a cross between a grunt and a snuffle, made a strong impression on me, opening up a place in my heart. It reminded me of listening to Ellie sleeping as a baby, that innocence and helplessness making me want to rise to better things. I'd taken · Venus for granted, as if she owed me, after our closeness as undergraduates, for daring to have a life of her own. Yet she'd always stuck by me, tried to help me have a life too. She'd taken a risk inviting Simon to her birthday party, and all I'd done was complain. She'd offered to go with me to the gay bars, and I'd snapped at her for even pondering my sexuality. Now she'd sacrificed a day she could've spent with her children to give me what she thought I needed to be with the man I loved. That she was wrong once again didn't alter the rightness of her intention. I was so lucky to have her as a friend.

"And when you're ready, open your eyes and give a nice

big yawn."

Of course the first person I saw was Venus, blinking like a child at the light. I would go through this for her sake. Commit myself to the exercises, take that flight and be released from my phantom phobia. It wouldn't make it any easier for me to go to Cairo, but I'd deal with that problem when the time came.

A COOL BREEZE billowed around us as we stepped out onto the tarmac, grabbing at the hem of Venus's cotton skirt and casting it above her bare knees. She pushed it back down with her free hand, the other clutching a buff clipboard with a scribbled list of uplifting prompts she could reel off to me should I lose my nerve.

Not a hundred yards from the airport building, our plane waited, the propeller churning the air in front of its nose. A stewardess in a blue skirt-suit stood to attention alongside the steel stairway parked beside the open door next to the wing, ready to welcome us on board. We knew exactly what was about to happen. Supine on the relaxation chairs, we'd mentally rehearsed every detail.

As the facilitator signalled us to move forward, a number of the delegates blanched. Others mumbled sotto voce the can-do mantras we'd generated in the class.

"Okay?" said Venus.

I nodded. It wouldn't do to appear too gung-ho about it, but I was excited. As a teenager I'd loved taking my first flight: the sudden thrust at take-off; the lofty perspective on motorways and mountains and patchwork fields; the meal trays with the doll-sized cups and the cubes of cheese in cellophane packets, all the bits laid out like the provisions in a child's toy shop. I knew today's experience would be on a smaller scale, but it still seemed an excellent way to spend my birthday. Venus knew me better than I thought.

The leader had almost reached the stairway when a sudden cramp sliced through my stomach, stopping me in my tracks. Prickly heat broke out on my forehead and a snake of sweat trickled down my spine. Venus looked alarmed as she ran her finger down the list clamped to her clipboard.

The facilitator thrust a brown paper bag into my hands. "Breathe into this. It's only a panic attack. You'll be fine in a couple of minutes."

My stomach lurched. A prawn-tinged stream gushed up my gullet and spewed into the bag. The bottom sagged for a moment before dissolving completely, releasing the vomit onto my sandals. Venus and the facilitator withdrew, but not far enough or fast enough to avoid the second wave from sprinkling them with the putrid liquid.

As we held our breaths for a third outburst, the sun crept from behind a cloud. That seemed to put an end to it. Venus wiped my chin with a tissue. "Let's get you cleaned up already and onto that plane." She spoke in a singsong voice I'd heard her use with Ellie.

My eyes stung and my mouth was like caustic soda. I was desperate to sit down, whether on the plane or off.

The facilitator looked me up and down. "Impossible. I can't let her board in that state, and there's no way I'm holding up the flight."

THINGS GOT PRETTY bad at home after our trip to visit our sisters in London. My mother found a stack of polaroids whilst cleaning my room: me and Geraldine and some of the nurses dolled up in our miniskirts and makeup. Instead of belting me, my dad threatened me with confession, but that was impossible: my mother would be mortified if Father Anthony got wind of it. I gobbled down a handful of paracetamol and ended up getting my stomach pumped at the infirmary. That got me an appointment with Chris Edmonds. I'd never even heard of a psychologist before and was fascinated by the tachistoscope flashing the images onto my subconscious.

The mere thought of these appointments gave my mother a headache, so my dad had to take me, and he wasn't happy about it. He didn't like Chris with his shoulder-length hair and smiley-face T-shirt, and I suppose he didn't like sitting in the corner without his pipe. I didn't think he would object to the treatment – after all, there was nothing namby-pamby about it – but, on the third or fourth session, he sprang from his chair: "This is barbaric! I thought I'd fought the bloody Nazis to put a stop to this malarkey."

Embarrassed, I expected Chris to stick up for himself and explain, yet again, the theory of operant conditioning, but he shrugged and set about detaching the electrodes from my chest.

"Yeah but I thought it was working," I mumbled. I'd believed in Chris, even more than I'd believed in St Bernadette of Lourdes.

"Let's see how things are next week," said Chris, but I knew there wasn't going to be a next week. If my dad said no, then no it was.

A FORTNIGHT LATER, Geraldine sent me a note asking me to meet her by the bus shelter. I didn't pause to wonder why.

It was early summer and no one asked where I was going when I left the house after tea. I wore my jeans and carried my London clothes and a bit of eyeshadow I'd filched from Woolworths in a duffel bag strung over my shoulder. Geraldine had asked me to dress up.

I got changed in the toilets in the park, juggling the garments away from the wet floor and squinting at my face in the cracked mirror as I smeared blue powder on my eyelids, praying all the while that no one would come in. I wasn't entirely happy with the result when I stepped out again, but Geraldine would redo my face if need be.

Stuffed with my jeans and plimsolls, the duffel bag dragged unevenly on one shoulder and, combined with the high heels and tight miniskirt, I must have looked quite ungainly as I hobbled to the bus shelter.

A group of lads were messing around but I saw no sign of Geraldine. I slowed my pace, undecided as to whether to wait elsewhere till she appeared. But, with my sandal straps rubbing against my heels, the bench inside the shelter seemed more compelling.

One of the lads stepped out from the shelter, placed his fingers in the corners of his mouth and gave a high-pitched whistle. Stubble shading his chin, he was old enough to have left school for a job at the pit.

Another lad joined him: "Give us a kiss, Darling."

Then a third: "Let's have a look at what you've got under your skirt."

They thronged around me, leering and laughing, poking and prodding, fondling my backside and lifting up my skirt. They pinched my cheeks and stroked my hair. Their breath smelled of beer and cigarettes.

"Leave me alone," I squeaked.

They laughed. "Meeting your boyfriend, was you?"

"Want me to give you a good time instead?"

Someone pushed me backwards and I tottered on my heels, crashing to the ground. Their fists were all over me, and their feet. I put up my arms to cradle my head, tried to offer it up as a penance to Jesus.

———— ————

VENUS SPONGED OFF the worst of it in the lavatories. Then she took me home and ran me a bath. I felt self-conscious undressing in front of her. All the years we'd shared a flat it had never come to this.

She took off her watch and pushed back the sleeves of her crocheted cardigan to stir the water with her hand. "What a dreadful way to spend your birthday."

"At least it was different."

"Of course it might have been the buffet that did it. We should sue them, in fact."

My stomach still felt somewhat fragile. "Nobody else seemed to be affected."

"As far as we know." She shrugged. "Either way, I can't

imagine I'm going to get you onto a plane in the next six months."

She was wearing the double-helix earrings she'd got for her birthday. I'd been a fool to miss the chance of complimenting her. I resolved not to let that happen again. "That was lovely what you did for me today. Just because it didn't quite work out, doesn't mean I don't appreciate it." Ridiculous of me to get so worked up about my birthday gift to her. Friendship couldn't be bought at a shop; it was built up from myriad moments of kindness like this.

She scooped up my clothes from the bathroom floor. "I'll put these in the washing machine. You'll want to go straight to bed after your bath. Can I get you some pyjamas or a nightie or something?"

I usually went naked under the duvet. "You could fetch my old galabeyah. I think it's in the bottom drawer of the pine chest."

While she was gone I soaped myself quickly and rinsed my hair. When she returned I was pulling the plug, a chunky towel screening my nakedness.

Venus draped the garment over a bentwood chair, gazing upon it like a relic of our younger selves. I wondered if, like me, she was remembering huddling around the gas fire in our galabeyahs with our mugs of cocoa and those rough army blankets pulled across our shoulders like shawls.

With a lacquered fingertip, Venus traced a pale blue stripe in the weave of the cloth. "Of course it's a tad worn already. We should get Simon to bring you a new one back from Cairo. How long till he goes?"

"Two and a half weeks, assuming Caroline's up to

looking after the kids on her own."

"Of course she will be," said Venus. "Now listen to me. Simon's going to be up to his eyeballs largely till the day he leaves. But he'll want some time with you. Invite him round for the last night, therefore. Give him a night to remember, Di. A night that will have him counting the days till his return."

Chapter 14

MY BODY ACHED in places I'd never noticed before, but at least this time they didn't have to load me into the ambulance on a stretcher. At least this time they weren't dealing with a self-inflicted wound.

My dad was waiting in the corridor when they wheeled me out of the x-ray department, a plastic carrier-bag in his hand. I pulled the hospital smock down across my knees, thankful he hadn't caught me in the torn miniskirt and frilly blouse I'd been wearing at the bus stop. I'd already wiped off the makeup with a flannel, but I gave my eyelids another rub over before I dared let him see my face.

When we got back to the cubicle a policeman was waiting, notebook in hand. "I can take your statement while you're waiting for the test results."

I'd expected trouble, but not as bad as this. "What am I charged with?" My bruised jaw made speaking a torment.

"There's a good one," said the policeman.

The chill of my dad's voice put a stop to his laughter: "There won't be no statement."

"I don't know about that," said the constable. "There was a witness. Old geezer who rang for the ambulance.

Claims he saw the attack from the bus. Even thought he recognized one of the youths."

"Interfering old busybody," said my dad.

"Lucky he was there. We could put them behind bars where they belong."

"Only if we take it to court," said my dad. "And what a fine spectacle that would be."

The curtains parted. Without a word to any of us, a doctor barged into the cubicle and picked up the cardboard wallet from the trolley where I lay. He slid out the x-ray plate and held it up against the lightbox on the wall. I looked at the doctor, buttoned up in his white coat, at my dad in his sports jacket and the constable in his belted uniform with its shiny buttons and epaulettes. Despite the cotton hospital gown, I felt naked.

"The consultant will have to check them over later." The doctor flicked off the light. "But there doesn't seem to be anything broken. I'll get a nurse to tidy things up and you can go home."

"See," said my dad, as the doctor made his exit. "Nothing to worry about. A bit of bruising that'll go down in no time."

"You won't be pressing charges?" asked the policeman.

In the ambulance, I'd felt reassured that, however much I was hurting, it wasn't my fault. Even the policeman seemed to think so. Yet stripped back to basics, Dad was right; I'd brought this on myself.

Dad swung the carrier bag to his other hand, revealing the red fabric of my miniskirt through the transparent plastic. "As far as I'm concerned, the less people get to hear about this the better."

———————

WHILE SIMON READIED himself, his children and his students for the day of his departure, I prepared for the night before. At lunchtimes, I pottered round Bainbridge's and Fenwick's, choosing a new duvet set to complement the raspberry pink of my bedroom carpet, a smart new dinner set to rival anything I'd seen at Venus's and Paul's. On Sundays, armed with a scrubbing brush and a bucket of soapy water, I excavated layers of grime from hidden corners of the house. In the evenings, I riffled through my CD collection and my recipe books while I waited for Simon to call to wish me goodnight. It was easy to set aside my anxieties when I was engrossed in orchestrating the finer details, like a bride mistaking a fairy-tale wedding for the challenges of married life.

I'd had enough to cope with at boarding school without worrying about losing my virginity. While some girls left the dormitory after lights out, shimmying down the drainpipe to meet their boyfriends, I had no desire to emulate them. When I teamed up with Venus at university, I assumed we'd find boyfriends together. With her exotic good looks, she was never short of admirers. But she hardly seemed to care. If a young man wanted to escort her home from the union disco, she'd make out she needed the toilet, only to drag me with her away into the night. I didn't complain; other people would only dilute our friendship. I could have carried on that way till we were a couple of old maids drawing our pensions. Venus, it turned out, could not.

During our final year as undergraduates we went out several times as a foursome, but as she led one young man into her bedroom, I was giving the other a peck on the cheek at the front door. By the age of twenty-five I had a PhD and a book in press but I was still virgo intacta. It wasn't until Venus had gone off to do postdoctoral research at Harvard that I took a man to my bed. And what a mistake that had been.

IN RETROSPECT, I was naive to lend so much weight to Simon's last night. Although we connived to construct an evening of romance and passion, the occasion had a waiting-room feel to it: however we filled the space beforehand, there was no doubt that Simon's leaving was the main event.

He was a proper gentleman, overgenerous in his praise of my barely-adequate culinary skills. I'd had the sense to eschew the fancier concoctions in my recipe books, but, when Simon arrived, I was still hacking away at the butternut squash for the risotto. I had to leave him in charge of the veg knife while I scurried upstairs to change into my dress.

The slightly stilted atmosphere made me all the more determined to end on a high note. When he'd cleared his plate and drained his glass and pushed away his coffee cup, I took his hand and invited him to come upstairs. He seemed surprised, and his hesitation made me question myself for a moment. I smiled away my fear.

While Simon was in the bathroom, I closed the curtains, shrugged off my dress and jumped into bed. I wished I'd composed a list of coping statements like on the Fear of

Flying course. *It needn't be like those other times. It doesn't hurt when you're in love.*

I didn't know the etiquette. Was I supposed to watch as he stepped out of his trousers and casually consigned his smoothly-ironed shirt to the floor? To appear excited as he approached me, his cock engorged with desire? Yet the thrill of his wanting me was enough to ward off my reservations.

He held me to him. We kissed. He cupped my breasts. He stroked my belly. He snaked his fingers through my pubic hair.

"I'll just …" I reached across and grabbed a tube of KY jelly from the bedside cabinet.

I'd been nervous about this part, but Simon seemed unfazed. He took the tube and squirted a dollop onto his fingertips. A beat later I felt it cool my genitals.

I lay on my back and pulled him on top of me. I took his penis with my hand and began to guide him inside.

"You sure you're ready?"

I jiggled my hips towards his. *It doesn't hurt when ….*

He pushed his way in. "You're a bit tight. Don't you want …?"

I stopped him with a kiss. He made small thrusting movements, abrasive against my inner walls. Simon looked uneasy, so I moved my hips with his even though it hurt all the more. He raised himself up, as if to withdraw, so I squeezed his buttocks and emitted a low moan. Simon smiled.

Ignoring my own discomfort, I concentrated on the vocals, panting and murmuring and whispering his name. Perhaps it was a form of self-hypnosis but I too began to relax.

Simon licked my nipple. "You like that, Di?" He was panting almost as hard as I was.

I cranked up the sound effects: *Ooh! Aah! Yes yes more!* If the soundtrack could be believed, we were about to climax in unison.

Yet Simon drew back. When I opened my eyes he was frowning. His cock seemed to have withered away inside me and my vagina no longer felt like a size-five boot hosting a size-six foot. "What's wrong?"

He rolled away onto his side. "You don't need to do that."

"What? What did I do?"

"You were faking it."

I withdrew my hand from where I'd been fondling his shoulder. "How can you say that?"

Tentatively, he touched my hip. "Di, are you a virgin by any chance?"

"For fuck's sake!"

"It's nothing to be ashamed of."

"I'm forty-five."

"Shit!" Grabbing my left arm, he brought the scribble of scars to his lips. "It's this, isn't it? Why didn't we discuss it first?"

There was no denying this would be a night to remember, although not in the way I'd hoped. "You'd better go."

"Come on, Di." He pulled me to him. "Don't you think you're overreacting?"

My body went limp in his arms. "It isn't working."

He laughed, more panicky than amused. "Of course it's working. Tonight was just a blip. Trust me, I'll be a whole lot gentler next time."

His cock swelled against my leg even has he spoke, as if lusting for a repeat performance.

"I'd like you to go now."

I thought he might object, but Simon rolled away from me and reached for his clothes. His pea-green shirt, so crisp and smooth when he arrived, had grown wrinkled in its time on the floor.

Simon laced up his shoes. Part of me wanted to call him back, but for what? I couldn't explain. All I could manage was to grab my dressing gown and follow him out onto the landing to watch him make his way downstairs.

In the hallway, he reached up towards the row of coat hooks. His hand hovered above the collar of his black fleece and then fell, brushing against the sleeve as his arm flopped to his side. "This is ridiculous, Di. We should at least talk about it."

WHEN, AFTER SIMON left that night, I held the Stanley knife to my arm, I wasn't thinking of much; just that, in the circumstances, it seemed the natural thing to do.

As a child, I'd drawn my own blood on two occasions: once, aged not quite eleven, with a breadknife in the bathroom; then, about eighteen months later, with a hacksaw from the woodwork room at school. But after Cairo I thought I was done with cutting. After Cairo there should have been no need.

WHEN VENUS APPLIED to do postdoc studies at Harvard, I was distraught. "In fact you could come too," she said. "It'd be a hoot to be there together."

I couldn't go abroad without a passport. I told her things were opening up for me in Newcastle; Colin Carmichael had plans for a research group on decision-making. I couldn't throw away such an opportunity.

I hadn't realised how lonely I'd be. I had other friends – more colleagues than friends, I suppose – but none could fill the Venus-shaped gap.

So I would've been particularly vulnerable when I bumped into Frank one Saturday afternoon in Fenwick's Food Hall. He'd had a short fling with Venus a couple of years earlier and asked for news of her. I was flattered when he suggested we go for a coffee. Coffees led to beers, the pub to a pizzeria, pizzas to nightcap until, in a manner that flowed so seamlessly I couldn't understand how it had never happened to me before, we ended up in bed. I was drunk enough not to care whether I fancied him but I thought he must be kosher if Venus had let him stick around for a while. Besides, it was time to cast off my virginity.

I can't deny I was confused that he turned away when I tried to kiss him. But his arousal was clear enough. Too embarrassed to admit my inexperience, I strove not to show how much it hurt. I'm not sure he'd have noticed anyway; from his glazed expression as he thrust into me, he was locked into a world of his own.

Fortunately it was over quickly: his pleasure, my pain. I

still believed it might end well, sleeping in each other's arms. But Frank rolled me onto my stomach, held me down and tore into my anus. This time I wouldn't have minded admitting how uncomfortable it was but, with my face buried in the pillow, it was effort enough to breathe.

When he pulled out I didn't know where I ached most. My mind was too numb to decide. Frank turned me back and, almost tenderly, kissed me long and deep on the lips. "Know something, Di?" He fumbled on the bedside cabinet for his cigarettes. "You have the tightest-arsed cunt ever."

Chapter 15

THE WORST THING about that night with Frank wasn't his lack of sensitivity. It wasn't that, when he'd gone, I rooted around until I found a knife sharp enough to slice through my forearm. It was that, after he'd spilt his seed inside me front and back without a thought of my discomfort, let alone my pleasure, I invited him back to do exactly the same again.

Perhaps I'd hoped it would be better the second time: easier for me and less frantic for him. But that doesn't explain the third time or the fourth.

Frank never questioned the growing network of scars on my arm. He never showed much curiosity about me at all. So long as he could lie me on my back and then on my front and barge in and out of me, he was happy. He gave me a kiss, smoked a cigarette, and left.

I didn't blame him for using me that way. He deserved to make love to a nubile young nymph instead of fucking an android.

The affair came to an end as casually as it had started. About ten weeks after that first meeting, he stopped calling round. I didn't realise what it meant initially: he'd always been erratic in his visits. I missed him, and then I didn't, and when, months later, I heard from a mutual acquaintance he'd got a job in Australia, I was relieved.

Things settled down at work too. Colin Carmichael jumped before he was pushed and Max Neasden did some budgetary juggling to manufacture a permanent post for me. I got a mortgage and, when I moved in, the whole department turned up to my house-warming. By the time Venus returned from Harvard the scars on my arm were less conspicuous, and I'd put all thoughts of Frank behind a heavily bolted door. Approaching thirty, I resigned myself to staying single and celibate, safe within the boundaries of the university, home and friends. Soon, I imagined, I'd complete the sad spinster stereotype with a snooty cat.

Simon may have been the antipode of Frank: mature, patient and the apogee of respect, yet he'd conjured up the darkness inside me as powerfully as Frank had. I tried to release it through the gash in my arm, but I should have known such respite could be only temporary. You can't obliterate one pain by creating another.

So I sit beneath the jumping ceiling lights, one hand tucked into a sling and the other balancing a styrofoam cup of pseudo-coffee, wondering if there's any point waiting for Tammy Turnbull, the psychiatric liaison nurse. It's almost morning but I've hardly had any night and my eyelids begin to droop.

IT'S APRIL, THE evening of Venus's birthday and my first encounter with Simon. I've gone upstairs to pander to Ellie's demand for a bedtime story. She's lying in bed clutching a furry orange rabbit, her mouth all pink gums as if she's lost not one baby tooth but a dozen. *Tell me a story, Di, about when you were a little girl.*

Someone sniggers. I'm not surprised to see Geraldine there in her green seersucker dress with puffed sleeves and smocking on the bodice. Indeed, due to the flexible geography of dreams, Ellie's bedroom is also the dining room, with the dinner guests assembled around the table. Fiona rubs her bare arms: *What were you, Di, a teenage vampire?*

Ellie wriggles across the bed to make space for me: *Take no notice of them, Di.*

Yes, says Ms Thompson. *Put it behind you, dear!*

Who invited the hippy? says Fiona.

Oh, don't worry about me, says Ms Thompson. *I'm only here to make up the numbers.*

Ellie pats the mattress beside her. *Once upon a time there was a little girl called Diana.*

I take a deep breath and go to join her. Even in the dream, I note the lemonade smell of her hair. "Once upon a time there was a little girl called Diana."

Geraldine sniggers. Ellie glowers at her: *I'll send you away if you keep interrupting.*

"Now Diana loved to dress up in her ballet tutu and cavort and caper all day long."

Relief sweeps over me as Ellie nods and grabs my hand.

"But something always got in the way of her dancing, and his name was Andrew. Diana and Andrew were twins. They shared the same birthday, and the same bedroom, and the same desk at school. In fact, Diana was forced to share her entire life with Andrew. Their bodies were joined together: they were Siamese twins."

Nobody calls them that any more, says Fiona. Conjoined twins would be a more polite way of putting it.

Yes, but this was the Sixties, says Simon. We didn't do political correctness back then.

"They were joined at the shoulder blades, back-to-back, so when Andrew walked forward Diana had to walk backwards, and she didn't like that at all. There wasn't much about Andrew she *did* like. He was always in the way, spoiling her dancing, distancing her from the other girls. Diana believed that where she was attached to Andrew was the place from which a little girl's wings would grow. Without her troublesome twin, she wouldn't just be able to hop and skip and jump more freely, she'd be able to fly."

Hang on a minute, says Venus. This story doesn't hang together. She's wearing the lace-trimmed lilac galabeyah she had on the night she first accosted me in the student halls of residence. *In fact conjoined twins are monozygotics who failed to separate. You can't get mixed-sex conjoined twins therefore.*

This is a true story, isn't it, Di? says Ellie. I don't want none of your lies.

It's a true story, right enough. Geraldine tosses her red curls and winks at me. *I was there at the time.*

"Diana tried to come to an accommodation with Andrew. She tried taking turns, one day doing things the girls' way, the next day the boys'. She tried being more like her brother, cutting her hair and dressing in miserable grey shorts and a shirt with a tie. She tried taking a knife and slicing through the sinews that held the two of them together. Each new strategy made her happier at first but, after a while, the old discontentment would come hurtling back. She'd never dance gracefully with Andrew clamped to her back.

"Finally, she asked Dr Hutton if he could help. But the doctor refused. He said she and Andrew had only one heart between them. If they were separated, one of them would die."

Fiona covers her ears. *This is gross! I'll blame you if I have a nightmare.*

"The doctors abroad were more optimistic. In Cairo, Diana found a surgeon who could be persuaded to give it a go. It's only fair to warn you, only one of you will survive the operation, said Mr Abdullah. I'm prepared to take that risk, said Diana. I may as well be dead as continue like this."

Geraldine grabs my forearm and twists the skin: *Death and resurrection, Romeo becomes Juliet.*

Venus purses her cinnamon-glossed lips. *Marvellous story, Di, but if you've set yourself free from Andrew already, why have I never seen your wings?*

I COME TO with a jolt. My arm throbs and there's a coffee-tinged damp patch down the front of my fleece. A middle-aged woman looms before me. "Diana Dodsworth? I'm sorry to startle you, but I believe you wanted to see me. I'm Tammy Turnbull. The liaison nurse?"

She was right, I *did* want to see her. I wanted to tell her about my primary school with the forbidden stairway, about Music and Movement and stealing Geraldine's clothes. I wanted to confess that *I* played Romeo and Juliet for real. I wanted her to know what I did with the breadknife, my mother's Valium, the hacksaw and the paracetamol, and how nobody suggested I see a specialist nurse like her. I wanted her to recognise how hard I tried to please Dr Hutton and Chris Edmonds and, especially, my mum and dad. I wanted her to empathise with the confusion, the yearning, the fear, loneliness, and disappointment that's never gone away. I wanted all of that, but of course it's hopeless. Because what can she say when I come to the end of my story except *Yes yes, all very poignant, Diana, but shouldn't you have put all that behind you, like your social worker said?*

I shake my head. "Who did you say you were after?"

"Diana Dodsworth. I was told she was sitting around here."

"Not me, sorry." I gesture towards a figure clad in black, intent on a hardback Harry Potter. "It might be that woman over there."

BACK HOME, I manage to change the bloodied sheet one-handed, but the duvet cover defeats me. I merely turn the whole thing over to keep the damp patch off my skin. I phone work on the mobile and tell Garth's secretary I've got a virus and will be taking a few days off.

"Do you want me to rearrange your appointments?" says Val.

She isn't usually so accommodating. Academic staff of my lowly status tend to do our own admin. "Okay. Thanks."

"Let me get your schedule up on the screen. I'm

assuming you keep it up to date?" She runs through the list of meetings. The new academic year's still over a week away, so there aren't many. "The one-to-ones should be easy enough and I'll do my best for tomorrow afternoon's."

"Tomorrow afternoon?"

"It says here Megan Richardson interviewing Susan Marlow."

As if I could forget. It was almost worth last night's various indignities to put that one off. "Megan can liaise with Dr Marlow." I wonder if Val knows what it's about. I wouldn't put it past her to have offered to reschedule solely to stop me bunking off something so dear to Professor Bradshaw's heart.

I finish the call and tuck the duvet around me. I'm dog tired but I can't switch off my brain. Besides, it's too bright for sleep. I keep turning this way and that, unable to find a comfortable position for my arm. Although it's only September, I'm cold and the duvet cover smells of an odd mixture of newness and stale blood.

I jump out of bed and tug at the bottom drawer of the pine chest. My stripy galabeyah is back where Venus found it after the ill-fated Fear of Flying course. I hardly wear it these days, and I'd squirrelled it away soon after she left. The colours are faded and the cheap cotton fabric fraying at the hems but, right now, it's exactly what I need. I pull it over my head and feed my arms through the sleeves. The tight fit across my chest doesn't feel restrictive, but fuels the illusion that my breasts are plump. I climb back into bed, finally confident of finding sleep.

IN CAIRO, I couldn't take my eyes off the men sitting outside dark cafés playing backgammon and sucking on the water pipes that were so much more tantalising than my dad's standard briar. Men with beards and moustaches dressed in loose long-sleeved shifts like Wee Willie Winkie's nightgown. My dad belonged to a different species.

I thought he'd refuse when I suggested going shopping, but we needed a souvenir to take home for my brother. I worked out which bus would take us to the Khan el Khalili.

We wandered along avenues of carpets too precious to tread on; strings of beads dripping like wisteria under canopies of fine cotton and silk. Ranks of brassware glinting up to the ceiling, plates and flasks of silver and gold; pyramids of blue pottery and woven baskets clinging to the walls; mountains of spices like children's powder paint, perfuming the air with ginger and cinnamon and other smells I couldn't name. I could imagine the Three Kings shopping here for their gold, frankincense and myrrh.

I held up a painting of funerary gods on papyrus. "Do you think this would do for Trevor?"

My dad made a face and walked away. The stallholder called after him: "I give you good price."

Confused, I ran after him. "Did you mean that?"

"I thought I might get it cheaper," said my dad. "Let's try it on another stall."

We worked it like a single organism, attuned to each other's movements like Butch Cassidy and the Sundance Kid, like Ginger Rogers and Fred Astaire. The papyrus for

Trevor, a turquoise scarab brooch for my mother and a vase shaped like a long-necked cat for Patricia. Me the excited child, Dad the withholding parent; I'd never seen him so playful. Yet, when I approached a stall selling traditional Arabic man-dresses, a cloud crossed his face.

"Galabeyah," said the stallholder. "This one for man. This one for woman."

The woman's version came in pastel colours with a narrow strip of lace around the front opening and collarless neckline. The man's was unadorned, the colours muted. I knew my dad wouldn't like either but, if there was one thing I was learning from being in Cairo, it was that I could decide for myself. I held one up against me for size: slightly large, but at fifteen I still had some growing to do.

The stallholder named his price. I looked askance at my father. Dad stepped forward and rubbed the fabric between his fingers, an off-white cotton striped like bedsheets in brown and blue. The front opening fastened with buttons fashioned from white cord, left over right, the man's way. I scrutinised my father's expression; underneath the disdain he was obliged to show the stallholder, did he approve of my choice?

Dad shook his head and backed off from the stall. But it seemed to take some effort. As if, behind his frown, he felt like jumping for joy.

Chapter 16

M Y EARLIEST MEMORY: three years old and dancing all alone in my sister's tutu. Twisting, turning, spinning, sliding, the tiny buds of my wings pulsing from my shoulder blades. Colours bright as a picture book, angels carolling in my head.

My mother's footfall on the stairs. Her singing put on pause.

Dancing, prancing, gallivanting, cocooned within my own childish dreams. No world for me beyond the walls of my sister's bedroom, no sense of other people, of disapproving minds.

My mother screaming. Her mouth a hole, her cheeks blood-red, her eyes devil-black. Long knobbly fingers snatching, grabbing, clawing the dress from me as if peeling a lamb from its fleece.

Crying, shaking, locked in a nightmare: my mother gone and, in her place, this witch.

"You've really gone and done it this time. You'll be for it when your father gets home."

I CARRIED ON racing my cars across the lino while the words

shot back and forth between my parents. *You should've got it done yonks ago. Isn't that your job?*

My mother fetched my coat and shoes. My dad led me out of the house.

I was proud walking up the terrace hand-in-hand with my daddy. Proud, but perplexed by the break with routine. Most days, we washed our hands for tea soon after he came home from the colliery. I never went outside when the sun was going down behind the headstock of the pit. I never went anywhere with just my dad.

The barber's door was closed and didn't yield when my father pushed it. He released my hand and chapped his knuckles on the glass. The barber peered through a crack in the doorway. A bell tinkled as he held open the door to let us in.

It was warm inside with photos on the walls of smiling men in roll-necked jumpers and a sweet smell, like our bathroom when my daddy had been shaving. The barber wore a white tunic with a comb poking out of the breast pocket. He piled some cushions onto a leather chair and hoisted me on top. He pumped a lever with his foot to make the chair rise ever higher till I felt like the king of the castle.

I watched in the big mirror as he took a lock of my hair between his fingers and scissored through it. The clippers whirred like a battery-powered car as they tickled the back of my bent head. When I looked in the mirror again, I couldn't find me. A miniature version of my father stared back, but where had *I* gone?

The barber ripped the cellophane from a yellow lollipop. My father handed him some money and back we went into the night. The wind blew cold about my ears as loneliness gathered at the bottom of my tummy. I sucked hard on my lollipop as I trotted to keep up with my father, hanging on to his big rough hand.

IN MY DREAM, Geraldine hitches up her skirt and squats. Urine streams between her legs onto the tarmac, all the way down Bessemer Terrace. I'm also aching to go, my bladder blazing with the weight of water, but I daren't expose myself in public. I hop from one foot to the other, pressing my hand between my legs to hold it in.

I'm not quite awake when I throw off the duvet and dash to the loo. I only just remember to gather my galabeyah out of the way as I drop onto the seat. Instead of the expected torrent, there's a shy, burning trickle. It brings no respite; the moment it stops I'm desperate to go again. I remember this from Cairo.

Cairo: like a slap in the face it shocks me awake. There's no forgetting a nanosecond of my shame. Cairo: no longer a physical place for me – someone's home, a tourist hotspot, the capital of Egypt – but a state of mind, a philosophical construct. A child too young to choose: hope raised and dashed, a problem solved giving birth to another. *Put it behind you,* Ms Thompson had said, and I'd tried, until Simon sent the past colliding with the present. Cairo again, bringing our affair to a ludicrous conclusion, the stuff of bedroom farce. Where was my brain when I imagined I could seduce him? When I took that knife to my arm? What I'd give to turn back the clock twenty-four hours.

As if to underline the futility of such fantasies, my

forearm starts to throb. There should be a law against such morbid acts of self-pity and indulgence. Like wasting police time.

That gentle doctor could have been attending to some genuine injury. She could have had ten minutes in the staff room with her feet up and a cup of tea.

Even as a kid, I never wanted to end it. Even at eleven when I took my mother's Valium and thought no one would find me, I only wanted a break. At fourteen, after that weekend in London when Geraldine kissed Suma, I didn't swallow paracetamol to kill myself. I took it because the contradictions were too much to bear.

I took it because I believed in all those stories of redemption. I thought Jesus really did rise from the dead. I thought Juliet would get up and walk, hand-in-hand with Romeo, out of the Capulet mausoleum. I thought that by taking it to the limit I'd be transformed into another person, reincarnated as someone I could live with. Not even Cairo did that for me.

Triumph over hope; that was what I sought. I sense it now, hunched on the toilet seat trying and failing to pass water, the relief of reaching rock bottom. It's a safe, familiar place, the certainty that things can get no worse. I've lost my boyfriend. I've deceived my best friend. My boss doesn't trust me. My left arm's a tapestry and I appear to have a urinary tract infection. Oh, and the new duvet set I bought is so thick with blood I'll probably have to chuck it in the bin.

Yet I've found myself again. I can't say I like this person, but least she's not a stranger. Cackling like a mad woman, I tear off a sheet of toilet paper and wipe myself. Why should I have expected anything better? Only those who've never left their beds believe their dreams will come true.

As I push through the kitchen door, Marmaduke leaps down from the draining board, clattering crockery with the sweep of her tail. She tiptoes across to her empty food bowl, mewling as she casts me a reproachful glance.

"I get it," I say. "I can't blame you for lapping up last night's leftovers if I've neglected to give you any dinner." I wonder if she'll acquire a taste for risotto.

I open a can of juicy rabbit chunks and scoop half into her bowl. My knives are still lined up as I left them on the worktop. How can I be so chaotic and yet so organised? Marmaduke whines as I tip the rest of the can into her dish.

I haven't the stomach to eat anything myself. I make a cup of Earl Grey and carry it through to the lounge. In the street, a car door slams. I try to keep my mind as blank as the television screen.

When the doorbell goes, I jump, only just avoiding spilling my drink down my front for the second time today. Simon cancelling his flight to come and check I'm okay? I strike out the thought the moment it appears, but not before I've registered the shame.

The doorbell chimes again. I want to creep away and hide but the man hovering at the bay window has seen me. He shifts a large bouquet to the crook of his arm and gives a wave.

It's lethal being at home in the daytime. The delivery people don't care where they dump their parcels, so long as they don't have to return them to the depot. I'm scowling when I open the door. "Sorry, I can't take anything in right now. I'm about to go out and won't be back till late."

The young man has tight, curly hair and piercings in his eyebrows. He considers my bare feet, my unbrushed hair and eccentric attire and thrusts the bouquet at me as if he doesn't believe a word. "Somebody loves you."

"I doubt it," I say, but, as if it's a conditioned reflex, I'm reaching for the flowers with both arms.

Laughing, he turns to go.

The cellophane crackles as I shift the weight away from my injured forearm. "Just a minute, young man. Who exactly are these for?"

The silver rings squeeze together as he raises his eyebrow. "Diana Dodsworth. I thought that was you."

ANOTHER ABORTIVE TRIP to the lavatory is needed before I can unwrap the flowers and settle them into vases. Possessing only one proper vase, I have to raid the recycling box for empty jam jars, but the flowers are exotic long-stemmed aliens that threaten to topple them. Waxy scarlet trumpets, pale green rosettes surrounding something resembling a freckled bee, white spikes and yellow spikes and green bamboo twists: I have to lean them against walls and windows for extra support. Still, I'm happier puzzling over the arrangement than the shock of Simon sending me flowers.

Nobody has ever sent me flowers before. Getting them now – and such an exquisite ostentatious banquet of them – when it's all over with Simon, makes the past omission so much more poignant. I pick up the card again, turn it over in my hand. It's a slip of a thing, like a business card, the message scrawled in what I take to be the florist's hieroglyphics: *Missing you already, Simon.*

Where is he now? In that nowhere land between airports or still waiting for take-off at Heathrow? *Missing you already, Simon.* Not *Love, Simon.* Just *Simon.*

What was in his mind as he placed the order, gave the florist his message? I can't bear to think of him still raw from last night, racking his brain for some way of resuming a connection. More likely he'd have set it up beforehand, a romantic gesture to complete our romantic meal. *Missing you already.* A pat phrase really, predictable. You can probably buy *Missing you already* cards at Hallmark.

Pressure on my bladder and that burning sensation again. I make my way up to the toilet, not anticipating much relief.

THE LANDLINE IS ringing in the kitchen as I stagger downstairs. Simon asking if I've received the flowers?

"There you are!" says Venus. "How come you've turned off your mobile?"

I yo-yo between relief and disappointment. "I didn't realise I had."

"I've been trying to contact you for ever. In fact I waited an hour for you in the senior common room at lunchtime."

"I'm sorry, Venus. I don't even remember arranging to meet."

"We didn't but of course I thought you'd be bursting to tell me about last night."

The wound on my arm begins to bite. A glance at a hothouse flower leaning against the window pane fails to soothe me. "Anyway," says Venus, "what are you doing home so early?"

No point lying. "Actually, I've not been in to work all day."

"Humongous hangover from too much champagne?"

"Nothing so sparkly, I'm afraid. I've got a UTI."

"Like I said, a night to remember."

"What?"

Venus laughs. "Obviously you're feeling dreadful right now, but a good Catholic girl like you must know there's a penance to be paid for the sin."

"You've lost me completely."

"Oh, you goose, haven't you heard of honeymoon cystitis?"

I relive the moment when Simon's expression morphed from spellbound to confused. I switch my attention to the makeshift vase on the windowsill, the label for reduced-sugar blackcurrant jam peeling away at the edge. "It's a new one on me." It certainly wasn't sex that triggered the infection in Cairo. "At least you gave him a good time," says Venus. "Of course, you've seen the doctor?"

"Do you think I should? I thought it would fizzle out of its own accord."

"Believe me, Di, these nasties need treatment, and sharpish."

I haven't seen my GP in nearly twenty years and I'm in no hurry to resume the acquaintance. Especially not after running away from the liaison nurse this morning. "Maybe I can pick something up from the chemist tomorrow."

"What? Cranberry juice or that obnoxious potassium citrate? You may as well dose yourself with liquorice allsorts. Get yourself to the doctor for some antibiotics. And don't let them fob you off with waiting three days for the lab report."

The prospect of negotiating another pocket of the health-care system fills me with dread, but it's clear Venus speaks from experience. "I'll see how I am in the morning."

"In fact you'll be ten times worse in the morning. Therefore you need to ring the surgery *now* and badger them to give you an emergency appointment this evening."

I glance at the clock on the cooker. It's nearly five. "Won't they be closing?"

"Obviously I keep a list of your doctor's opening times in my head." Venus sighs. "In fact I'd make the bally appointment for you if I didn't have to scoot off right now and pick up the kids."

"Sorry," I say, "I didn't mean …"

"And I'm sorry I snapped. Especially when you're under the weather. But there are times I want to shake you, Di. It's like you think taking care of yourself is a mortal sin."

Chapter 17

A T THE AGE of five, I couldn't understand why I wasn't allowed to enter the school by way of the left-hand staircase. "Don't be such a baby," said my mother. "That side's for girls. And don't scuff your new shoes."

I stared at the two flights of stone steps, the only distinction the letters embossed in the lintel above them, finished off on both sides by a snaking S. The boys' route had the tubby B and O and the joyful Y with its arms reaching up to the sky. The girls' the awkward G and R, flanking a vertical line that hardly merited the distinction of letter, followed by the angular L. Did it matter that the girls' path contained more letters if both led to the same place?

My mother relaxed her grip on my arm. "Look, Miss Bamford's waiting."

What was the point of school if not to explore the entire alphabet? How could I learn to read and claim the treasures reading would bring if some avenues were out of bounds?

That morning my mother taught me the correct way to enter my school. She taught me the only way she knew: with shouting and scolding and slaps around the legs. Then she humped me up the boys' stairway like a bag of coal.

THE WOMAN ON the adjacent seat flashes me a disapproving look as I readjust my position for the sixth time in as many minutes. I won't apologise. I'm sure she has her own problems – not least the pregnancy she looks far too young to handle – but I'll bet she hasn't had last night's sleep interrupted every half-hour by the duplicitous urge to urinate. Venus had been right; I should have tried to get an appointment yesterday.

The doctor I'm due to see is called Libby Dean. I don't recognise the name, but then my last visit was twenty years ago when I transferred to the practice from the university health centre.

When the receptionist calls out a name, the woman beside me humps herself up and waddles away. I take advantage of the extra space to have a proper fidget. Behind the desk the staff are chewing over last night's TV. I felt so rotten I actually watched the garden makeover programme they're getting agitated about.

"I keep nagging Brian to do us a water feature."

My stomach lurches. In her slate-grey fitted jacket and with her hair teased into a severe ponytail, the speaker looks remarkably like Tammy Turnbull. I narrow my eyes to see her better but, almost as if she knows I'm watching, she turns her back on the waiting area and ducks behind one of the computers.

Is it the liaison nurse? I was given to understand she was based at the hospital. Could she be so concerned we missed our chat she's traced me to my GP surgery? No, that's ridiculous; NHS resources wouldn't stretch to that. Sleep deprivation is making me paranoid.

I shuffle into a new position. If they don't call for me soon I'll have to nip out to the loo.

Of course, Tammy Turnbull wouldn't need to come in person. Every hospital attendance generates a letter or two to the GP. At this very moment Libby Dean could be reading about how her next patient had the audacity to lacerate her own arm before cold-shouldering the one person who might have helped her. Dr Dean might require an explanation before doling out the antibiotics.

I squeeze my legs together from the top of my thighs to my knees, but it makes no difference. I'm letting my mind run away with me again. Barely more than twenty-four hours has elapsed since I fled the hospital. Hardly time for a busy A&E doctor to dictate a letter, let alone have it typed, signed, and forwarded to my GP.

MY DAD WAS furious when I got a urinary tract infection in Cairo. At first, when I said it hurt to do a wee, I assumed he was angry with *me*. Complications meant more time in hospital, more expense and more time away from home. But when he began haranguing the staff, he revealed a side of him I hadn't known existed: he'd never been the kind of dad to fight my corner.

He'd been a different man in Cairo. Alone together in the Khan el Khalili, it wasn't only the Aladdin's-cave set-up that made it seem like a fairy tale. It was as if he'd been magicked into the dad of my dreams. All those years I'd been longing to be transformed into a more lovable person, it had never crossed my mind to pray for my parents to change.

Delicious as it was, it made me anxious. If the dream fell apart, I'd be doubly disappointed. So I had mixed feelings when he packed my mother off on the plane to England and said that he'd wait with me in Cairo. Instead of setting off from Bessemer Terrace each morning to the wages office at the pit, he left his grubby boarding house to walk the dusty streets to the clinic, to sit quietly at my bedside, telling me stories while I cried.

Perhaps the infection in my waterworks gave him a sense of purpose. Perhaps it justified his decision to stay: "Your mother would've let them walk all over her."

I'm not sure his fuming made much difference. The nurses would have cottoned on soon enough. In Arabic-inflected American accents they insisted that an infection wasn't uncommon on removing a catheter, and I'd be fine in a couple of days.

"If it's not uncommon," cried my dad, "why didn't you bloody well give the kid something to prevent it?" He seemed almost euphoric in his indignation.

"I THINK I'LL try you on Macrodantin. Four times a day for five days. But you *must* complete the course and leave a urine sample with reception before you leave the surgery."

Dr Dean smiles sweetly as she turns back to her computer screen. With her snub nose and blonde hair dropping in two plaits to her shoulders, she looks about sixteen. But what do I care? In a couple of minutes I'll be out the door with a promissory note for the drugs that'll grant me a pain-free piss.

She chuckles as she taps at the keyboard. "It's ages since we had the record digitised, but we're still finding gremlins. Is this really your first visit since 1987?"

"That sounds about right."

Her gaze pierces the screen. "That'll account for it then. Nobody's picked up that they've got you down as male."

I feel an urge to rush out to the lavatory, but I can't go without my prescription.

"It's easily sorted," she quips. "Only it would make quite a difference, you see, with what you've got." She misreads my look of horror for curiosity. "A UTI is a lot less common in a man but much more serious. Basic anatomy A woman's shorter urethra is more susceptible to everyday infections."

It's not only her childish hairstyle but her openhearted enthusiasm that makes me think of a little girl playing at being a doctor. I'm about to rob her of her innocence.

Her eyes widen as she scrolls down the screen. I struggle to interpret her expression as she turns to appraise me. "You certainly wear it well."

Even though it's not the ridicule I've dreaded, I'm cringing inside. She's not likely to dismiss this as another of those pesky computer glitches.

Nor does she. Without discarding her childlike fascination, she becomes more doctorly: "I guess I'm going to have to let it stand, then. But just to be sure, given what I said about the sex difference, you went all the way?"

I give her the slightest of nods.

"Well, I assume you'll be okay on the Macrodantin."

As the printer whirrs into action, I begin to relax. Yet it doesn't stop me imagining Libby Dean picking up the phone to summon a bunch of medical students to join us. *Listen up, kids! This might be your only chance to see one of these in your whole career.*

She takes the green printout and reaches for a ballpoint. "1974. You must have been terribly young."

Libby Dean probably wasn't even born. "I was fifteen."

"I guess it was pretty basic in those days. Are you having any follow-up?"

Sweet as she seems, this is not a conversation I care to continue. I incline my head towards the prescription and, to my relief, she signs.

"One thing at a time, eh?" Smiling, she hands me the script. "But do consider it, Ms Dodsworth. We've made tremendous advances in surgical procedures in the last thirty years. It wouldn't do any harm to get yourself checked out by a specialist. Especially as you had it done at such a young age."

Forcing a smile, I stuff the chit in my backpack. "Thank you for your time, Dr Dean."

"Why don't you come back and see me anyway once you've got rid of that nasty infection? You'd be overdue a general health screening even without such a complex history."

———————

I WAS SANDWICHED between my parents in the back seat of

a taxi, creeping along the Corniche with the Nile to our left. We'd wound down the windows but there wasn't even the promise of a breeze. The driver hit the horn with the heel of his hand and growled in throaty Arabic as he pulled past a camel cart laden with builder's rubble. My mother flinched.

My father fanned his face with a tourist map of Cairo. "It's not too late to change your mind."

My mother broke off from raking through her patent leather handbag. I tried not to squirm on the tacky plastic seat. I knew what had sparked the quiver in her voice.

Not too late when they've told the driver to take us to the clinic? Not too late when they've spent money they never had to get us here? Not too late when I've missed the start of my O-level year at school?

I'd thought my dad was beginning to understand me. Thought he agreed that this would put things right.

Chapter 18

I WAS SEVEN years old when Geraldine announced that she was going to teach me a new game. "It's called doctors and nurses."

She wriggled out of her knickers and lay down on the grass, pulling up the hem of her dress and tucking it under her arms. She indicated the rubber gloves she'd filched from her mother's kitchen: "Now you've got to examine me."

I hung back. "That's dirty." I wanted to look and, at the same time, I didn't. My dad would wallop me if he found out. But it wasn't only that. "Where's your …?"

Geraldine rolled from side to side, chuckling. "Girls haven't got one, silly. Don't you know nothing?"

I'd never imagined we'd be different underneath our clothes. I thought we'd be like sticks of rock: some plain, some striped, but all with *Made in Skegness* running through the middle. "How does your wee get out then?"

"It just comes. Out of a little hole."

It did look neat, like a rosebud or a drawstring purse. Yet even through the marigolds I didn't dare touch her.

"This is what your mammy looks like," said Geraldine. "Except she's got a hairy bum."

"Have you seen it?"

"Course not."

"Then how do you know?"

"I just do." She'd stopped laughing and seemed rather cross as she got up and snatched her knickers. Her dress was wrinkled at the back from the grass. "Now you lie down. I'll examine you."

I shook my head, crossing my hands in front of my crotch.

Geraldine stamped her foot: "Come on! I showed you mine."

The confusion made me want to cry. Like in church, trying to make sense of *For ever and ever, Amen.* I began to walk away.

Geraldine called after me: "Scaredy-cat!"

Just as I feared she might be right, the answer came to me, perfectly formed, like a prayer. "I don't want to make you jealous, that's all."

"Why would I be jealous?"

"Cos I've got both, that's why. A boy part and a girl part."

"You're fibbing. You can't have both."

"Yes you can."

"No you can't."

"Can."

"Prove it then!"

I wiped my nose on the back of my hand. "I don't have to prove it." Like all the Jesus stuff at church: if you were good, you'd believe.

"Liar liar liar!" screamed Geraldine. "If you had two

kinds, you'd show me."

I couldn't let her win. I had to be everything she was and all she could never be. Not heads nor tails but the rim holding them together. "I hate you, Geraldine Finch." I punched her on the arm and skipped, jogged, sprinted away.

I FOUND OUT later that some people really did have two sets of genitals. The evidence was in the textbook Suma showed me in the nurses' home although, by then, I had no interest in showing it to Geraldine. I thought hermaphrodites could embrace the best of both worlds. Suma put me right about that. Yet, hearing the whispers in the playground about what we had coming to us at puberty, I thought one set more than enough.

Thirty-five years on, I'm unclear of my exact intention when I took the breadknife up to the bathroom, removed my pyjama bottoms and drew blood. Perhaps I needed to act out what couldn't be spoken, the fear and confusion, the terror of growing up.

It didn't strike me as strange at the time that nobody asked me why I did it. I was probably relieved: my inability to give a decent answer would have brought an extra layer of shame.

I shared my mother's greater concern. "Don't say a word about this," she said. "If your father gets wind of what you've done he'll slice them off with a bit of cheese-wire."

I suppose he didn't look at me enough to notice I was walking like a cowboy, or that I winced when I sat down. When my mother told him the bolt on the bathroom door had burst when I'd been trying to force it into a neater alignment, he swallowed the story as smoothly as his mug of tea. "Silly sod," he said. "I'll have to dock your pocket money for that."

NOBODY ASKED ME why I took my mother's Valium about a year later, but when I cut myself with a hacksaw another year on there were so many questions I could hardly keep track. Perhaps because I'd been fool enough to do it at school, and people *had* to take notice. Perhaps because the injury was severe enough to keep me in hospital overnight. Perhaps because harming myself had begun to look like a habit.

The questions made me anxious at first. But when I realised my parents were no longer bothered by what had gone before I almost relished the attention,

First they took me to a tiny room with nothing in it but a desk and two chairs, like an interview room from Z-cars. The psychologist there had waist-length hair parted down the middle and wiry John Lennon glasses. In the gentlest of voices she asked me to tell her the meaning of various words and how much change I'd have left from a ten-shilling note if I bought five apples at thruppence apiece. She arranged some wooden blocks in a pattern on the desk and asked me to copy it, and got me put some pictures in order to make a story. I imagined I was auditioning for a TV quiz show and got so carried away I forgot I'd been caught doing something unmentionable in the woodwork room.

The psychiatrist, Dr Hutton, was an older chap, older even than my father, with tufts of white hair sprouting from his ears. He wore a tweed jacket with leather patches on the elbows and a tie with a coat of arms below the knot. He wanted to know how I got on with Patricia and Trevor, and if I had any friends at school. I reeled off a list of names from the register and pretended I preferred PE and woodwork to English and maths.

His eyes twinkled behind his half-moon glasses when I mentioned woodwork. "Ah yes, an extremely valuable skill, don't you agree? I imagine they start off by teaching you the safe use of tools, is that right?"

Dressed in my school shirt and blazer and hospital-issue pyjama bottoms I'd never pass the audition, no matter how well I'd done in the psychologist's tests.

Dr Hutton steepled his fingers. "Why don't we stop beating about the bush and approach this man-to-man? How about telling me what drove you to take a hacksaw to your testicles?"

I'd never heard that word spoken aloud before. It was embarrassing, especially from a grown-up.

It was as if the psychiatrist could read my mind. "Come, come, it's nothing to be embarrassed about. You could've done yourself a serious injury. If I'm to help you, I'm going to need to know why."

Dr Hutton opened a buff file on the desk. I knew he'd need to report on me, but I hadn't thought of it as help.

"How do you feel about your genitals?"

I shrugged. It was like asking how I felt about my big toe.

"They make you uncomfortable?"

I remembered Geraldine ripping off her knickers and laying down on the grass. I couldn't tell Dr Hutton I'd wanted both kinds, and now I wanted none. I'd be like my sister's Sindy dolls, no holes or dangly bits.

"You'd like to get rid of them?"

To my horror, I began to sob. I expected Dr Hutton to tell me to pull myself together, but he stayed silent for a while, before sliding a box of paper hankies across the desk.

"Do you find it hard being a boy?"

I mopped my eyes and nodded vigorously.

"Have you ever wished you were a girl?"

I didn't think Dr Hutton would understand if I said I'd wished I was Geraldine. After all, he didn't know her.

"Perhaps you feel torn, not sure whether you'd be happier as a boy or as a girl?"

"It does feel a bit like that."

"It's not easy being the middle child," said Dr Hutton. "And with one brother and one sister, you're pulled in two different directions."

I nodded. I'd never thought of that.

"And all the mixed messages young people get these days. This permissive society has everyone confused. Those pop groups with boys who look like girls. Manes of long greasy hair and bell-bottomed trousers."

Remembering my mother mistaking Geraldine's twin cousins, Paddy and Pete, for girls, I laughed.

"That's the spirit," said Dr Hutton. "Now I'm going to have a chat with your parents, but I'll tell you what I'm going to recommend. We can't have you performing self-surgery every time you get a wee bit upset, can we? Ugly ducklings don't turn into swans, whatever the story says. They grow up to be handsome ducks and are happy with it.

And you'll grow up to be a man just like your father. But you need to start training for it right now. So we're going to toughen you up a bit, get you out on the football pitch with all the other lads. You're going to join the Scouts and learn to make campfires. And you're going to get a proper haircut instead of that girly mop."

Chapter 19

I'M WHEELING MY bike down the hallway, about to leave for work when I see the picture postcard on the mat. I can tell straight away it's from someplace sandy. I pick it up, my hand shaking.

The Sphinx backed up by the two pyramids at Giza, a fiery ball of sun behind. I flip it over, already disappointed at the economy of words. Yet how kindly he's assembled them.

I won't cry. I don't cry. I can't cry and, besides, I'm almost late for work. I let the card drop back onto the doormat and lug my bike outside.

It seems you were right about the sunrise (as always)! B/W Simon.

I can't afford to be sentimental this morning. I'm sitting in on Megan's interview with her transvestite father and I don't know how I'll get through it without giving myself away.

"WAS THERE A specific point when it hit you that you were really a woman," says Megan, "or was it a more gradual realisation?"

She's sitting opposite her father, an antique tape

recorder on the low table between them. I've given them the two upholstered seats and perched myself on the desk chair, slightly apart. I ought to have told Megan to avoid asking two questions in one, but it's hard to stay focused on the pedagogy when I'm bursting to hear her father's reply.

Susan Marlow is dressed less flamboyantly than when I first saw her, in a black pencil-skirt and a buttoned-up blouse with self-coloured embroidery on the bodice. The bouffant wig has been discarded in favour of what I take to be her own hair: salt-and-pepper threads hanging limply about her ears and barely managing to clothe her pink scalp. "A bit of both, to be honest. I always had a sense, right from being a toddler, that I didn't really fit as a boy. But as a kid, you have to get on with it. Contort yourself whatever way you can into the space you've been allocated, however much it hurts. And it's not to say there weren't compensations. For instance, I married a dream of a woman, inherited two of the finest kids ..."

The ghost of a smile passes over Megan's lips. She's not doing so badly in terms of professional distance; indeed, she's holding it together better than I am.

Susan Marlow crosses one leg over the other. It looks almost painful in that tight skirt. "Then my brother had a heart attack. Shook me up something rotten. He was only fifty-two. He's recovered now but there were a few days when we were convinced we'd lose him. And I thought, *What the hell! You only get one chance at life and, if you can't live it your own way, what's the point?*"

"Thing is," says Megan, "how would you feel if you went through all that only to find out it wasn't your way at all?"

A good question, although I'll have to speak to her later about deviating from the script.

Susan Marlow uncrosses her legs. She rises slightly from the chair, smoothes her skirt across her backside, and sits down again, sending a puff of musk in my direction. "I'd be surprised and profoundly disappointed. And wracked with guilt for the pain I'd caused other people. Yet despite all that, I'd be glad I'd given it a go."

Megan smiles. "Even so, you must have some qualms. Such an enormous decision."

"Of course, but I'm not making it in a vacuum. I've a huge support team. Not just my family, but the professionals involved in my care. They have to work within strict guidelines."

"Guidelines?" says Megan, with enviable sangfroid.

"The Benjamin standards, they call them. You have to get assessed by a psychologist and prove you can live as a woman. People complain it's demeaning and slows down the process, but it's a safeguard against going into something you might regret."

I want her to ask more about the Benjamin standards – imagining some kindly but firm experimenter insisting we examine more balls before deciding whether they come from the jar with mostly white or mostly black – but Megan turns the page. "Do you believe surgery can really transform a man into a proper woman?"

"Well, it's not just surgery. It's the hormones and the clothes and the demeanour, and how you feel inside. But if you're asking, am I deluding myself into thinking I'm going to be the equivalent of a natural-born woman, then the answer has to be no. I'm well aware that people look at me now and think I'm neither one thing nor the other. All I can say is that this feels one hell of a lot more authentic than how I used to go about."

"But you *will* get to look more feminine, as the treatment goes on!" I detect the tiniest squeak of desperation in her voice, the first departure from objectivity.

Susan Marlow smiles. "I sincerely hope so."

Megan clears her throat: "But you'll always be male on official documents, won't you? Passport, driving licence, that kind of thing. Do you think that will make things difficult?"

"Well ..." says Susan, eyes gleaming between lashes clogged with mascara.

The tape recorder emits an ear-piercing squeak. "Hang on a minute!" Megan leans forward and presses eject. Dr Marlow waits, entirely relaxed, as though she could wait all day if she had to. Her expression, as she watches the girl, shines with parental pride. As if Megan were performing open-heart surgery rather than changing a tape. It hurts to admit it, but this mixed-up man-woman understands more about being a father than mine ever did. I have a strange urge to jump up from my chair and embrace them both.

Megan resumes the interview before I can make an ass of myself. "We were talking about still being male on official records."

"That's certainly how it used to be. Being reminded of the mismatch every time you had to produce your passport or your driving licence. The humiliation if you went to hospital or applied for a new job. Especially in recent years –

you need ID to cross the road almost."

"But it's not like that anymore?" Megan's wide-eyed enthusiasm dispels any suspicions that they're playing out a conversation they've rehearsed in advance.

"The Gender Recognition Act 2004. Seems I've timed my transition perfectly. From now on, anyone who has lived for at least two years in the other gender can apply for a revised birth certificate. Officialdom doesn't need to know I was ever a man,"

I'm almost falling off the edge of my chair: "You're saying you can get a birth certificate identifying you as female?"

Father and daughter turn to stare at me, open-mouthed, as if they'd forgotten I was there.

"You have a problem with that, Dr Dodsworth?" The fatherly concern has disappeared. This Dr Marlow sounds as prickly as Professor Bradshaw.

Heat floods my cheeks. "No, no, I think it's a great idea. I didn't mean to interrupt you. You're doing a really professional job, Megan. I guess it's so interesting, I got carried away."

DR HUTTON'S PRESCRIPTION wasn't easy to follow, but it did have some benefits. That my dad was less crotchety I might have predicted; that I'd stop missing Geraldine became an added bonus.

First off, Dad marched my brother and me off to the barber's for a military-style short-back-and-sides. Then he enrolled me in a junior league soccer team recently established by the mineworkers' union.

I hardly slept the night before the first training session. Games at school meant humiliation after humiliation: from being among the leftovers when the captains were picking teams through turning seemingly invisible whenever I might be in position to take a pass, to the raw nakedness of the communal showers. I had no reason to expect this to be any different.

Yet it was. Maybe because they were desperate for members, I immediately felt part of the gang. Maybe because the coach was a good deal gentler than the screaming former paratrooper who took us at school. Maybe because I could go straight home afterwards and have a bath in privacy.

It shouldn't take a psychologist to work out that such conditions would bring out the best in me but, back then, we were all surprised at how I blossomed. Not that I reached the lofty heights of captain or anything, but nor did I ever sit out a match on the bench. Unexpectedly, I enjoyed jogging up and down a muddy field with a ball and twenty-one others. It was like being four or five again, merging with the pack that flowed up and down Bessemer Terrace. I belonged because I was there.

It was almost as good at Scouts. The songs around the campfire were as free flowing and anarchic as Music and Movement at infant school: nobody cared if you forgot the words or the tune as long as you did it with gusto. Even the cold damp nights under canvas were bearable, when there were baked beans and sausages for breakfast.

Within the walls of Dr Hutton's therapeutic regime, I

grew in confidence, if not in stature. I remained a pariah at school but, with football and Scouts as stepping-stones across the week, I managed. Now, if Geraldine turned her back on me or looked through me as if I wasn't there, I hardly noticed. I didn't *want* to hang around her any more. I felt no envy of girls chattering in covens or walking arm-in-arm across the playground. Their closeness seemed not to feed but suffocate. How much freer were the anonymous bands of boys who connected through grunts and punches and the trajectories of balls?

I understood then that Geraldine hadn't abandoned me because I was unworthy. She'd moved on because boys and girls needed different things. She might not have been able to articulate it, but Geraldine had recognised that earlier than I had. It was nothing personal.

IT WAS A stinking day in midwinter, hail needling our shoulder blades and our knees burning with cold. My hair had grown out of the military cut and lay plastered to my head, my heavy fringe channelling rain into my eyes. Some of the boys seemed more intent on avoiding hypothermia than taking possession of the ball, but I was fizzing with energy and never more determined to win. I dreaded the referee abandoning the match before time.

I had a couple of shots on goal: one hit the post and the goalie dived to catch the other. Each time a cheer rose up from our supporters it faded away to a sigh. I caught a glimpse of my dad under his black umbrella. Even if I didn't score I still might get a *Well done, our Andrew! Man of the match!* when I got home.

Not long to go but, despite feeling weary, I didn't want it to end on a goalless draw. Richard Mansfield had the ball, but I could see that he'd never make the distance to the goal. I screamed at him to pass to me but he didn't seem to hear.

Then all at once the ball was coming and I hardly had time to stop it, let alone think. The goalie leaped, a roar went up from the dads as the ball came to rest against the back of the net. A piercing whistle, another roar and the whole team were on top of me, shouting, cheering, a huddle of cold wet arms and legs: a single organism, with me its beating heart.

The coach raced over and raised my arms in the air. Blinking the rain from my eyes I peered across the pitch to the row of proud fathers. As my teammates clapped me on the back and the coach urged us into the pavilion to get dried off, I stared at the gap in the line.

The changing area buzzed as boys rubbed their wet hair with old towels and stuffed their soggy strips into drawstring duffel bags. I laughed as long and loud as any of them but I couldn't make myself feel it inside.

My teammates met up with their fathers to climb into the passenger seats of cars or to walk home side by side. Someone offered me a lift but I declined.

Outside the barber's, I jangled the coins in my pocket, hoping they would be enough. The bell tinkled as I pushed into the fuggy perfumed heat. I'd never been for a haircut alone before, but I took my seat among the men on the bench with as much bravado as I could muster.

The shop was busy that Saturday morning, giving me ample time to ponder my decision. I ran my hand across my damp hair. It had grown in at the back and sides although still wasn't long enough to be in fashion. My resolve thickened as I thought of my dad leaving the match prematurely. This would give him something to talk about when I got back.

I didn't know what the cut was called. Although short, it wasn't dated like that last cut, but nor was it as trendy as the long mane to which I'd been aspiring. It was worn by the type of scowly youth who patrolled the town in turned-up jeans with braces and thick-soled boots, looking like trouble. I'd shied away from them before. Did I dare join them?

I thought of my dad missing my winning goal as I settled myself into the leather chair. The barber wrapped a cape around my shoulders and jacked the seat higher. Our eyes met in the mirror as I outlined what I wanted,

Chapter 20

I WATCH MEGAN galumphing down the corridor in her suede pixie boots, her father tottering behind in her too-tight skirt. I knew I'd be relieved once the interview concluded, but I never suspected I'd feel as euphoric as this.

When I turn back into my office and close the door behind me, everything looks different. The red of my bike as it rests against the bookcase seems more vibrant, as if someone has been in with a brush and a pot of paint whilst my back was turned. The four-drawer aluminium filing cabinet seems more sturdy; the computer that sits in the middle of my desk looks as if it could be the latest model. It's as if I'm looking at the old familiar objects through a prism.

I flop down on to the seat recently vacated by Susan Marlow. Her musky perfume still hangs in the air. I want to cry and, for the first time in thirty years, I think I could manage it, were it not for the fact that I've got a PhD student due for supervision in half an hour and I might not know how to stop.

I'd never have dreamt a middle-aged man dressed as a woman could release me, that a person the wrong shape for her clothes should hold the key to setting me free. The door of my cage is finally open and I'm ready to fly.

I wrap my ankles around the chair legs to anchor me to the practicalities. I need to check the details of the Gender Recognition Act. Find out exactly *how* to get a birth certificate in the name I gave myself thirty years ago.

I get up and go across to the computer, switch it on, type in my password and wait for it to execute its login routine. Yet as the university insignia with the rampant lions flashes onto the screen, I hesitate. The powers-that-be have been threatening to monitor internet usage since a lecturer in the geography department was discovered surfing porn sites. Perhaps it would be better to look this up on my computer at home.

While I'm trying to figure out whether I'm being appropriately cautious or plain paranoid, I check my inbox. Between the minutes of the faculty meeting and a plea from a colleague to swap the times of some second-year lectures next semester, there's an email from Valerie Armstrong enquiring if I'm going to meet the deadline for the APA conference applications, and one from Simon Jenkins giving his Cairo address.

Both make me groan initially, until I remember I've nothing to hide anymore. While I'm sure Professor Bradshaw's secretary's offer to assist with the typing – *given how snowed-under you must be after having those few days off sick* – is more of a bid to prevent me defaulting on my appraisal objectives than burning out from overwork, I can see it from her point of view. She'll only be badgering me because Garth's been onto her and – while it would be wonderful if he were as laid-back as Max Neasden and could deflect the corporate bullshit of ratings and targets into the gutter where it belongs – he has to have free rein to fulfil his job description as he sees fit. They'd probably both rather not have to chase after lecturers as if we were school kids. What a pain it must be to manage people who refuse to follow through with what they've promised.

When I shuttle off a reply to say I've got it in hand, I'm not lying. With a new birth certificate and passport, and Marmaduke in a cattery, I can tootle off to a conference anywhere in the world. I can claim my share of the departmental travel budget and garner brownie points for forging transatlantic links. A five-hundred word abstract shouldn't take more than an afternoon to write.

With this in mind, I revisit Simon's email. *To Diana Dodsworth and undisclosed recipients*: a quick note to his university contacts to say he's now fixed up with an email address. I won't waste time bemoaning the fact that he hasn't seen fit to email me personally; I'm grateful he's kept me on his list. Poor Simon, what I've put him through these past five months! I'm lucky he's so tenacious: he might have pulled away a little, but he's never let go.

I keep my reply light and focused. After all, I'm sending it from work. *Good to know you're now online in the land of the Pharaohs. Am thinking of coming out for a visit if your offer still stands. B/W Diana.*

That's it: I'm going back to Cairo! Thanks to the Gender Recognition Act I've found the confidence to confront my demons and complete the transformation that began there thirty years before.

I presume I'll need to get my original birth certificate from my parents. A visit to Bessemer Terrace is always awkward, but at least this provides a sense of purpose to lift me above the tangle of memories that await me there. I should check how they're doing for money. A colliery pension won't go far and I can't imagine Trevor or Patricia being in a position to tip them a hand-out.

I never asked how they paid for Cairo. I never thought till now to offer to pay them back. It's as if, for all these years, I've been frozen in childhood, full of grief for what I haven't had instead of grateful for what I have.

I'm so absorbed in these reflections, I don't notice a knocking on the door until a young man pushes it open and edges in. "Did we have a meeting, Dr Dodsworth?"

"Come in, come in! Sorry, I was miles away. Have you been waiting long?" I spring from the desk chair and indicate the seat from which Megan Richardson conducted her interview with her father, while I settle myself onto the other, still perfumed with Susan Marlow's musk.

I WAS AT the table eating my cornflakes, less than a fortnight after I'd had my hair buzzed right down to the scalp. I had a French test that afternoon, but my sister kept disturbing my revision, springing from the table and darting out into the hallway every couple of minutes, only to return moments later looking as bitter as her breakfast grapefruit.

My mother held a sheet of newspaper against the chimney to draw the fire. Flames leapt behind it like shadows on a cinema screen. "The postman doesn't always come before you've left for school, duck."

"I know that, Mam." Patricia slid her teaspoon between the pockets of sallow juice and the white pith of the fruit.

Je sais, Maman.

Trevor scuttled into his seat and scattered cornflakes into a blue-rimmed dish. He fluttered his eyelashes and blew kisses at Patricia. "He loves you. He loves you not. He loves you."

Il t'aime.

"Shut it!" said Patricia.

Ferme la bouche!

My mother left the fire spitting and cracking in the grate and joined us at the table. We heard the clatter of the letterbox as she was pouring the tea. Patricia yelped and dashed from the room, Trevor at her heels calling *Darling, darling, darling!* I took advantage of the momentary quiet to re-read the list of words in my book.

Patricia flounced back into the room and flung a manila envelope onto the sideboard. She tossed a batch of square white ones onto the table beside my dish. Her hair veiled her face as she hunched over her grapefruit.

"Nothing from Nigel?" asked my mother.

"All for the skinhead," snarled Patricia.

Toutes pour le garçon aux cheveux tres courts.

I'd regretted the haircut immediately. Instead of looking tough, it had given me the veneer of a concentration camp inmate. On the journey to school I'd hidden under my hood to stave off both the cold and the taunts of my schoolmates.

But other people were so unpredictable.

As I'd walked between classrooms, I'd been bombed by

screaming girls fighting to stroke my hair, as if I were Donny Osmond. The news about the winning goal had served to fuel the hysteria. It was like being in a story where a fairy grants the hero three wishes and every single one goes wrong. I'd wished not to be an outcast only to become so much in demand I belonged more to other people than to myself. Now I squinted at an envelope that had landed, katey-cornered, on my textbook and pushed it away.

"It'll probably come in the second post," said my mother. "Or he'll give it you at school."

Trevor snatched an envelope from the jumbled heap beside me. "Roses are red, violets are blue, let me watch you do a poo!"

As I wrestled the envelope from my brother's hand, it splashed into my cereal bowl. I picked it out, dripping milk, and placed it along with the others.

"Why don't you open them?" said my mother. "Let's see who's your secret admirer."

"It's no secret," said Patricia. "All the third-year girls are after him, the divs."

I hadn't realised it was Valentine's Day. Why should I? No one had ever sent me a card before, not even as a joke. Not even Geraldine when we were kids.

"I wonder who that one with the curly writing is from," said Patricia. "It looks ever so romantic."

I'd have been far happier if the stack of envelopes on the table had been for her.

"Open your cards and let's have done with it," said my mother.

I loosened the knot in my tie and tugged at my collar.

"They're private."

My mother snatched a card from the pile. "Don't take it so serious. It's no'but a bit of fun."

As I tried to grab it back, Patricia and Trevor seized the rest and portioned them out between them. They ripped off the envelopes and tossed them in the fire.

"Listen to this," said Trevor, flourishing a card with a couple in silhouette, hand in hand on a beach at sunset. "Roses are red, violets are blue, I want your body and I'll give you mine too. Signed – Your Sweetheart."

My mother frowned. "Isn't that a bit risqué?" She must have decided it wasn't, because she laughed and held up a card with a picture of two teddy bears cuddling. "Oh you are gorgeous, Oh you are sweet, You are the boy I so want to meet."

"That's nice," said Patricia. "Who's it from?"

My mother paused and widened her eyes, like an actress playing a simpleton on the telly. "An admirer." She was giggly like that time we played pitch and putt with the ginger-haired twins.

"This is a belter!" Trevor held out a card depicting a young couple side-by-side on a swing. "Kiss me in the morning, Kiss me at night, Kiss me when you want to but always kiss me right."

I felt embarrassed for them. It was all very well for my brother to mess about, he was only a kid, but Patricia was in the sixth form and my mother was ancient. I gulped down my tea and slapped my book closed, but none of them were paying me any attention.

"My turn," said Patricia, inspecting a hand-made card

dotted with silver-foil hearts. "All the girls may want you, All the girls may try, When I get my hands on you I'll never let you go."

"That's rammel," said Trevor. "It doesn't rhyme."

Patricia laughed. "Proper poetry doesn't."

Why did I feel this thing clawing at my stomach? It wasn't as if I'd wanted the cards in the first place. I picked up my book and drifted off into the hallway, where I grabbed my coat and my duffel bag and headed off to school.

WHEN THE GIRLS were fighting to pat my head, like I was a cross between a pop star and a seaside donkey, Geraldine kept herself aloof. I thought at first she didn't approve of my hairstyle. Later, I came to realise that she didn't like to share. Geraldine, who had played the leading lady in all our dramas, and sometimes the leading man, wasn't prepared to demean herself with a bit-part in a crowd scene. She'd bide her time until she could commandeer the starring role.

So it was that she took me to the pictures to see *Love Story*. Or rather, took me to the back row of a darkened auditorium to finish off the game we'd started many years before.

Her hand across my furry scalp was mesmerising; her gentle sighing like a lullaby in my ear. As our lips met, my cock began to stir. Had she been content to leave it at that I'd have been happy, sitting with my arm around her shoulders while the grown-ups showed us how to do it on the screen. But Geraldine forced her tongue between my teeth to explore parts of my mouth I'd never even visited with a toothbrush. She tugged my shirt out of my jeans and squeezed her hand into my underpants. My cock shrivelled with shock.

I didn't understand what she wanted, but it would have been rude to ask and rude to pull away. At either side of us couples were canoodling. I didn't realise that this would be part of the package when I'd accepted her invitation to go to the flicks. It seemed doubly unfair when I'd been obliged to pay for our tickets.

Eventually, she withdrew her tongue from my mouth and her hand from my pants and settled back into her seat. I hoped she'd taken all she wanted from my body and would now sit back and enjoy the film. But even in the dim light reflected from the screen I could see she was scowling. I could hear her disappointment in every breath.

When the film was over, everyone but Geraldine stood for the national anthem. She clambered past dishevelled couples to the aisle and, ignoring the usherettes' disapproval, stormed out of the cinema. She didn't speak to me again until, six months later, she found another use for me, to keep her company on a visit to her sister in London.

"IF ANYBODY ASKS," said my mother, "tell them you're twelve."

We were in one of those eternal queues that seemed to epitomise Lourdes. This one, near the grotto where The Blessed Virgin had first appeared to a young and ignorant Bernadette, was distinguished by sitting rather than standing, shuffling our backsides along a wooden bench, like at the barber's.

My mother fingered her rosary. "No, eleven's safer. What's French for eleven?"

"But I'm thirteen."

A wizened nun in a sackcloth habit with a belt of rope looked up from her prayers.

"Keep your voice down," said my mother. "If you tell them your real age they'll make you go in with the men."

It made me think of the separate stairways when I first went to school. "Do the women and children get in quicker then?"

My mother squinted when she looked my way. Was it me that was too much for her or was it the sun? "What are you on about now?"

I'd been granted a week off school but this was no holiday. Twenty-four hours on a coach with my mother's head lolling on my shoulder and strange animal noises emanating from the deformed creatures languishing on stretchers at the back. Late nights and early mornings filled with prayers and, in between, sharing a bed with my mother and a solid sausage-shaped thing masquerading as a pillow. I kept forgetting you couldn't drink the water and dreaded having to do my business in a toilet consisting of a hole in the ground. Improving my French was out of the question, since it was impossible to pick it out from among all the other languages. As for a miracle, it seemed as likely here as at Skegness. "You know," I said, "do women and children not have to wait so long? Like the cripples."

My mother sighed at my stupidity. "There's separate baths for men and women, obviously. Do you think I'd let a strange man see me without my clothes on?"

This was getting scary. If I stayed in this queue would I have to see my mother in a state of undress? Would she see me? In the hotel we changed into our nightwear one by one in the bathroom down the corridor.

A wooden door opened in the rock and three nuns were summoned inside, along with a woman in a bright yellow trouser suit. The rest of us slid along the bench. "I don't think I'll bother," I said. "I'll light a candle in the basilica and see you back at the hotel."

My mother seized my wrist as if to give me a Chinese burn. "Don't you dare try and wriggle out of this. What do you think I brought you for? Your dad's been working overtime to pay for this. You'd better start off saying your act of contrition so you'll be ready when they let you in. Like I told you, keep your eyes on the statue of the Virgin Mary and pray for her to put you right."

At junior school there had been a craze among the more adventurous kids to hyperventilate to make themselves faint. I thought how convenient that would be right now but it needed an assistant, someone who would clutch me tight around the waist to stop the air getting in. Instead I made do with reciting a prayer over and over until it served to shut down my mind. *Oh dear God because thou art so good, I am heartily sorry that I have sinned against thee and by the help of thy holy grace I will not sin again.*

In time, my mother and I were summoned through the wooden door and stripped of our clothes, wrapped in a damp sheet and lowered into the icy water. I had no thoughts of my mother's nakedness, nor of her or the attendants seeing my cock. Despite my best efforts, I had no thoughts, either, of the power of the mother of Jesus to grant me a miraculous cure. All I knew was the shock of the water and the sting of the sheet, and fear of contamination from all the lepers and cripples and imbeciles who'd been dipped there before me.

Afterwards, we wandered around the souvenir stalls, damp and dazed. I kept stealing glances at my mother but, apart from the water lending a frizz to her hair, she didn't seem to have changed. I wondered how I'd know if *I* had, but couldn't think how to ask.

Changing into my pyjamas late that night in the chilly bathroom, I finally realised what we'd come for. I looked down, I felt between my legs, but my cock was still there, exactly as it had always been.

Chapter 21

TWENTY TO SEVEN and the Skinner building is eerily quiet. Outside the light is fading, the traffic lulled on Queen Victoria Road. My office floor is strewn with old-style computer printouts: blue-backed concertina-style paper with perforations down both sides. Half an hour ago, perhaps longer, the cleaner tapped on the door, scoped the obstacle course around the bin and, with a curt "I'll come back later, doctor," made a hasty retreat. I don't know if she was in awe of the rampant creativity or appalled by the mess.

My stomach grumbles. I navigate between the stacks of paper to rummage in my backpack. I retrieve a piece of dried-out orange peel and a few grubby tissues, but there's nothing to eat. Yet I'm reluctant to call it a day and go home to Marmaduke. I haven't felt so passionate in years.

It was midway through a supervision session that I had my brainwave. I could hardly wait to evict the student from the room so I could go back to the data from my own PhD. There'd been one rogue experiment I hadn't included in the book, the results so out of kilter with the rest it hadn't made sense. Twenty-odd years on, it's time for a rethink. If my hunch is right, it's going to make a great paper for my debut at the APA. I can almost hear the thundering applause as I bring my presentation to a close.

My thesis showed that the adolescent's intolerance of ambivalence peaks around age fifteen. Yet in every experiment one or two subjects had resisted the urge to make a snap decision to escape the discomfort of not knowing. Such outliers are commonplace in psychological research; we are dealing with people, not standardised blocks of wood. In retrospect, I am surprised neither I nor Colin Carmichael thought to investigate what distinguished these individuals from their peers. We didn't even analyse the data for sex differences.

Revisiting the data this afternoon, the central tenet still holds: kids in mid-adolescence tend to prefer things cut and dried. But not all of them. I'm going to need to take advice from a statistician before I can be absolutely sure, but it's looking as if the most rigid thinkers tend to be boys rather than girls, and a particular type of boy at that: those recruited through church youth groups and military cadets. I'll be interested to see what they make of that in America.

My stomach growls again. I'm reluctant to interrupt the creative flow, but I need to refuel. Perhaps I could grab something quick nearby and then come back for another couple of hours.

I decide on Luigi's. It might feel strange to go there in the evening, and without Simon, but the more I think of it, the more it appeals. Like going on a date with myself, a celebration of all that's gone on today. Hard to believe it was only this morning that Susan Marlow sat in my office, oblivious to the effect her words were having on me. Had it not been for her midlife crisis and her daughter's missing labs and Garth Bradshaw's truculent management, would I ever have known about the Gender Recognition Act? Would I have been able to commit to visiting Simon in Cairo, to finally presenting a paper at the APA?

Shrugging on my jacket, I lean over the computer to check my inbox. Still no response from Simon to my earlier email. I refuse to let it put a dampener on the day. Poor soul, he's probably still reeling from the shock.

———————

THE BEST THING for me about Patricia leaving home was that I could move into her bedroom. As long as I agreed to move back into the bunk beds with Trevor whenever she came home on leave. For the first time since I was a toddler, I had a room of my own.

Despite the purple psychedelic wallpaper and the forlorn gaps from where Patricia had taken her things, the room felt much warmer and welcoming than mine and Trevor's. If it hadn't been for school and my early-morning paper round, I could have stayed holed up there for weeks on end.

I searched through the leftovers in her cupboards and drawers for things I could borrow: a stumpy lipstick; some dregs of perfume; that strange contraption, the sanitary belt. I took to sleeping in her baby-doll pyjamas, powder blue trimmed with lace along the edges and puffed sleeves. Then I graduated to her chiffon nightdress with a ruffle round the neckline and, for daywear, her old school shirts that buttoned right over left. If I asked myself what I was doing, I'd have said it was my way of maintaining the connection while she was away. It was that her school shirts and night attire were less shabby than mine.

When Geraldine explained I'd have to dress up to stay in the nurses' home, it was like she knew I'd already begun the process in Patricia's room. As if she'd rigged up a hidden cine camera, or she could read my mind. I knew it would lead me into dangerous territory, but I couldn't refuse Geraldine. I couldn't refuse that part of myself.

We took our clothes and wash bags with us to school that Friday morning and, ripping off our ties, hot-footed it to the station straight after lunch. We agreed it was too risky for me to put on the red miniskirt at the station in case we bumped into someone from home. So we boarded the London train and got off again at Leicester and headed for the toilets. Then we caught the next train for St Pancras dolled up to the nines.

I'd daubed myself with Patricia's makeup in the privacy of her bedroom, but this was the real thing. When I took a swig from the lemonade bottle, my waxy lips left their imprint on the glass. When I blinked, my eyelashes, claggy with mascara, would hesitate before peeling apart. My goosebumped legs felt dreadfully exposed in the miniskirt and, crossing the station, I tottered in my borrowed platform shoes, but Geraldine linked arms with me and half dragged me to the train. It didn't really matter how awkward I felt because every time Geraldine looked at me, her face lit up with a smile.

"What are we going to call you?" said Geraldine.

"What about Andrea?" I said. "It's nearly the same as Andrew."

Geraldine wrinkled her nose. "It's not you."

"Juliet?" I blushed at the memory.

"Nah." She stared through the murky window, as if she might find inspiration in the grim backyards flanking the track. "You've got to be Diana."

"Diana?" How would I ever have breasts like Diana Dors? Be as brave as Diana the huntress?

"Die-Anna, get it? Like a new person rising from the dead." Geraldine looked quite pleased with herself as she rifled through her leather schoolbag.

"But I'm not called Anna."

"I can hardly call you Diandrew, can I?" said Geraldine. "Now give me your hand, I need to do your nails."

NO-ONE CHALLENGED PATRICIA when she introduced me as her groovy kid *sister*. No-one mentioned the *No men overnight* rule. Bessemer Terrace seemed much farther than a hundred miles away; it was as if we'd crawled through the back of the wardrobe into a different world.

We first met Suma when she was coming off shift, prim in her striped uniform with her hair flattened behind her nurse's cap. When she joined us in the common room a little later, she wore a brocade caftan with her thick hair hanging loose about her shoulders, and she smelt like a melange of pinecones and church. Desperate for something to say to this goddess, I asked what her perfume was.

"Frankincense."

She took me to her room to show me the vials of scented oils from the market in Cairo, along with her photographs from home.

"I could imagine Tutankhamen's tomb smelling like this," I said.

"You should go there," said Suma. I thought at first that she was going to kiss me, then it looked more like she might cry. So it was a relief when she did neither. "You're a beautiful child. Promise me you'll never let anyone make you think any different."

She reached for her medical book, as big and heavy as a double-volume encyclopaedia. I was impressed: "This must have cost a bomb."

Price tags were as nothing once the book fell open at page 371. I forgot London, forgot the dreams of Cairo, forgot Suma as I scanned the text.

Years before, when Geraldine had wanted to play doctors and nurses, I'd run away in a sulk. I'd been fibbing when I told her I had both male and female genitals; I never imagined anyone actually did.

I took the book to Patricia's room. There was a name for the condition, a beautiful word that might be a synonym for a nymph. I envisioned a super-race ruling through logic, physical strength and love. But the book made it clear this vision was romantic tomfoolery. Hermaphroditism was a personal and social disaster. Without medical treatment, such people were trapped in a psychological no man's land, unable to take part in society, driven mad by being neither one thing nor the other. No one could live a satisfying life with ambiguous genitals. As with the separate stairways at my first school, you could follow only one route.

I hefted the textbook back to Suma's room. Why had she shown me this? Why be so cruel?

When I saw her kissing Geraldine, I wanted to slam the book down on the desk and push myself between them. But I couldn't let them see how much I cared. Taking the book with me, I rushed back to Patricia's room and bolted the door. With my hands over my ears to keep out the hammering, I flopped onto the bed and began to read in earnest.

The treatment for hermaphroditism was the surgical removal of the least prominent genitals. From the medical perspective, it wasn't overly complicated to convert an anatomically ambiguous individual into a woman. Even with my pre-O-level knowledge of biology, I recognized that if surgeons could transplant a heart from one body to another they could amputate a man's cock and testicles without him bleeding to death. Wasn't there a time when the most celebrated singers were castrated boys?

At the end of the section there was a picture of a glamorous woman, a model and society hostess who had started life as a boy. I stared into her eyes, trying to fathom what lay underneath. She didn't look like some misfit, a freak of nature, neither one thing nor the other. She looked proud and powerful and more feminine than any woman I'd ever seen. But she was scary, too. I couldn't imagine following in her footsteps.

I rinsed my face at the basin, scrubbed off my makeup with Patricia's flannel. Then I removed the peasant skirt and blouse I'd borrowed from my sister and got dressed again in my school shirt and jumper and grey flannel trousers. Geraldine had given up banging on the door some time ago, but I still felt the need to check the corridor was deserted before stepping out.

It wasn't until I was on the northbound train, and the guard was checking my ticket, that I felt safe again. But it wasn't to last. I followed his gaze to my hand, to the tips of my fingers, each nail a buffed-up pearly pink. Geraldine had come equipped with varnish remover, but Geraldine was still in the nurses' home and the shops were closed till Monday.

―――――――

I'M THE ONLY person with a candle to myself at Luigi's tonight, but I don't feel lonely. I've ordered a small carafe of house red and, each time I raise the glass to my lips, I silently toast the people who've helped me get where I am today.

So here's to my parents who, after all, did their best: they never asked for such a troublesome child. Here's to Geraldine for befriending the oddball and indulging my penchant for morbid role-play games. Here's to Miss Bamford who taught me to read, despite repeatedly banishing me to the corner of the classroom, so that, in books, I could discover the world beyond our street. To Trevor and Patricia, for showing me how boys and girls were meant to be. To the twins for teaching me keepy-uppy; to Suma for teaching me what I was not.

Here's to St Bernadette, to Dr Hutton, to Chris Edmonds, for failing to fix me, and letting me find my way to Mr Abdullah who, on the surface at least, did. To Ms Thompson who plucked me from the comprehensive and set me down amongst the young ladies at Dorothea Beale.

Another toast to Venus Najibullah for finding me on our first weekend at university and never letting go. To

Colin Carmichael and the two-jars procedure; to Max Neasden for having such scorn for paperwork, he gave me a job without scrutinising mine. To Frank who, for all he was such a bastard, never promised more than he could give. To Venus again for coming back from America and never forgetting our friendship.

Here's to Garth Bradshaw for sending me Megan, to Megan for forcing me to meet her father, to Susan Marlow for sharing her knowledge of the Gender Recognition Act, to the lawyers who wrote it for setting me free. (Must make sure to look it up on the internet when I get home.)

To Caroline for divorcing Simon, to Giles for wanting to bring him to the party (I'll gloss over the fact that he insisted on bringing Fiona as well). To Simon, to Simon, to Simon who, for some strange reason, seemed to like me and, stranger still, kept on liking me even when I backed away. To Venus, to Simon, to every single person across the forty-five years of my life.

I drain the glass. Should I order another or am I already too pissed to return to work?

I've placed my phone within arm's reach on the gingham tablecloth, primarily to avoid appearing too much of a social isolate among the couples and groups of friends. I'm startled when it jerks into life with its strident chime and the flash of the little screen. I pick up and press the button with the green phone icon. A shiver goes through me as I hear his voice.

Luigi brings my main course. I'm conscious of leaving Simon hanging while I decline ground black pepper and accept a sprinkling of parmesan.

"Where are you?" says Simon. "Is this a bad time?"

"I'm at Luigi's and the timing's perfect."

"Who are you with?"

Do I detect a smidgen of jealousy? "No one. Except now I'm with you."

There's a pause while he takes it in. "A virtual date."

"If you like."

"I do." He wants the details: where I'm sitting; which Luigi is tonight's waiter; what I'm having to eat. "Don't let it get cold," says Simon. Fortunately, I can eat my pasta marinara one-handed while the other holds the phone. He sounds quite chuffed that I've come out to our special restaurant, that I've done so alone. I'm reminded that Simon used to see me as feisty; perhaps, from now on, I will be.

He tells me about his flat, his office at the university, the bustling city, sounding somewhat overwhelmed. "I got your email. Are you really planning on coming out?"

I swallow a mussel without chewing. "If you'll have me."

"Of course I'll have you. There's nothing I'd like better than to have you to stay."

As my gaze hovers over the couples at the other tables, I'm convinced their happiness can't match mine.

"Although I have to say I was surprised," says Simon. "What about Marmaduke? What about your fear of flying?"

"It won't kill Marmaduke to have a spell in the cattery. And they run courses at the airport. Relaxation, coping statements, exposure, that kind of thing."

"Exposure?"

"Not as exciting as it sounds. It's the behavioural term for confronting the thing you fear."

"So they actually get you on the plane? When can you get on the course?"

This is getting tricky and neither of us has even hinted at what happened, or failed to happen, on our last night. With a series of hand gestures I summon Luigi and order another glass of wine. "I'll have to see. It might be a while. Don't forget, I'll need to apply for a visa and I haven't even got a passport yet." *Or a birth certificate in my current name.*

"That shouldn't take too long," says Simon. "Well, whatever works for you, I'll be here, waiting."

"Thanks, Simon. By the way, the flowers were gorgeous. Still are, most of them. That was really sweet of you."

"The least I could do."

Is he referring to our last night being so dreadful or merely that we wouldn't be able to see one another for a while? We need to clear the air but it's hardly a suitable topic for discussion in a bustling restaurant. Besides, I'm enjoying this date so much I don't want to spoil it. As Luigi approaches my table with a goblet of red wine, I postpone my decision until after the first sip.

The wine tastes of brambles, with a hint of the hibiscus drink I remember from Cairo. Plus a faint metallic tinge, like blood. It's been quite a day: the Gender Recognition Act, my abstract for the APA and now the surprise phone call from Simon. I'm supposed to be celebrating tonight. I refuse to be dragged down by memories of failure. I take another slug of wine. "So I was right about the sunrise all along?"

Chapter 22

I'M LEAVING FOR work the next morning when I spot the official-looking letter lying on the mat. My first thought is that I've been issued with a revised birth certificate, without even registering that I need one or checking what the process involves.

My head throbs as I stoop to grab the envelope: the payback for an evening of phone romance and red wine. Let's hope I can hold it together to finish my abstract for the APA. Despite beavering away in the department till nearly midnight, there's still a fair bit to be done.

I rip right through the confidential frank on the envelope and extract the single sheet of A4. It reads as if I've been sent someone else's letter by mistake. It's less than a fortnight since the revelation that my GP's computer had me recorded as male, but the young doctor with her pigtails and snub nose might have been part of another life.

Dear Ms Dodsworth,

I trust that you have now recovered from the infection you consulted me about recently. I was wondering if I might be able to help you with the other matter we discussed. As I said, there have been major advances in the field over the last 30 years and I would be very happy to help you explore whether any of these might be of benefit to you.

I do hope you would like to make an appointment to come and discuss this with me.

With all best wishes,
Dr Libby Dean, FRCGP.

Did she labour over draft after draft in an effort to hit the right tone? Did she delegate the task to a secretary who would puzzle over what went unsaid?

With my new birth certificate I'll be able to leave such concerns behind. I crumple the letter into a ball and hurl it onto the stairs, a new toy for Marmaduke to toss between her paws. I won't need an appointment with Libby Dean to have the system register me as female. In a couple of weeks, or months at most, I reckon, it will be as if I've never been anything but.

———

IT WASN'T THE nail varnish that gave me away, but the polaroids. I'd been so careful to hide the red miniskirt among Patricia's things I forgot about the snaps of girls having fun in the bar. Blurred as they were with camera-shake, it was clear to my mother when she discovered them on one of her cleaning blitzes that one of those giggling girls in the photos was me.

My dad hit me so hard he gave me a nosebleed. My

mother spent hours on the phone to my sister, weeping the whole time. Trevor complained that no one had listened to him when he said I was a fruitcake. I gobbled up a load of paracetamol and surfaced in Casualty. No-one was happy, but one thing we all agreed on was that it was time to go back to Dr Hutton.

The psychiatrist peered at me over the top of his half-moon glasses. I could see straight away he didn't like what he saw. "Looks like you're overdue a haircut, young man."

My dad squared his shoulders. "This has gone way beyond the length of his hair."

Dr Hutton arched his eyebrows. "Oh?"

My mother looked down at her lap, twirling the wedding band on her finger. At least she wasn't crying. Not yet, anyway.

"Isn't it obvious," said my father, "there's something seriously wrong with his brain."

My mother nodded. "It's not like we've molly-coddled them or anything. His younger brother's as right as a cart."

"And what do you think might be wrong with his brain exactly?"

Dad stared across the desk at Dr Hutton. They looked like kids in the playground sizing each other up before a fight. "You're the expert."

Dr Hutton smiled thinly and turned to me. "What do *you* think is the matter?"

My stomach was in knots. I stared hard at a chip in the tiled flooring exactly midway between Dr Hutton's desk and my right shoe.

"Come on, Andrew," said my mother. "Surely you've

got some idea."

"We all know you're far too old to be playing at dressing up," said Dr Hutton.

It was as if they were trying to pick at the knots in my intestines, but the more they probed the tighter they got. I felt like Juliet after she's imbibed the poison, being buried alive with no Romeo waiting to plant the kiss that would set me free. I'd have to call out, even if it meant betraying our secret, even if they'd hate me for what I had to say.

"What's that?" Dr Hutton cupped his ear with his hand, but my mother had heard me all right. She was reaching for the box of paper hankies on the psychiatrist's desk.

"I said I wished I'd been born a girl."

My dad looked surprisingly satisfied. "There now. I said there was something not right with his brain."

"Isn't there anything you can give him, doctor?" wailed my mother.

No one had punched me. No one had accused me of having them on. It was as if the Blessed Virgin had finally acknowledged I'd been dipped in the holy water of Lourdes, and read what was written on my newly-washed soul. "Pills to make me a girl?"

Dad was nearly out of his chair. Fortunately for me, my mother was sitting between us. "To stop all these horrible thoughts and feelings, I meant. To make you normal again."

Dr Hutton raised his hand like a policeman holding back the traffic. His voice was calm and gentle: "Is that what you want, Andrew? Are you telling us you really want to be a girl?"

CHRISTMAS 1973 WAS unlike any other. We put up the same paper streamers as every other year, the same nativity scene with the shepherds and the Three Kings. We still decorated the tree and arranged the presents around it. We still had roast turkey and brussels sprouts, Christmas pudding and mince pies. We went to early mass together as we had always done, heading off before sunrise in heavy coats and hats and scarves. It didn't feel like Christmas was *supposed* to feel, however, more like a wake than the highlight of the year. If it hadn't been for Trevor, we might not have bothered. The rest of us were more concerned about what was to happen on the thirty-first of December, rather than the twenty-fifth.

Dr Hutton had promised a treatment more effective than tablets. The postman delivered my appointment for the clinical psychology department along with a batch of Christmas cards.

Patricia was appalled. "Don't you realise it's brainwashing?"

She was only home for two or three days, but we suffered the aftershock for weeks. It wasn't merely a matter of her turfing me out of her bedroom and foisting me once again on Trevor. Patricia had changed since leaving home that summer and she couldn't have slotted back into the role of dutiful daughter even if she'd wanted to. Her kohl-rimmed eyes, and her attitude, which I'd found so attractive in London, didn't work this far north. She found fault with my mother over everything and anything: the way she made the gravy; that she'd stopped her ballet lessons more than a decade before. Many of their disagreements began with me.

"Brainwashing?" said my mother. "They'd hardly do that on the national health."

"What would you call it then?" snapped Patricia.

"Dr Hutton called it aversion therapy."

' *You* do realise …" Patricia glanced across at me as she lowered her voice, I pretended to be absorbed in Trevor's *Beano* annual. "You realise it involves electric shocks?"

"I don't think so." My mother sounded alarmed and I felt my own flesh tingle. "Dr Hutton would've said."

"What did he say then?"

"That it would put a stop to your brother's silly ideas."

"You can't force him to be something he's not."

My mother laughed. "Well, he's certainly not a girl."

"He might be happier living as one."

"That's fine down London," said my mother. "But he'd never get away with it here. And you should keep your nose out of it. It's your meddling got him into this mess in the first place."

I DON'T KNOW whether it was because of this conversation with Patricia, but my mother got a headache the day of my appointment, so my father had to take me to see the psychologist.

I'd been expecting to see the woman who had administered the IQ test when I first met Dr Hutton. Over a year had passed since then and I could hardly remember what she looked like, let alone her name, but it was clear Chris Edmonds wasn't her.

Mr Edmonds – Mr, not Dr, *But why not call me Chris?* – had shoulder-length blond hair parted in the middle, and wore a purple tie-dye granddad shirt without a collar. I knew from the start Dad wouldn't approve.

Chris explained the treatment: a closed-in slide projector called a tachistoscope would present me with a series of photographs, all of them of me but in some I'd look like a boy and in others a girl. Each time the machine presented an image of me as a girl, I'd get an electric shock. Over time my brain would learn – be *conditioned* – to associate being a girl with what Chris was careful to refer to as *discomfort* – and therefore – big fanfare – I'd stop wanting to be one. The treatment could start as soon as the technicians could make up the photos.

Dad reached into the pocket of his gabardine. "Are these any use?" He handed Chris the polaroids from London. I blushed.

Chris looked delighted as he shuffled through the pile. "These will be perfect."

DESPITE THE UNEXPECTED premium from meeting her, an email from Susan Marlow pinging into my inbox still makes me shudder. Haven't I paid my dues in getting Megan through her course requirements? I'd be happy if I never had to see either of them again. But I don't dare delete her message unread, so I double click it and let her words commandeer the screen.

Dear Dr Dodsworth,

I very much enjoyed meeting you yesterday and would like to thank you again for all the support you have given to my daughter Megan Richardson. I hope I am right in assuming that you also found the interview enlightening regarding LGBT issues. To this end, I am forwarding you the links to some websites that you may find of interest, including the Gender Recognition Act. Do get in touch if you have any further questions.

All the best,
Dr Susan Marlow, Senior Lecturer in Microbiology.

Fuck fuck fuck! Is she as evangelistic with everyone she meets or just me? Does she suspect that my curiosity might be more than professional? On the other hand, not having found time to check out the Gender Recognition Act at home last night, she's given me the opportunity to do it legitimately from work. But, scrolling down her message, even delving through the corporate bumf at the bottom, I can't find the links. Perhaps it's for the best. I'd feel freer exploring it without the shadow of Susan Marlow looming over me.

An envelope icon flashes in the bottom right-hand corner of the screen. A couple of clicks and Valerie Armstrong's reminding me of the deadline for my abstract for the APA. Poor Val, she's persistent if nothing else, and I didn't even toast her in the restaurant last night.

I swivel on my chair and gaze across the stacks of computer printouts to the whiteboard on the opposite wall. Amongst the storm of red and green squiggles is the outline plan for my conference paper. All I have to do is weave them into a couple of orderly paragraphs and they'll be ready to submit.

Chapter 23

THE SHOCKS HURT, but it was pain with a purpose and my inquiring mind was fascinated by the science and the finely-tuned technology. Shocks strong enough to hurt but not to harm. Images flashed so quickly I couldn't describe them, yet still registering on my brain. After three or four sessions I was back scoring goals regardless of whether my dad was watching from the sidelines, and I'd lost interest in Patricia's wardrobe. My mother seemed happier, singing as she set the table for tea. Until out of the blue my dad bellowed *Stop!* the way you might shout *Fire!* in a burning picture-house and Mr Edmonds switched off the machine.

"What's the matter?" I said. "We've only just got going."

The psychologist set about detaching the electrodes. I crossed my arms like a toddler having a tantrum.

"I'm afraid we've got to stop for today," said Chris.

"It isn't fair," I said. "I'm the one who has these feelings. It should be up to me."

Chris turned to my dad. "Would you like a quiet chat about it?"

"There's nothing to discuss," said my dad. "I simply

can't permit you to administer any further shocks to my son."

"Not even to cure me?" I cried.

"It could help, you know," said Chris. "Perhaps I didn't explain it properly?"

"I've made up my mind," said my dad.

I KEPT MY head down as I shuffled behind my dad down the hospital corridor. Just short of the revolving doors at the exit, he laid a hand on my sleeve. When I pulled away, he winced: "Let me buy you a brew."

Generally I went straight back to school after my sessions with Chris. "I've got English lit."

Dad inclined his head towards the WRVS counter in the corner of the waiting area: "Come on, our Andrew. A cup of tea will pick you up."

I wanted to say I didn't need picking up, but I'd exceeded my quota of protestation in the psychology department. I didn't dare risk any more without another adult to referee.

Brown liquid slopped in the saucers as Dad deposited our drinks on the table. I scooped a soggy malted milk into the ashtray.

Dad spooned sugar into both our cups. "You were born in this here infirmary."

"I know." If he was planning to remind me of the four times I'd been rushed to Casualty, I'd walk straight out.

"Did you know that while your mam was having you, I was down south at a funeral?"

I stirred my tea with a plastic spoon. What was that to

me?

"It's a rum old world," said Dad. "A birth and a death in the same day."

I could've pointed out that whoever it was couldn't have died the day I was born. I'd never been to a funeral, but I knew it took a few days to arrange. But to comment, even to criticise, would betray more interest in his story than it deserved.

"My old army pal, Wilf Pettigrew. Took everything the Jerries could wang at him only to go and pop his clogs when everything was back to normal. Hadn't even hit forty."

Forty? He thought forty was young? I stole a glance at my dad, his sunken cheeks and leathery skin. He was older than my mother, although I didn't know by how much. I might have been interested when I was little, but not now, not here in the hospital coffee bar soon after he'd scuppered my chance of redemption.

"I wanted to call you after him, but your mother wouldn't have it."

I almost spilled my tea. Life had been hard enough without being saddled with the name Wilfred. I registered a new respect for my mother.

My dad stretched out a sigh. "Seems you turned out like him anyroad."

I had no idea where this was going, but I knew I didn't like it. How dare he veto my treatment, and then try and make up for it with a heart-to-heart? If I didn't get away I'd be overturning tables like Jesus in the temple. I'd be punching my own dad.

My eyes misted over as I trudged through the car park.

What did I care about this Wilf character? Why couldn't my dad just see *me*? It was almost lunchtime when I walked through the school gates. A sizzling hatred had flared up as if from nowhere and I didn't know how to turn it off. But it helped me come to a decision about my future. I was determined to do whatever it took not to grow up to be like my dad.

———————

I'M IN THE kitchen, hacking at a lemon with a carving knife, when Marmaduke makes an entrance through the cat flap. She gives me one of her looks. *Drinking in the daytime, Diana! Where will it all end?* The liquid in the tumbler effervesces as I feed it the wedge of lemon, sucking it down to the depths before releasing it back to the top. I can't see me ever bouncing back so smartly.

The ice rattles as I carry my gin and tonic to the front room, Marmaduke padding behind me at a safe distance. When I flop onto the sofa, she curls up in the armchair in the bay window. "Don't judge me, O Daughter of Isis. At least I'm not drinking straight from the bottle. At least I'm not slashing my wrists."

Marmaduke demonstrates her disdain by licking her paws. I show mine by gulleting half the contents of the glass in one go. I savour the sour-sweet taste of the tonic, the way it fizzes in my mouth. Anything to avoid admitting my life's careering towards a brick wall.

I gaze at the clock on the DVD player. It's less than three hours since I emailed my abstract to the APA conference committee. How pleased I was with myself. How smug.

It was too early for lunch but, after all that mental effort, I thought I deserved a break. After playing around a while on the conference website, a little disappointed they hadn't yet posted the programme of extracurricular activities, I decided I was safe to google the Gender Recognition Act. Garth should applaud me for informing myself of equality and diversity issues, as well as for my dedication to his star student's assignment.

I guzzle the rest of my drink and wander back to the kitchen for a refill. Tonic water sloshes onto the worktop as I add a dash to the gin. I don't bother with fresh lemon or ice, and the bottle comes with me back to the sitting room. Marmaduke spreads her claws and yawns.

"*Two thousand and four,* she said. *The Gender Recognition Act two thousand and bloody four.* What would you make of that, Marmaduke? If it said two thousand and four would you ever expect for one moment you'd have to wait till two thousand and effing five before you could do anything about it?"

At first I thought I must have missed something. The website, crammed with legalese, seemed designed to confuse rather than inform. I got bogged down in definitions, determinations and evidence, until I finally came to understand that those who had transitioned more than six years previously would not be required to produce documentation they might not possess. This bit of common sense cheered me so much I didn't even mind their referring to it as the grandfather clause. I actually laughed when I read on to discover that such old-timers would be allowed to jump to the front of the queue and have their applications prioritised during the first six months of the Act. I needed to check when the six months started to see if I might get in with the early birds. With October looming, it was a slim chance.

I take a slug of gin. I hardly taste it. "I never imagined I'd be six months too soon."

Marmaduke purrs like an idling motor. How can she sleep at a time like this?

"Why did they call it the Gender Recognition Act 2004 if it wasn't going to come into effect till April 2005? Where's the logic in that?"

Where's the compassion? It's all very well for Susan Marlow but *she* won't be eligible for another couple of years. What does *she* care about the difference between four and five?

I can't hang on till next April. Simon will be back by then and, unless they can turn around my application and issue me a passport and American visa in under a month, the APA conference will have been and gone without the dazzling paper from Dr Dodsworth on adolescent tolerance of ambivalence.

Marmaduke raises her head. I feel myself welling up as she plunges from the chair and struts towards me. I must've exhausted all my nine lives with Simon; he won't forgive me if I let him down again. Garth Bradshaw will surely hound me out of the department if I don't redeem myself at the APA. My marmalade cat is all I've got left. I set down my glass on the carpet and invite her onto my lap. But she thrusts her nose in the air and saunters from the room.

Chapter 24

I FIXED MY gaze on the chipped tile on the floor between my chair and the psychiatrist's desk. It was in a slightly different position to when I'd last sat there but, of course, it must have been the furniture that had moved and not the chip.

My mother dabbed her eyes: "I can't take it in."

"Perhaps you'd like to enlighten your parents, Andrew," said Dr Hutton.

Ploughing through medical books in the library, scribbling down notes and assembling it like an essay for English Lit, my argument had seemed clear and irrefutable. Now, laid out on the desk, the two double-sided sheets of my best italics seemed as shameful as Mr Worrall's discovery of the petition in junior school. "There's an operation," I mumbled. "It could turn me into a girl."

"You're asking to be castrated?" growled my dad.

"Like that model," whimpered my mother. "What was her name again?"

"April Ashley." At least the concept wasn't entirely unknown.

"I can't believe we're discussing this." My dad glared at

Dr Hutton: "You were supposed to fix his brain."

Dr Hutton sat back in his chair, stretched out his hands with his fingers interlaced. "I wonder where this notion has come from," said Dr Hutton. "Might it perhaps be an attempt to gloss over the fact you've chickened out of your treatment? Aversion therapy, if I may remind you, Mr Dodsworth, was exactly what you asked for – an opportunity to fix his brain."

My dad shifted in his seat, but he said nothing.

"Didn't you have the backbone for it, Andrew?" continued Dr Hutton. "Were the shocks too much to take?"

"They weren't too bad," I mumbled.

"What you've done is to demonstrate you've no backbone." Dr Hutton winked at my mother. "And I do believe that girls need their backbones quite as much as boys."

I looked across at my dad, but I was on my own. "It wasn't working," I said.

"You haven't given it sufficient time," said Dr Hutton.

At my age, both my granddads had been doing shifts underground. They said we had it soft, but maybe we just had it different. I wasn't a coward. I cleared my throat. "As I put in my letter, psychology and psychiatry are trying to change my mind to match my body. I don't see why it has to be that way. Why can't you change my body to suit my mind?"

"Well for one thing," said Dr Hutton, "I'm not a surgeon."

My mother smoothed down the skirt of her summer dress, smiling at the psychiatrist's feeble joke.

"Look," said Dr Hutton, "I'm not unsympathetic but, you know, life doesn't always go the way we want it. We all have moments when we'd rather things were different. I'll bet your father doesn't always feel like going to the office. I'll bet your mother doesn't always feel like shopping and cleaning and putting food on the table. And I can tell you …" Dr Hutton chuckled, "… I certainly don't always feel like listening to people's problems. But we get on with it, because we're realistic. We know we can't always have our own way. And, once you set your mind to it, it'll be the same for you. You might wish you'd been born a girl, but the fact is you weren't. We've all got to make the best of things. That's what growing up means."

My mother nodded, but what she said next surprised me: "But suppose an operation was the right thing for Andy, how might that come about?"

"Over my dead body," said my dad.

"Have you ever heard of taking a sledgehammer to crack a nut?" asked Dr Hutton. "Surgery's an extreme remedy for a problem that's bound to go away of its own accord."

My mother persisted, despite her quaking voice: "In theory, though. If that April Ashley had it done …"

"In Morocco," I said.

"So not on the national health?" said my mother.

Dr Hutton sighed: "I believe some cases have had surgery abroad for vanity reasons."

"Must be crackers," said my dad.

My legs were shaking and I felt light in the head: "What if it wasn't for vanity? What if a person couldn't go on living the way they were?"

"Speaking hypothetically?" said Dr Hutton.

Crossing his arms over his chest, my father shook his head. My mother and I nodded.

Dr Hutton composed his words carefully: "Such a person, if he were an extreme suicide risk and all other avenues had failed, might, in certain special circumstances, be referred to the Gender Dysphoria Clinic in London for assessment."

I laughed: "So can you refer me to this Dysphoria Clinic?"

Dr Hutton shook his head. "As I said, I was speaking purely hypothetically. But I have to tell you that in your particular case, even if it did fit the criteria, which I very much doubt, you'd have a long wait. They wouldn't consider you until you were at least eighteen."

"DON'T THINK IT'S a bed of roses, being a woman," said my mother.

Since Patricia left home, I'd taken to helping out more with cooking and cleaning. I didn't mind, but I was embarrassed that my mother would think I was hankering after a future as a housewife. It seemed to me that a bed of roses was exactly what my mother's life was like: perfumed petals imprisoned within a tangle of thorns.

She was battering fish while I was attending to the chip pan on the stove, calmed by the melting dripping, a waxy, cheesy island gradually being consumed by a bronzed molten pool. I'd been fizzing with anger since the meeting with Dr Hutton and scared of where the feelings might take me; twice I'd been in detention for cheeking a teacher. It was as if another me had moved into my body and, like the new fat washing into the old, it was threatening to take over. My doppelganger was bold and spiky and determined to lead me astray. He was brave but he hadn't the brains to temper his bravado: in my dreams he got me into fights with brawny men with skull-and-crossbone tattoos across their knuckles; he had me getting arrested for filching fags from the corner shop. If I didn't manage to rein him in he'd have me leaving school to join the army, he'd have me labouring down the pit. My alter ego would drag me into all kinds of dangerous scenarios and then, exactly when I had most need of his confidence and courage, he'd abandon me, leave me to face the consequences of his rash decisions alone.

I didn't want to grow up to be my father, or any other man I knew, apart from perhaps the psychologist, Chris Edmonds, But his world was too confusing: the tachistoscope; the electric shocks; the T-shirt with the yellow smiley face.

My sister's was the only adult situation I could freely aspire to. She wasn't hemmed in by domestic drudgery like my mother or, like my father, escaping to the hills. She had a room of her own to serve as either retreat or launching pad, with people around who understood her, other girls who enjoyed and wanted similar things. It would be like when we were little, streaming down the street at one with the Bessemer Terrace gang. I couldn't imagine a parallel world for men. Men might try to create such a life but, sooner or later, it would self-destruct in the competition to lead the pack.

Some days I thought I'd do anything to secure a future

like my sister's. Yet the transition from boy to girl seemed terrifying. The pictures in the medical books had made me quickly turn the page. Yet whenever I thought it might not be worth it, I'd remember Dr Hutton's scorn when I presented my case. All those hours of research dismissed as a passing phase. I'd show him. Him and my dad.

How could I wait more than three years to be referred to the clinic? It was over a fifth of my lifetime, over a thousand days. A thousand days of hating my body, of being shut out from the only place I could be myself. I'd be a man by then, with a deep voice and a wayward cock. How many freakish erections would I have succumbed to, how many wet dreams?

Or maybe, like my mind, my body would stay in limbo. While even the dunces and retards tackled puberty, I'd be the runt at the back. I'd be a perpetual schoolboy, Peter Pan without Wendy. I could probably cope if I could hide away like a hermit, but I'd need to rub along with other people, get a job to pay my way. All I could envisage for the next three years were different versions of impossible.

I sneaked out of school one lunchtime to pick up a bumper bottle of paracetamol from Boots. If they asked, I'd say they were for my mother's headaches; which was true, except that her headache was me. I was waiting in the queue, delving into my duffel bag for my money, when I came across a crumpled pink envelope with my name typed on the front. Someone must have put it there at breaktime. My stomach clenched as I recalled the stack of Valentines I'd been sent the previous year. But Valentines fell in February and we were well into May.

I paid for the tablets and darted out of the shop. Leaning against the wall where no one could peer over my shoulder, I ripped open the envelope and took out a sheet of flimsy white foolscap. The message was short and simple, typed on a machine with a smudged letter e. *Meet me tomorrow 7:30 p.m. at the bus shelter. Wear your mini skirt. Love, Geraldine.*

It didn't matter that we hadn't spoken since I'd caught her kissing Suma in the nurses' home. This was an opportunity to confide my hopes and fears and disappointments. Geraldine wasn't academically inclined, but she was more worldly than I was, with a down-to-earth common sense that would cut right through the doubt and confusion plaguing my mind. She'd be a hundred times more helpful than Dr Hutton with his pompous pontifications.

Back at school, I made straight for the lavatories and locked myself into an empty cubicle. I unscrewed the top of the medicine bottle and tipped the tablets into the toilet bowl, keeping back a scant half-dozen in case my mother got one of her headaches.

IN THE CURTAINED cubicle in the Casualty department that evening, the policeman shrugged and put away his notebook: "You know where I am if you change your mind."

After he'd gone, my dad grabbed my duffel bag from beneath the trolley. He exhumed my jeans and T-shirt and stuffed the plastic carrier with the harlot-red miniskirt inside. "Them youths didn't interfere with you, did they?"

I slipped the hospital gown from my shoulders, snatched

the T-shirt and pulled it over my head, but it didn't seem substantial enough to hide my blushes. I knew what it meant to be interfered with, but only for a girl. "Not really."

I swung my legs round to the side of the trolley and shuffled into my jeans. My dad turned away and examined the lightbox where the doctor had shown us the x-rays. "The day you were born I was down south at a funeral," he said.

I froze, my fingers pincering the tab of my zip. "I know, Dad, you told me."

"Wilf Pettigrew. We were in yon prison camp together."

Please, Dad, not now! I tugged at the zip, but it jammed halfway.

Dad droned on, like he was in the confessional at church. "I could see from the off he was different, but I didn't think much of it at first. He was gentle, sweet-natured. His ma used to send him cigarettes and chocolate and he was always willing to share."

He made it sound like a boarding school in an Enid Blyton book. I tried to make myself comfortable on the trolley, resting my back against the wall as I pulled the hem of my T-shirt down over my fly. He was determined to tell his story and I was compelled to listen: with my cuts and bruises, I was relying on him to get me home.

"I was gone-out when I got the telegram. I'd heard nothing from him for nigh on fourteen years. It never occurred to me not to go and pay my respects. Your nannar was happy to watch Patricia while your ma came in here to have you.

"I thought I'd be meeting up with my old army pals again but, when I got to the church, I was left to croak through the hymns with a bunch of strangers. I wasn't planning on going back to the house but his ma was adamant. Like she needed someone who remembered him from the war. I could hardly refuse a grieving mother and the snap would set me up for the train.

"At first I thought they were acting funny because they were southerners. They gave me a right earful. I didn't even notice nobody mentioned how he died. I had his brother-in-law boasting about their wonderful family doctor. *Signed the death certificate, you know.* As if that weren't a standard part of the job. And his sister trying to quiz me about the prison camp, as if she hadn't the manners to know there's stuff goes off that's better forgotten. And then his ma, taking me by the arm to the shed in the garden. *This is where I found him*, she said."

I thought Dad must have finished, he stood there so long. His story might as well have come from the time of pharaohs, so little relevance it had for me. Yet I was grateful for the distraction from thinking how Geraldine had let me down.

My dad turned round, fixing his gaze on a spot on the wall just past my left shoulder: "It was a criminal offence, back then, you see. The suicide act didn't come in till a couple of years after."

I shivered: "Suicide?"

"Could've been thrown in the slammer for it. That's why they kept it hush-hush."

My laughter was half mocking, half hysterical: "They couldn't send a dead man to prison."

"Them as didn't succeed got tried and sent there. And

their families sometimes, for aiding and abetting."

I was five years old again, swinging my legs on a wooden bench in church, grappling with the concept of eternity, the *For ever and ever, Amen.* Then and now, the world was too big and too terrible to comprehend, my place within it too small. I needed to go home, wrap myself in Patricia's nightgown and sleep off my fears.

The rail jingled as a nurse whisked the curtain aside. "Still here? Didn't Doctor tell you you're free to go?"

———————

THE REAR WHEEL sings as I push my bike down the second-floor corridor of the Skinner building. I weave it through the fire doors and press the button for the lift. The aluminium doors ping apart almost immediately and a young man squeezes himself into the corner to make room for me and the bike. It's Tom Leaside, one of the postdoctoral research assistants. He throws me a cheesy grin: "Sloping off so early?"

"Doctor's appointment." I'm as embarrassed by where I'm heading as much as by my compulsion to reassure him I'm not shirking my duties. Four o'clock was the only time Libby Dean could fit me in.

The lift shudders as we reach the ground floor. Tom keeps his finger on the button while I reverse my bike into the lobby. A moment later he joins me. "I hear you're coming to the APA conference."

Word certainly gets around. "I've only just submitted my abstract. It's got to get accepted yet."

"Surely you've no worries on that score?"

Fortunately my colleagues can't begin to imagine my worries on the matter. "Don't count your chickens, and all that."

"I reckon it's going to be quite a party. Clare Sutton's got an invited paper in the sports psychology section and we've got a whole symposium on autobiographical memory. It'll be the first time I've presented abroad."

"We can't all get funding." It's perfect: Garth will have to come grovelling, full of apologies for raising expectations he's not able to finance. I can appear mature and magnanimous, and go the following year on a proper passport.

"Don't worry about that," says Tom. "Ours will be funded through the research grant and wouldn't Clare get her expenses through the APA?"

"I suppose so."

"Don't sound so happy about it!" Tom starts to laugh and changes his mind. "Sorry, I forgot you're not well. I'd better let you hit the road."

Chapter 25

M Y PARENTS' ATTITUDE shifted after I was set upon at the bus shelter. It gradually became clear, without anything being said, that they'd given up trying to force me to be the boy I couldn't possibly be. As long as it was never referred to, and I kept it confined to the bedroom, I was free to daub myself with makeup and dress in girls' clothes. They made no comment when I hung up Patricia's floral skirts and cheesecloth smocks on the line along with the rest of the weekly wash. It seemed as if Geraldine's note had fixed it for me after all.

My mind focused and, whether in blazer and flannels in the classroom or in a frilly pink negligee sprawled on Patricia's bed, I was finally getting to grips with simultaneous equations, iambic pentameters and oxbow lakes. My mother seemed grateful for my help around the house and would even accede to some of my wilder culinary suggestions, such as mashing a pinch of mustard in with the potatoes or a sprig of mint with peas. Perhaps I *could* hang on till I was eighteen, whether or not puberty grabbed me by the balls.

When Patricia came up for a few days in June, she

didn't only take over my boudoir, but my role as deputy chef. Fearing a repeat of the fireworks we'd had at Christmas, I was on edge when she and my mother were alone together. Doing my homework at the dining-room table, I couldn't help overhearing their conversation in the kitchen through the partition door. I was surprised when Patricia invited my mother to join her and Suma on a visit to Cairo in the summer. My mother seemed surprised too, "Africa? In August? We'll be burnt to a frazzle."

Patricia replied that Cairo was nearer the Mediterranean than the Equator and, besides, the heat would be relaxing, good for her nerves.

"Won't do my nerves much good to go to a war zone," said my mother.

My stomach clenched, as I recalled the pictures on the news the previous year, Men with guns in desert camouflage uniforms, the shameful reminder that I'd never be that brave. On that weekend visit, Suma hadn't mentioned the conflict in her country, or perhaps I'd been too wrapped up in my own concerns to hear.

Patricia was yet more dismissive: "That was over and done with last October. And besides, the dispute was in the Sinai, miles from the capital."

"Makes no odds," said my mother. "I couldn't leave your dad and the boys."

"So you're going to be tied to the kitchen sink for the rest of your days? Just because my dad thinks it's beneath him to mash a brew."

"Don't you start with that women's lib malarkey! A couple of months in London and you think you know it all."

It hadn't taken long for another argument to flare. I considered taking my books up to the bedroom, although it wouldn't be much quieter with Trevor up there.

"Why do you think I invited you?"

"Well, it can't be for the pleasure of my company, can it?"

In the pause that followed I pictured them, hands on hips and matching scowls, determined not to be the first to back down. I gathered up my books and screwed the top back on my fountain pen.

Patricia was only just audible: "Don't say anything to Dad, but Suma knows a place that could help our Andrew."

I froze. Above the clatter of pans, my ears strained for more. Holding my breath, I put down my books, scraped back my chair and tiptoed to the door.

All I could hear were two out-of-tune sopranos backing Donny Osmond on *Puppy Love*. How could they be friends again so quickly and, if they were, why wasn't my mother pumping Patricia for more information about the place that could put me right?

ABOUT A MONTH later, a few days before school broke up for the summer, my mother made her announcement. It was teatime, and the four of us were gathered round the dining table with plates of cold tongue, and new potatoes glistening with butter. "I've booked my ticket," she said. "I'm off on holiday next week."

Trevor scowled: "You're going to Skegness? Without us?"

"Egypt. Patricia's treating me." A visit to the hairdresser

had left her with frothed and lacquered hair like a doll's, her forehead flayed from the heat of the drier.

Dad's knife scraped across his plate. Nobody we knew went abroad on holiday. They might go on pilgrimage to Lourdes or, at a pinch, Rome, but nobody's wife or mother took off for Egypt, even if her daughter was paying. "A bit of salad would've gone nice with this," said my dad.

I took that as a signal not to ask questions. But Trevor was indignant. "Who's going to make our tea?"

"I was going to ask your nannar if she could help out," said my mother. "Failing that, you'll all have to muck in."

Dad at work, Trevor out with his friends, the whole house to myself: "I could do the cooking." My cheeks burned with the heat of their gaze and I stared at my plate.

"There's not just cooking," said my mother. "There's washing and cleaning and shopping on top."

"It wouldn't bother me," I said.

"That's women's work," said Trevor.

I felt a tingling in my groin, half excitement, half fear. For the past month, the thought that Suma knew a place where they might be able to help me had been soothing me to sleep. But my hopes had to stay secret; to speak of them would be like admitting I'd discovered my presents hidden in the wardrobe long before Christmas. But now my brother had broached the subject, I thought my mother might seize on the opportunity to open things up. *Andrew's going to need to get to grips with women's work*, she might have said. Instead, my mother shook her head. "Times are changing, young lad. Haven't you heard of women's lib?"

I EMBRACED THE role of housewife with gusto. Returning from my morning paper round soon after seven, I'd rustle up a plate of eggs and bacon for my dad. While he was seated at the table, accompanied by some orchestra on Radio Three, I'd make up a couple of sandwiches for his snap, and some for Trevor while I was at it, although he needed little incentive to stay out all day. As soon as they'd gone, I'd retune the transistor to Radio One and take it upstairs while I chose my outfit for the day.

I was too busy to feel lonely. I didn't want to just keep the place ticking over, I wanted to excel. I scrubbed between the tiles in the bathroom and shampooed the carpets upstairs and down. I patched sheets and trousers and sewed on buttons that had been missing for years. I retrieved the red miniskirt from its hiding place and put it through the wash, mended the tears till it was wearable again. I poured over recipe books and scoured the shelves in the supermarket for exotic tastes to surprise my dad and brother at mealtimes.

In the heat of the afternoon I'd lie on my bed with a cup of tea and one of my mother's magazines. I'd doze off to the voice of Jenni Murray on *Woman's Hour*. I was content, almost happy. Yet now and then I'd be ambushed by a feeling I couldn't fathom: a sense of loss, nostalgia for the childhood that was about to end. A sentimental song on the radio might spark it off, or a story out of *Woman's Own*. It kicked me in the stomach, winding me and I'd collapse in a heap, doubled up, and wait for it to pass.

My mother was gone a week, then two weeks, then a little more. Even Trevor seemed to find this odd. "When's Mam coming back?" he demanded one teatime, disgruntled with my watery cauliflower cheese.

We usually had the radio on to mask the silence, although neither Trevor nor I could appreciate classical music, and Dad wouldn't countenance anything else. Today it was an orchestral piece that jumped unpredictably between a whisper and a thunderburst. Trevor had raised the question in a quieter sequence but we had to sit through a few clamorous bars before Dad deigned to reply: "When she's finished what she went there to do."

"And when's that going to be?"

"I really don't know," said Dad.

Any minute now Trevor would be asking what it was she'd gone for. He'd have worked out it wasn't a holiday.

"Will she be back in time for us to go to Skegness?"

"Nobody's going to Skegness this year," said Dad.

Trevor was momentarily speechless. Then he started chuntering about how it wasn't fair until I thought my dad was going to dob him one. Instead, he got up from the table without finishing his tea and went out to sit on the front step with his pipe, leaving my brother dangerously close to tears. He was right, it wasn't fair. I knew he'd feel worse if he set off crying in front of me, so I racked my brain for something that might cheer him up: "I was thinking of making a chocolate cake tomorrow."

He stuck out his tongue: "Fruitcake would make more sense."

LIBBY DEAN SLOUGHS off her gloves and tosses them into a bin below the sink. "It doesn't look too bad."

I can't believe I've just exposed myself to a woman with a child's turned-up nose and pigtails. I climb down from the couch and jiggle my legs into my knickers and trousers.

Dr Dean takes a seat at the desk and gestures for me to join her: "But you're right, it is rather narrow, and with no natural lubrication …"

My ears are ringing and my eyes refuse to focus. I want to run out but my legs are like lead. I lower myself onto the chair and try to look demure.

"Didn't they tell you about dilatation?"

I feel like a kid, chastised for dodging my homework until I realise Libby Dean must perceive me as a surgical patient denied proper after-care. I remember feeling judged by the social worker, Ms Thompson, assuming she wanted to send me to Borstal rather than the swanky boarding school for young ladies she had in mind. I've never been any good at recognising empathy.

She turns aside, brings up a search engine on her computer screen. "I suppose it was prior to the Benjamin standards …"

I laugh, recalling Megan's interview with Susan Marlow. Everyone I meet seems more genned up about this than I am. My worst nightmare is slowly developing into a farce. Dr Dean eyes me quizzically. I shake my head, hoping I'll eventually settle on a mind-set outside the triumvirate of terror, hysteria and shame.

Her fingers clatter on the keyboard. "I could refer you to the Gender Identity Clinic at Charing Cross. Or if it's really more the physical side you're concerned about, we might start with one of the gynaecologists at the RVI."

The buzzing in my ears gets louder. "I don't know."

Libby Dean swings round in her chair, poised to give me her full attention. Her palms are flat on her thighs, but I fear she really wants to give me a hug. "We'll do this at your pace, Ms Dodsworth. Now, next month, next year, or never. However you want to play it, I'll be here for you."

If she's wondering why I bothered to make the appointment if I'm going to chicken out of everything she suggests, she's not the only one. It's ironic really: I emailed Simon about a week ago to say I'd come down with a cold and wouldn't be in contact. A stupid lie, but the only thing I could think of to buy me some time. After the bombshell about the Gender Recognition Act, I couldn't keep pretending I was coming to visit but nor could I bear to bring the relationship to an end. Nobody consults the doctor about a cold, yet here I am in my GP surgery. Maybe Simon does have something to do with that. "My boyfriend ..." I fix my gaze on the stethoscope coiled on her desk.

Dr Dean smiles: "Would you like me to see you both together? Or I'm sure any of the other services would be only too happy to include him. There's clinical psychology, if you'd like to talk things through."

"He's abroad at the moment."

"So you'd prefer to hang on till he's back? Or is it that you were hoping to get things moving for yourself when he's away?"

She's bubbling with good intentions while the best I can do is sit here like a sulky kid. It's like one of those guessing games where you're restricted to yes and no answers. But how can I explain I've made a pact with a God I no longer believe in that, if I go through the motions, if I act like there's a happy-ever-after waiting round the corner, I'll be rewarded with a new birth certificate and passport straight away?

Dr Dean hasn't yet exhausted her reserves of goodwill: "I'm wondering if a chat with a psychosexual counsellor might be a good place to start. You could see them on your own first, if you like, and then follow up with your boyfriend when he gets back."

It's almost as bad as when they tried to get me to see Tammy Turnbull that night in A&E. Come to think of it, is it due to discretion or NHS inefficiency that Libby Dean has made no reference to that? Whichever way it is, I can't admit to a counsellor how little I know about sex. A cold sweat washes over me as it strikes me that Dr Dean might think Simon gets turned on by all that gender-bending stuff. "My boyfriend's perfectly normal. I mean, he was married, he's got two kids."

Libby Dean swallows a giggle. "Then he'll know there are other ways of making love that don't involve penetration."

I push back my chair. If this is a taste of psychosexual counselling, I don't want it.

Dr Dean reaches out. Her fingertips graze my knee. "I don't mean to offend you. You've not had an easy time of it, and change is always scary. But you *are* entitled to a sex life. Things could be even better, you know, if you take the risk and let people help you."

I grit my teeth: "I'm fine, honestly. I shouldn't have wasted your time."

"I don't consider it wasted, and I'm happy to give you all the time you need. Your boyfriend, he doesn't know, does he?"

"Like I said, he's normal."

"Then he'll want to love you as you really are."

Chapter 26

"YOU KNOW YOUR ma wants you to see a doctor when we get there?" said my dad.

I was roused from my doze to the smell of his pipe and a deadness in my right leg. "Like Dr Hutton?"

"I reckon he's a surgeon."

I was too tired to get excited, but I couldn't let this one go. I rubbed my leg and gazed across the ranks of bucket seats, trying to see beyond the wall of blackened glass to the planes warming up on the runway: "Does he know I'm not eighteen?"

He sucked on his pipe. "I doubt them Arabs bother about stuff like that."

"He knows about me though, does he, Dad?" I jiggled my leg, life creeping back into the muscles. "He understands about my ... problem?"

"Let's wait and see when we get there, shall we?"

People sat slumped around their luggage, drinking coffee and smoking, and grumbling now and then in languages with zero overlap with English or French. An acrid smell drifted across from the toilets. I'd thought it would be fun to travel to Cairo via a communist country, but that was before I understood we'd taken this route because it was half the price of flying direct, and before I realised we'd be corralled overnight in this dismal transit lounge, with no chance of venturing outside to explore. My body ached to be horizontal but the design of the room conspired against it: a run of seats had curves in all the wrong places and the tiled floor, strewn with sweet wrappers and cigarette butts, was too cold and grimy for anything but the soles of our shoes. I could understand why my father might not want to talk.

Yet it seemed that he did. "I was about your age when the war started. Thought I was right grown-up at fifteen."

It would be like my granddad telling me about going down the mine when he was barely into his teens. *Youths these days don't know you're born.* Perhaps if I kept my eyes closed and didn't say anything he'd give up.

"So pissing desperate to fight for my country. Couldn't wait to join up."

I felt his disappointment curdling in my stomach. We both knew I would never have been so brave. "You're a right fossneck at that age. Nobody can tell you nowt. As far as I was concerned, it was all a glorious adventure. Me and my pals were going to give Hitler a bloody nose."

I thanked God I hadn't been born in America. In a couple of years they'd be shaving my head and dressing me in camouflage and shipping me out to Vietnam. My fear of fighting, if nothing else, was proof I wasn't meant to be a man.

"Three years felt like an eternity. We were all praying it wouldn't be over and done with before we reached eighteen. Most of us lied about our age and enlisted a year early. Even a scrap of a lad like Wilf Pettigrew who looked about twelve and a half."

Not the funeral the day I was born again! How many times did I have to hear about that?

"Well, we'd not even done with basic training when we realised we'd been had. Nobody was letting on, mind; didn't want to come across as some milky pacifist. And what was the point of moaning about it? We were already trapped.

"I was angry at first, the way they treated us. Like we didn't have a brain to think for ourselves. Like we'd had to be press-ganged instead of volunteering. If an officer didn't like the look of you, they could make your life hell. If you had two left feet like Pettigrew or were a bit lairy like me."

Was this a new story or another version of the one I'd heard before? Either way, it was more than I wanted right then. I tried to think about something else, set off trundling through the *Our Father* in my head, but when I got to *Thy will be done* my mind was shunted back to my dad.

"I was like you, you see, too tupheaded for my own good …"

Like me? I'd never seen myself as stubborn. I sat up then and opened my eyes, blinking at the harsh fluorescent light.

"Of course, I'd have had to go eventually, but it wouldn't have done me no harm to hang on another year, to do a bit more growing at home. Your grandpa tried to tell me but of course I wouldn't listen. Thought I knew best."

A hiss of static burst forth from the tannoy. I heard the word Cairo. "Dad?"

"There was no telling me, never is at that age. Had to learn the hard way."

People were beginning to shake off their sleepiness and gather up their things.

"Had to see for myself before I knew what war meant. But if there'd been some way, if I could have joined up for the day and then gone home to think it over, it might have brought me to my senses."

High on the wall behind us, a speaker crackled. Passengers started to congregate beside the plate-glass doors. The world beyond had moved on from black to navy blue. I looked at my watch.

Dad put his hand in his jacket pocket and brought out our boarding cards. "Do you think that's our flight?"

I'D EXPECTED TO see pyramids as the plane dipped towards the airport, expected Suma to meet us and whisk us away to her family home in an oasis of palms. I'd expected men in red Tommy Cooper hats, with a black tassel swinging from the crown.

As the bus coughed its way towards the city, I wiped away the naiveté of my expectations as I rubbed the sleep from my eyes. I was fifteen, too old to believe in fairy tales, and yet my dad must have brought me here for something. Cinderella got to marry her handsome prince. The ugly duckling grew up to be a swan.

We got down from the bus in the main square and Dad asked for directions to the hotel. Men dressed in long white caftans held hands as they studied the headlines at the newsstands. Women dressed like nuns head to toe in black chatted to long-legged dolly birds, their voices stretching shrill and guttural above the blare of the traffic. Heat seared the paving and my skin felt sticky beneath my T-shirt and jeans.

We met up with Patricia and my mother at the hotel, with just enough time for a shower and change of clothes before the four of us headed off to the clinic. Mr Abdullah was a compact figure, no taller than my mother, but very suave with his Brylcreemed hair and clipped moustache, his three-piece chalk-striped suit in defiance of the heat. I found his demeanour reassuring: I'd been half expecting him to greet us straight from surgery in a bloodied butcher's apron.

Nevertheless, I was embarrassed when he took me off to a more clinical room and bade me strip down to my socks. Most of the questions he fired at me were familiar from my meeting with Dr Hutton, yet his accent, with its pleasant lilt, made me self-conscious about my own rough vowels, so I kept my responses brief.

When we rejoined the others, Mr Abdullah summoned his assistant to bring us some refreshments. Dad and I had eaten nothing since the plane, and my stomach rumbled in anticipation. Yet it seemed odd to be tucking into tea and cakes while the doctor sat writing notes at his desk. The pink perfumed tea was served without milk in straight-sided glasses that scorched our fingertips, and the tiny cakes oozed syrup as soon as you touched them. For a moment, I wondered if they were part of the treatment, but it would have been a strange kind of medicine that was prescribed for the entire family.

When we'd wiped our hands as best we could on the napkins, and the plates and glasses had been cleared away, my sister asked Mr Abdullah if he considered me a suitable case for treatment. Patricia'd had a shaggy perm since she had last been home and, though it wasn't particularly flattering, it did make her look older, so it seemed right when she took the lead. Mr Abdullah took his time in answering and, when he did, his reply left much to be desired: "Is still very young."

Patricia stole a glance at my parents, although she seemed to be doing fine without their support: "Isn't that an advantage? He's fit and healthy, and there's no sign of puberty so far."

The book-lined room was impossibly hot, the electric fan on the surgeon's desk clattering away to little effect. Puberty wasn't talked about in our family.

Mr Abdullah nodded sagely: "Physically, is very good. Mentally," he tapped a stubby finger on his temple, "is not clear."

My dad leaned back in his chair, arms crossed, looking smug. My mother glanced uneasily at my sister. "He can't bear to live like this," said Patricia. "He tried to castrate himself with a hacksaw. Had half a bottle of paracetamol pumped out of his stomach."

I hoped that would be enough for Mr Abdullah. He leant towards me: "Tell us, my son, what is it you truly desire. Do you hate so much to have a boy's body? Are you sure you want to give that up to be a girl?"

I didn't hesitate: "Yes, yes please, Mr Abdullah. I want to be a girl."

My dad shrugged. My mother wiped a tear from her eye. Mr Abdullah sat back and knitted his fingers: "Insha'Allah I can make that happen. But you must be entirely sure. Mr Dodsworth, please speak to my assistant about the financial side. And then I ask that you will all go away and pray that indeed this is the right path."

I stifled a yawn. Sleep deprivation and prayer, just like Lourdes, except that this time I wasn't leaving without my miracle.

─────────

THE WIND WHIPS at my fringe as I approach the pelican crossing. In the gaggle of students waiting on the other side is a girl in a red coat. I haven't seen or heard from Megan since the interview with her stepfather. She should have got back to me with her report by now, but I've been too wrapped up in my own affairs to chase her about it. I hope she's all right.

As the beeps go and the green man flashes, I prepare my smile for when we meet in the middle. But as soon as the student steps off the pavement, I can see it's not her.

For now, I've got other things on my mind than Megan's wellbeing. I've been avoiding Venus almost as much as I've been putting off Simon but she caught me off guard this morning and persuaded me to meet her in the senior common room for lunch. "In fact, Giles has a proposition to put you," she said. I wasn't seduced by her air of mystery. Giles can proposition me all he likes but nothing could entice me to attend another dinner party with Fiona.

"SO WHOSE IDEA was that exactly?" Amid the thrum of conversation and the patter of cutlery, my voice sounds shrill.

Giles puffs up his chest and glances across the table at Venus: "We cobbled it up between us, if you get my drift."

Cobbled being the operative word. Taking a sip of water, I remind myself they mean well.

Venus places a manicured hand on my sleeve. The cuts I made with the Stanley knife have healed now, but even that slight pressure on my arm makes me wince. Venus takes her hand away and wraps her fingers round her water glass: "Come on, Di. We're your friends. You can't stop us being a tad concerned about you, and wanting to help."

"Simon was over the moon when you told him you were going out there," says Giles. "But nobody wants you having a panic attack halfway across the Sahara."

Much as I hate the idea of Simon discussing me with Giles, I try to look grateful. It's been a week since I got an email from Simon trying to pin me down to a date for my visit. Better he assumes I'm getting cold feet at the thought of boarding an aircraft than he guess at the real reason I haven't been able to bring myself to reply. "I don't think that's very likely."

Venus's eyes widen. "Says the woman who sicked up her entire stomach at the prospect of a half-hour flight."

"That wasn't anxiety," I insist. "It was those bloody prawn vol au vents."

Giles goes pink as he pushes his glasses up his nose: "We wouldn't cramp your style. As soon as Simon picks you up at the airport, we'll be on the next flight to Sharm el Sheikh."

I gaze out at the trees skirting the walkway down to the Playhouse. The breeze ruffles the branches, culling the crispest bronzed leaves and parachuting them to the ground. I can't tell them I'm not going until I've told Simon. I can't tell Giles his wife is the last person I'd want holding my hand on a plane.

"Take a couple of days to think it over," says Venus. "Although of course everything gets booked up awfully quickly around Christmas. You'll have to decide soon therefore."

"That's the trouble," I say. "I can't commit to anything until my passport's sorted."

"You haven't got your passport already? Oh, Di, you goose, what have you been doing these past weeks?"

"You might not have noticed in the maths department, but it's rather hectic in psychology at the start of a new academic year. And I've been slaving over my submission for an important conference in America ..."

"While obviously the rest of us have been sitting on our butts reading *Hello* magazine."

Giles makes a clawing gesture reminiscent of Marmaduke when another cat trespasses on her territory. "I'm sure we can hang on another couple of weeks."

"It's really sweet of you, Giles, but it's too much to ask. You shouldn't have to plan a family holiday around me and, besides, the journey's impractical. It would take you twice as long to go to Sharm el Sheikh via Cairo, and I imagine it costing at least three times as much."

"That's okay. We want to help you. Fiona's adamant about it, and anyway we'll need to go to Cairo at some point. He'll give you priority, but seeing Simon was part of our plan."

"Yes, but It isn't necessary. Don't forget, I've been on that Fear of Flying course. I'll be perfectly fine on my own."

Venus lurches forward, eyes twinkling as much as the jewels strung round her neck. "Of course. Why didn't I think of it already?"

We can't fail to give her our attention, although Giles' gaze skims her cleavage before reaching her face.

"Obviously we did the course, got all the skills and coping strategies, but we didn't put it into practice. In fact we can finish it off ourselves. Let's book a little plane journey right now so we can wave you off to meet your lover without having to worry whether you're safe."

"And you don't need a passport for a day trip to London or Edinburgh," says Giles.

"Flying to Edinburgh?" I say. "It'd be quicker by train."

"But not necessarily cheaper," says Giles.

"In fact let's do it this Saturday. Paul can ferry the kids to judo and ballet on his own."

"A bit of shopping and somewhere smart for lunch," says Giles. "Can I come?"

"Sorry, girls only," says Venus.

"I can't do Saturday, I'm afraid. I've arranged to go and see my parents."

"Your parents?" says Venus. "You never visit your parents."

Giles' hand shoots to his mouth. "Never mentioned them to my knowledge. I assumed they were dead."

"What's brought this on? Getting them ready to meet Simon is it?"

"I thought I should go and see if they've still got my old

passport." Plus, I realise, I'm hoping to pluck up the courage to follow Megan's example and put a couple of questions to *my* dad about some of *his* past decisions.

Whatever story Venus has concocted to account for the distance between me and my family, my proposed visit clearly refutes it. There's a note of malice in her voice as she turns to Giles: "In fact all the years we shared a flat I never once met Di's parents. I used to wonder if they'd ever existed."

"She might have been a changeling, if you get my drift," says Giles.

"I guess we don't live in each other's pockets like some other families."

"Obviously you'd feel different if you had children of your own."

It feels like a slap. Venus never plays the Madonna card when I'm around.

Giles giggles: "Can you teach Fiona not to live in her mother's pocket? She drives me dizzy, the way they oscillate between bitter enemies and bosom friends."

Chapter 27

W E'D BEEN CREEPING along the Corniche for what felt like forever, when the driver spun the wheel and zipped into the narrow street. The sudden jolt tipped me sideways, my shoulder grazing my father's upper arm for a moment before I managed to rearrange myself on the tacky plastic seat.

He was fiddling with a tourist map of Cairo, concertinaed into a fan. *It's not too late to change your mind,* he'd said. But it was, of course it was too late.

I'd seen the sun come up behind the pyramids; I'd gawped at Tutankhamen's treasures in the Egyptian Museum. I'd shopped for souvenirs in the Khan el Khalili and stuffed myself with Egyptian cuisine. But none of these were what we'd come for; surely he realised that?

It *was* happening quicker than I'd expected, but there was no point putting it off. Each day's delay meant another notch in our hotel bill; another headache holding my mother hostage to the heat of the afternoon. Another day lost from my O-level year at school.

Through the windscreen of the taxi, I could see the whitewashed walls of the clinic up ahead. My mother was sobbing quietly into a pink paper hanky. *Honestly Leonard,* she'd said, *you certainly choose your moments!* I thought I might cry too, but a calmness washed over me. Perhaps it was hearing her address him by his Christian name but, right then, I felt the equal of my dad.

I turned towards her, away from him. "It's all right, we're all a bit nervous. But it's for the best, you'll see."

———————

"YOU'RE SURE YOU won't stay for dinner, Diana?" says my mother, looking past my shoulder to the framed picture of the Sacred Heart on the wall. Twirling the gold wedding band on her finger, she corrects herself: "Lunch, I mean."

From the matching armchair at the other side of the gas fire, my father glowers at her: "Leave off wittling, woman."

I'm seated between them in the middle of the sagging sofa, the apex of an isosceles triangle. Even in this faded, wizened state, slipping intermittently into a senile fugue, my father's irritation sparks off palpitations in my gut. I take another sip of the pale brown liquid that tastes more like gravy browning than coffee: "Thanks, but I really should get back."

"Of course," says my mother. "You'll have heaps to do before you go off to America."

I smile noncommittally as we watch my father ease his creaking bones out of the chair. I haven't been able to bring myself to confess I've been thinking of going back to Cairo, telling them instead that I needed my birth certificate and my old passport for the APA conference next year. I'm not sure now if I've misled her or it suits her to believe I'll be flying out quite soon. Unlike Dad's, my mother's brain is as sharp as it's ever been, but she hasn't mentioned the fact that neither of the documents she's ferreted out for me bear the name Diana.

My father shuffles past my knees to the formica unit in the alcove between the fireplace and the window, and starts clattering china figurines and portraits of grinning grandchildren back and forth across the shelves.

My mother springs from her chair and hovers at his elbow. "What is it, duck?" The expression on her face, if not quite love, is much sweeter than the resignation I'd expect.

I lean back, careful not to entangle my hair in the lace-edged antimacassar on the seat back. I feel foolish now, thinking of everything I'd hoped to ask them. I could have done this less painfully for all of us by post.

My father snatches a bluish vase from the teak-effect shelving and hugs it to his chest. "Oh, that old thing!" says my mother. She taps his shoulders and nudges him back towards his seat. He's no taller than she is, shrunken as an Egyptian mummy.

Before collapsing into the chair, he gathers up a clutch of teaspoons from the coffee table and sets down the vase in their place. When he meets my gaze, his eyes are completely lucid.

Beneath my new silk blouse, sweat snakes down my spine. I'm fifteen again, shopping for souvenirs in the Cairo bazaar. I can almost smell the incense, hear the cadence of the Arabic voices, feel the intoxication of my father's attention as we work in harmony to haggle down the price of a vase in the shape of a long-necked funerary cat.

"Doesn't it just go to show?" says my mother, with a nod towards the Egyptian vase.

What would she know about it? I wonder, surprised by the anger burning in my throat. *She was locked in her hotel room with a headache for most of the trip.*

My mother's mind is on a different track: "They insist he can't take in new information. Well, how would they explain this? I told him you had a cat and doesn't he go and fettle out the only thing in the house with a cat on it? Some bit of junk your sister got at a church jumble sale years since."

I laugh: "No, she didn't. Dad and I picked it up at the Khan el Khalili."

"The Khan el Khalili?" says my mother. "Sounds like some foreign place."

I glance at my father for confirmation but his eyes have glazed over. "It was the market in Cairo. We got a turquoise scarab brooch for you."

My mother looks genuinely nonplussed: "You came to Cairo? I thought it was just me and Patricia and that Egyptian pal of hers. Zuma I think her name was."

I reach out to touch the woven nylon of my backpack, resting on the sofa cushion beside me. It feels like the only thing in this room I can rely on right now. "Of course I came to Cairo. That was the whole reason you went."

"It was a holiday for the girls," insists my mother. "A treat for passing their nursing exams. You can't have been with us, duck. You'd have been far too young."

Is this madness, forgetfulness or complete fabrication? The academic in me is fascinated, thinking what an interesting contribution it would make to Tom Leaside's symposium on memory distortions at the APA conference. The child in me, however, feels sick: "I can't believe you don't remember. It was where I had my operation."

My mother's jaw drops. I feel as if I've punched a frail old woman in the face. A shiver goes through me as I remember how she was when I got back from Cairo. As though, if we acted as if nothing out of the ordinary had happened, people would think I'd been Diana since birth.

There's a mewling sound, but it's not my mother. I turn aside to see my father stroking the vase as he tries to imitate a cat. "This is your inheritance," he says. "From Wilf Pettigrew's estate."

Once I start to shake, I can't stop: legs, arms, even my upper lip. Wilf Pettigrew: it seems I can't escape his legacy.

My father's intervention might have disturbed me, but it's brought my mother back to herself. "How could Wilf Pettigrew leave something for Diana?" she says. "Wasn't he the chap who died the day she was born?"

OUTSIDE, IN THE crisp October air, I can breathe freely again. Head down, I stride up Bessemer Terrace, the strength returning to my muscles with each step I take away from my childhood home. My backpack tugs on my shoulders, freighted with the ferment of memories and the blue-green vase in the style of the Egyptian goddess Isis, a gift from Wilf Pettigrew according to the wild logic of my dad.

As I turn the corner a bus eases away from the bus stop. I put out my hand but it cruises on by. A child on the back seat sticks out his tongue.

Feigning nonchalance, I make my way towards the bus stop to consult the timetable. Halfway there, I freeze. A group of youths in ripped jeans and hooded sweatshirts are messing about in the shelter, setting fire to scraps of paper and watching them burn out on the ground. Reason says they'll have no interest in a middle-aged woman like me, yet my gut's telling me not to put it to the test.

I nip down the nearest street, away from the bus stop, gulping air as if my lungs have sprung a leak. As my rucksack bounces against my back, I tell myself I'm not really running away. There's unlikely to be a bus out of town for another hour, and I might as well explore a little while I'm here.

The houses end abruptly in a stockade of iron palings. There's a tarmac yard with a low-rise building beyond. I fancy I see a dual stone staircase with the stern inscription B-O-Y-S and G-I-R-L-S carved into the lintel above. But they've demolished the imposing nineteenth-century schoolhouse and replaced it with a squat confection of glass and brick and a sign in child-friendly comic sans boasting of *St Teresa of Avila Community School* and a unisex, wheelchair-accessible entrance with a covered porch.

I turn away, almost colliding with an old woman pulling a tartan shopping trolley. I apologise automatically but she seems not to hear, or not care. "Nice morning," she says, although it's well past noon. *Nice morning*, and walks on, the wheel of her trolley squeaking in her wake.

In an instant, I'm no longer stooping, weighed down with fear and guilt and shame. The air is fresh and the sun casts shafts of light along the terrace while, up above, cotton-wool clouds scroll across the blue. I'm not fleeing my past, my parents or the boys at the bus shelter; I'm reconnecting with my roots. Nobody is going to challenge my right to be here. Nobody will recognise me or demand to see my ID. Whatever they thought of the boy who went to Cairo thirty years ago and came back a girl, no one here is going to bother me now.

Fear flips into curiosity, the wish to discover what has and hasn't changed. The pit would've been directly ahead of me, but the headstock has long been dismantled and all that's left of a century of coal mining is a grassy knoll in the far distance, the slag heap reclaimed for children's play. How peaceful it seems now without the clanking machinery, although I'm sure that's no consolation to the men who lost their livelihoods, their sense of who they are. Walking on, I pass boarded-up houses, litter-strewn alleyways, evidence of poverty and neglect. Yet I can't share the sense of deprivation and bereavement. This may be the only home I knew, but it never gave me a secure base. I wonder how it would be for a kid like me to grow up here nowadays; whether it might be easier in a community so much less certain of itself.

Before I know it, I'm at the park, kicking through a sludge of fallen leaves towards the pavilion where I queued behind the long-haired twins for a ticket for the pitch and putt. But the geography has me in a muddle: the dingy toilet block where I swapped my jeans for Geraldine's red miniskirt is in the corner where I thought the swings should be; the soccer pitch where my dad failed to witness my rain-swept winning goal is right across the other side by the bowling green. I spin round, trying to piece the different bits together, almost reliving my mother's panic attack while I blithely played footie with Paddy and Pete.

The clouds have darkened, closing in across the sun. My *nice-morning* feeling has abandoned me; in its place a jumble of emotions that drift away before I can name them, a formless bulk of wrong. Despite my efforts, despite the torment of Cairo, I can't reach the woman I want to be.

My shoulders are aching from the drag of all that passed, unprocessed, in my childhood, all that went unspoken in my parents' house today. All three of us faithful to convention, colluding in upholding the family taboo. My mother's selective memory as much as my father's dementia, my own cowardice and shame, all conspiring to ensure that nothing important would be said. In the middle of it, the ghost of Wilf Pettigrew. The shadow of Mr Abdullah's scalpel and Ms Thompson's statutory powers.

By the window in the pavilion there's a scribbled list of hot drinks and cold sandwiches on sale. I reach for my purse in the pocket of my backpack; perhaps this oppression is due to nothing more than low blood sugar. But the thought of a plastic cup of instant coffee and processed cheese layered between white bread does nothing to raise my spirits. I put away my purse and head back towards the town centre. I'm not terribly hopeful, but if I'm going to find a decent cup of coffee in this place, that's where it will be.

IT WAS AS if they'd flicked a switch: one moment oblivion,

the next a searing pain unzipping my body from my groin to my chest.

"My cock hurts." As soon as I heard the whine in my voice, I wished I'd kept it to myself. They'd think me pathetic, a whinger. Uncouth and ignorant. The proper word was penis and the whole point of this agony was that I no longer had one.

A stirring to my left, a tobacco smell above the sour hospital antiseptic. "Your cock?" My father's voice, quivering with expectation.

A high-pitched groan that seemed to sail right round the world before coming to port in my throat. I sensed my father rise from his chair.

Behind my eyelids passed a procession of the crippled and maimed, soldiers wearing uniforms of open wounds, amputees holding aloft their severed limbs like trophies, marching to the music of their moans and screams.

A needle piercing my thigh. The two sides of the zip knitting together. The pain washed away, tossing me on a wave towards the ceiling. The voices of the wounded turned to song, a hymn to our Lady of Lourdes holding me safe above them.

Did I say cock in front of my dad?

"Sleep now," said my dad, through the fog of my drug-fuelled dream.

In the moment before I was flipped back to nothingness, the echo of my father's *Your cock?* What kind of hope embedded within that question? Had he truly believed, at the last minute, I'd change my mind?

Chapter 28

SQUASHED BETWEEN A run of charity shops and the old-fashioned ironmongery adjoining the barber's, *The Pit Stop* doesn't look very promising from the outside. Yet, when I push through the door, I'm greeted by a mass of sparkling glass and chrome, and a hissing Gaggia machine dominating the far wall. I select the *Guardian Weekend* from the rack of courtesy newspapers and settle myself at a table a little way back from the window.

A teenager in a long linen apron and a spotted kipper-tie takes my order. As she scribbles in her notebook, I ask if she knows the times of the buses to Chesterfield. She looks forlorn, says she'll have to ask Jerry and disappears into the kitchen while I, still too dazed to read, leaf through the magazine.

After a while, an older woman approaches, wiping her hands down the front of her heavy apron: "You were asking about buses?" She's big boned with a cap of kinky auburn hair cropped close to her skull and a gold stud glinting in her right nostril. Beneath the lived-in skin, beneath the veneer of makeup, I can still make out the freckled ten-year-old with the wide-open smile. I'm tempted to flee but she holds me with her gaze. I've never been able to deny Geraldine Finch.

She pulls out a chair: "*But soft, what light through yonder window breaks? It is the East and Juliet is the sun.*" She laughs: "Right little bugger you were. Had me wrapped round your little finger. I must have been at least thirty before I tummelled that Shakespeare made up that story and not you."

The young waitress comes over with my cappuccino and toasted panini, gifting me a bit more time to think of something suitably momentous to say. Geraldine asks the girl to bring her a latte.

"I was supposed to go for my break," moans the teenager.

"I'll let you off at four if you work through it," says Geraldine. We both watch the pouting teenager as she calculates whether the odds are in her favour. "Suit yourself, I'll shut up shop if I have to." Geraldine squeezes my hand. "This is my best friend from primary school. I haven't seen her for thirty years. It's like Lazarus back from the dead."

The girl lopes back to the kitchen. Grinning from ear to ear, Geraldine releases my hand.

"Nice place you've got," I say. Embarrassed at the banality of my contribution, I bite into the panini. Hot cheese oozes out onto my cheeks.

Geraldine hands me a red paper napkin: "Yeah, it's not so bad. But what about you? I hear you're a bigwig at the university. Psychology professor, isn't it?"

"Just a junior lecturer, I'm afraid."

"It's all one to me." Geraldine shrugs. "But isn't that typical of Renee? Constantly bigging things up."

I smile thinly. I haven't thought of my mother as the kind of person to accentuate the positive, but perhaps Geraldine sees a side of her that's been hidden from me. I've only ever viewed her from a child's perspective.

The waitress delivers Geraldine's frothy coffee and goes off to clear the table behind us.

"I suppose it's no bad thing," says Geraldine. "Seeing how things are."

I'm shot through with adrenalin: part thrill, part terror. I wouldn't dare broach the subject myself but it might help to get her perspective on the past. But Geraldine's thinking of my mother's current tribulations, not those she suffered on my account: "She brings him in here sometimes. He likes a hot chocolate, does Leonard, but he can't sit still long enough to finish it. She gives me a ring when they're setting off. Saves him getting agitated waiting to be served."

Geraldine laps a blob of foam from her upper lip. She seems so together, so uncomplicated, as she tells me about the simple way she cares for my parents. Surely that's my job, looking out for ways of making their life easier. Yet I'm inadequate to the task: it only took an hour or so in their company before I had to escape, overwhelmed and suffocated by the past. Geraldine may think I'm almost a professor but, in the real world, I'm still acting like a child. Shifting the focus, I ask: "So what about *your* family?"

I'm expecting a litany of sisters whose names I can't remember, but Geraldine dives into the pocket of her trousers and produces a worn leather wallet. She extracts a crumpled photograph and pushes it my way.

I wipe the grease off my fingers before picking it up.

There's a red-haired girl on a swing with a blond boy standing behind her, both hands on the chain. At first, I think it's a photo of Geraldine and me, but the clothes are wrong for the Sixties. I'm assaulted by another blast of failure as I realise these must be Geraldine's kids: "So you're married?" I can't keep the whiff of envy from my voice.

"Of course not." She exchanges the picture for one of a plump woman on a sandy beach: "We thought about having a civil partnership when the act comes in next year but Elvira's determined to hold out for gay marriage. How about you?"

I laugh pathetically: "Too busy with work." The gobbled-down panini lies like a brick in my stomach. Whenever I've fantasised about running into Geraldine I've assumed the biggest barrier would be unfinished business from the past.

"A bachelorette as my mum would have it," says Geraldine. "How's the LGBT scene in Newcastle?"

Blame it on emotional exhaustion, or merely the context of the café, but I've pondered over the G ensconced within the lettuce, bacon and tomato before I get what she means. "I've never really been one for groups," I mumble.

"I guess not." She's put a brave face on it, but Geraldine's enthusiasm for our encounter has been draining away along with the coffee from her cup. She gazes around the room but there's only one other table occupied. "It's been lovely to see you, but I'd better get back to the kitchen. But, hey, why not pop in next time you're in town?"

I pass her my cup and plate as she rises to her feet. "I'll do that." It's not a completely empty promise. If I ever feel able to face my parents again perhaps I might also find the courage for a proper heart-to-heart with Geraldine.

———————

MY PARENTS ARGUED about who would stay with me. I heard them at it when they thought I was asleep. My mother knew it was her job, but she was terrified to stay on in Cairo without Dad or Patricia as a buffer against the peculiarities of the foreigners, the flies, the strange food, and the heat. She was worried what would happen if my dad overstayed his fortnight's leave, already half over, yet Mr Abdullah had insisted I wasn't going anywhere soon.

It didn't surprise me they hadn't planned this far. Neither had I. It was like the happy-ever-after of a fairy tale, no need to enquire beyond. Except that neither of them seemed terribly happy, especially my dad. Yet he was the one who stayed.

He moved into a basic guesthouse closer to the clinic, arriving every day at my bedside as if reporting for work. For hours he'd just sit there, feeding his pipe and watching me doze. Mostly I lay in bed, a splint spanning my ankles like some mediaeval torture contraption, stretching my legs apart to protect the skin graft. Time was segmented by the murmur of the meal trolley, the medication trolley and the muezzin from the nearby mosque. When the pillows were plumped up a certain way, I could see, through the window at the far end of the ward, pigeons coming to roost on its gilded dome.

Nurses arrived erratically to inject me, to inspect the catheter, to wipe the sweat from my skin with a flannel.

Being a patient was hard work; I felt more like a medical textbook than a nubile young girl. I tried offering up the pain to God, but it didn't stop the tears falling. Some days, crying seemed all I was able to do.

"What is it, duck?" said my dad. "Do wish you hadn't had it done?"

"No, no, I'm glad."

"So why are you crying?"

He sounded more curious than frustrated with me. Such uncharacteristic tenderness catalysed a convulsion of tears. "I don't know."

THE TEARS KEPT on flowing, as regularly as breathing, insistent as the urine drip-dripping from my bladder to the plastic pouch clipped to the side of the narrow hospital bed. Part of me, and yet separate, beyond my understanding or control. "Why can't I stop crying?" I asked my dad.

He scratched a mosquito bite on his ankle as he thought it over: "Because you're a girl now. Crying's what girls do."

My smile stretched to laughter but it didn't stem the tears. Laughing and crying together like I was harmonising the top and bottom lines of a song. I remembered my first trip to the barber's at around three years old. The shock of my reflection in the mirror, as if my head had shrunk. My eyes stinging and my father's sharp words. He'd been right back then as he was right that day in Mr Abdullah's clinic in September 1974: *Boys don't cry.*

"REMEMBER I TOLD you about Wilf Pettigrew?"

It wasn't clear if it were a statement or a question,

whether he thought me awake or asleep. I kept my eyes closed and my mouth shut. "The problem is, that if you're a bit soft, people take you for a nancy-boy. And once they've decided you're a nancy-boy you can kiss your peace of mind goodbye. Maybe it's not right, but there's nowt you or I can do about it. You can't change how folk think.

"They made up their minds about Pettigrew right from the off. He talked about lasses back home like the rest of us and he knew how to dismantle a gun, but it wasn't enough. There was something that marked him out. Maybe we needed someone who was different. Someone to take it out on, locked up in that prison camp like lions in a cage.

"First it was the officers coming and banging on the door of the hut. Said they needed Private Pettigrew for one of their special commissions. Even if we hadn't guessed what it meant we'd have known from how they sent him back with his underpants in his pocket, fit for nothing but to lie crumpled and snivelling on his bunk.

"Don't get me wrong, we all felt for him, but the way he took it, it wasn't good for morale. If he'd only kept quiet about it, borne it like a soldier, we could've let him be. But you couldn't ignore him, that was the trouble. He caterwauled like a girl, but weren't we all suffering, lice-ridden and half-starved and not knowing if we'd ever see Blighty again? We were trapped in that bunkhouse with him and none of us able to get away. And of course, most of the older fellas were married and missing their wives."

When he stopped, my stomach started to settle again. He'd poured out almost as many words in fifteen minutes as he'd given me in my whole fifteen years. I told myself that was all they were: words. My dad had served them to me in that particular order but I didn't need to accept them his way. I could arrange them in my head any way I chose.

When I opened my eyes, his cheeks were glistening. Quickly, I clamped them shut, wishing I could close my ears as easily.

"We couldn't help ourselves, you must see that? We weren't evil, just kids manking about. And it killed him – not then, but more than a decade later – and we'll all have that on our consciences till the day we die."

———————

AFTER THE DRAMA of visiting my parents, and the unexpected encounter with Geraldine that followed, all I want is to get home and snuggle up on the sofa with Marmaduke. I'm contemplating a microwaved gourmet ready-meal as the train skirts the backyards of Gateshead, a chill glass of chardonnay as it shunts left to traverse the Tyne. Automatically, I look to the right, where the window frames the homecoming view of the lines of bridges high and low. Just beyond the farthest bridge, a pennant hangs down the side of the former Baltic flour mill, billowing in the wind. It's too distant to make out what exhibition's being advertised; besides, for me, the building will always mean the rooftop restaurant more than the arts centre. Hard to believe it's less than six months since I dined there with Simon. If I don't brave the flight to Cairo, I doubt I'll ever see him again.

Alighting from the train, I cut across the concourse. My rucksack bobs against my back as I trot down the steps towards the Metro, scoping for the ticket machine with the shortest queue. I pay scant attention to the people around me; weighed down with luggage or shopping bags or the anticipation of a boozy night out, mere obstacles along my route home. Yet I can't ignore a man barging through the barrier with a cello-shaped case strapped to his back. He looks quite dashing, dressed in full evening dress: starched wing collar; dickey bowtie; and tails. Once released through the turnstile, he looks my way and smiles.

He seems familiar, but I can't place him. He could be a newsreader from *Look North*, a neighbour, or one of my former students grown up. As he strides buoyantly towards me, I hope I won't make too much of a fool of myself. The man adjusts the shoulder strap of his cello case and stretches out his hand: "Dr Dodsworth, good to see you again."

His hand is warm, his grip firm, his smile brimming with bonhomie. He's good-looking and his hair, thinning on top, is clipped short at the back and sides, a style from my early childhood become fashionable again for men, although not perhaps for one in the process of transitioning into a woman. "I would never have recognised you," I say.

Dr Marlow strokes the stubble at the back of his head: "A bit drastic, isn't it?"

I have to stop myself jiggling from foot to foot like a kid who's desperate for the toilet. I'm grateful for the passengers surging past us to and from the turnstiles for the need to keep it light: "You've changed your mind?"

"Just taking a break." He smiles, as if he's referencing a weekend in Paris, and shakes his head: "It's bloody hard work trying to pass yourself off as a woman, you know."

Beneath the layers of embarrassment, I skirt around the edge of a bottomless pool of sorrow. For a beat, I'm on the verge of collapsing into tears on his shoulder, but I can't mess up his gorgeous tailcoat any more than I can renege on thirty years of reining it all in. "I don't know what to call you."

"Susan's fine," he says. "Chopping and changing just confuses people."

I nod, remembering Geraldine asking me about the LGBT scene. Like his tie and tails, there must be someplace this makes sense. "What's with the penguin suit and the cello?"

He slips the case from his shoulder and rests the base on the tiles. The sleeves of his jacket ride up his forearms as he clasps his hands over the top of the narrow neck, exposing snowy-white shirt-cuffs clamped with exquisite emerald links. He tells me he plays in an amateur orchestra, performing a couple of pieces I've never heard of at the cathedral tonight. "Why don't you come along? I can get you a free ticket if you like."

"That's really kind of you, but I'd better be getting home." My voice sounds wooden, but I can hardly begin to explain the day I've had.

Dr Marlow leans in closer. I can smell the beer on his breath. "No probs. After all, the programme's not to everyone's taste."

It hasn't occurred to me till now that he might be somewhat inebriated. I hope he hasn't gone and hacked off his hair on a drunken whim. I step away, but I don't back off completely. I owe him something, and not only for the invitation to the concert. Even if the Gender Recognition Act can't resolve the ambiguity of my travel documents for this year, it's given me hope for next. "Is Megan going?" I ask, brightly.

"Have you seen her? Is she all right?" For the first time in this conversation, he seems to have lost his poise.

"You mean you haven't? I thought she lived with you?"

"Moved back in with her friends a month ago. I'm sure it's better for her than hanging out with an old queen like me, except she hasn't been in touch since that interview."

I don't know if I should tell him I haven't seen or heard from her either. My heart sets off thumping as I cast my mind back to when Garth Bradshaw refused to spell out her vulnerabilities. Had Megan ever harmed herself? Would she now? "She's gone missing?"

Dr Marlow's laugh is too deep to pass for a woman's. "Nothing so dramatic. She's in touch with her mother, it's just me she's sent to Coventry. But that's the way it is with stroppy adolescents, as I'm sure you know."

Chapter 29

ON MONDAY LUNCHTIME I queue at the post office at St Mary's Place for a passport application form, then cross over to the Metro station for a quad of serious-looking head-and-shoulders snaps. I do it robotically, still not certain where it's taking me, like I'm meticulously following the recipe for a gourmet meal I might end up throwing in the bin.

Walking back through campus to the Skinner building, my next job is getting someone to confirm the pictures are a reasonable likeness. Any of my colleagues could do it but, for such a significant event, it has to be Venus. I need to see her anyway; we haven't spoken since I declined her invitation to take a phobia-busting plane ride.

Sweeping through the autumn leaves on the approach to Newton Court, I glance up at the mosaic of lighted windows, like an advent calendar in the run-up to Christmas. Seeing the light in Venus's office, I reach into my backpack for my phone. I've got her number on speed dial so, in a matter of seconds, I hear it ring.

As if I need to double-check my recipe, I press the red phone icon before she answers. It doesn't give me much thinking time, but it'll do.

My phone buzzes and Venus's number flashes on the screen. "Di, did you call me already? Fancy a spot of lunch?"

"Sorry, Venus, I haven't got time. I was wondering though if you'd sign the photos for my passport ..."

"Obviously I'd be delighted. In fact pop up and I'll do it now."

I can't tell if this is the equivalent of a culinary innovation or adding too much spice to the dish. Opportunity or disaster, it's an experiment I can attempt only in the safety of my own kitchen. "You couldn't call round after work, could you? Like an idiot, I've left them at home and I want to get it in the post as soon as I can."

VENUS SCRIBBLES ACROSS the back of the photos and puts down the pen: "Well, that was humongously straightforward."

She hasn't commented on the blue-green vase stationed in the middle of my kitchen table, a few withering stems from Simon's bouquet poking out from its elongated feline neck. Perhaps, like my mother, she'd consider it a piece of tat from a jumble sale, or, like my father, assign it some symbolism of her own. Is it asking too much to hope for her to see it from my point of view, as a relic from the defining moment of my life? "Would you mind checking over the form?" I say, trying to make it casual. "In case I've missed something."

Venus raises a sculpted eyebrow: "It's hardly quantum physics." As if indulging one of her children, she picks up the form, holding it at arm's length, squinting.

"You need reading glasses."

She silences me with a playful flap of the hand: "Shh, you goose, let me concentrate!"

The kettle has boiled but I'm too shaky to scoop coffee grounds into the cafetiere. My entire body is on vibrate as I lean against the worktop, primed for the slightest hint of a change of mood, trying to savour what might be the last moments of our friendship. I remember as a child at the baths at Lourdes, catching my breath at the shock of icy water, not knowing if it would kill me or set me free. In the end, it did neither, but Venus holds more power in my mind than the mother of the Catholic Church.

Her lacquered fingernail hovers over the entry for *all previous names*. She scowls: "You were married before I ever met you? But child brides in Britain are outlawed." I wait for her to register that there are other types of previous names. Her voice rises to a squeak: "Andrew?"

I nod, but she's not looking at me. Her gaze darts back to the top of the sheet, to the box she skimmed over initially, the box with a tick beside the word *male*.

"You're joking me!"

I imagine the lonely years to come, skidding friendless, jobless into old age. It isn't hard to picture it. "I wish I was."

"What happened? Did your parents make the same mistake you made with Marmaduke?"

"It's a long story."

She blinks hard. I've never seen Venus so discombobulated. It unnerves me: mathematicians like things cut and dried.

"Forget the coffee," she says. "This calls for a

humongous gin and tonic. In fact I'll have to ring Paul. Tell him I'm going to be home a tad later than I thought."

———————

WHILE I WAS sobbing my heart out in Mr Abdullah's clinic, my mother had been preparing to welcome me home. Patricia's room was officially mine now, the walls adorned with lily-of-the-valley, the woodwork a light lavender gloss. I was thrilled at first at the treats she'd assembled for me like an early Christmas stocking: hair-slides and bangles and rose-scented body lotion; nail varnish and lace-edged knickers and American-tan tights; an address book, rainbow-hued notebooks and a chunky pencil with a tassel on the end. Yet there was something not quite right about it, the exuberant excess rendering me a visitor in my own home.

I tried to find comfort in the familiar: the smell of fresh-baked cobs in the baker's; newsprint, chip shops and the smoke of English cigarettes. Trees, their leaves on the turn like a smouldering fire, and the joyful whoops of kids throwing up sticks to spark off a shower of conkers. Cream crackers with cheddar cheese and Horlicks melting into a cup of hot milk. The music of church bells and chatter in a language I could instantly understand. I wanted to believe I could be myself here, but I didn't feel it in my heart.

I spent a week convalescing: me, my mother, and a brick wall of unmentionables. I camped out on the couch mostly, with a stack of magazines and library books she'd chosen for me, and the transistor tuned to Radio One. She brought me hot drinks and Lucozade, steaming bowls of tomato soup. My mother seemed in awe of me, approaching like a lady-in-waiting in the service of a despot, bombarding me with votive offerings in lieu of love. If I tried, in my pathetic way, to talk about what had happened in Cairo, my mother carried on as if she hadn't heard me, cut right across me with the offer of a nice mug of Oxo, a strengthening slice of cheese on toast.

The day before I was due back to school, I opened my underwear drawer to find a pamphlet from the Catholic Truth Society, a sanitary belt and a packet of Dr White's. My first thought was that Patricia had left them there, but I knew my mother had packed the remains of my sister's things away when she decorated the room. I didn't want to upset her, or embarrass myself by explaining they were no use. So I sat on my bed, learning about the mechanics of menstruation from the pages of *My Dear Daughter*. Learning that, despite Mr Abdullah's creative sculpting, I'd never be a woman on the inside.

I TRIED TO tell myself it would be like going back to school after that skinhead haircut: despite my fear and trepidation, people would think it cool. But I knew this was more serious. For a start, my coat might cover my hair, but wasn't long enough to hide the fact that I wasn't wearing trousers but white knee-length socks and a skirt.

My mother had tried to ease my way, sending a note with my brother for the headmaster: *Andrew Dodsworth will henceforth be known as Diana. Regards, R Dodsworth (Mrs).* She'd done her best – heaven knows where the grandiose *henceforth* came from – and it wasn't her fault both she and the letter were inadequate to the task.

I thought I could ride it out: two and a bit terms and I could leave the trials of the schoolyard behind me. My main priority was keeping the extent of my difficulties from my parents. They'd already sacrificed more than I could ever have imagined. It was up to me to deal with school.

Trevor, still smarting from being deprived of an exotic holiday, or any kind of summer holiday at all, wasn't willing to have humiliation heaped upon him through the happenstance of being my brother. Unlike me, he didn't hesitate to make his feelings known at home: "You know what they sing when he goes by?"

My mother tightened her grip on her knife and fork. My father sliced through the liver on his plate: "I've told you, Trevor. Diana's a she."

"When he goes in the toilets all the girls hold their noses and run out."

"And what do you do when your schoolmates make fun of your sister?"

"My sister finished school over a year ago."

"What you do when they make fun of Diana?"

Trevor shrugged. "I don't do nothing."

"A brother should stand up for his sister."

"It's nothing to do with me. I didn't tell him to go and get his willy chopped off."

WITH OR WITHOUT Trevor's intervention, my parents were going to have to face reality sooner or later. The day the school secretary interrupted the O-level history class to say I was wanted in the headmaster's office, I wondered if the moment had come.

Hovering outside in the corridor, I could hear my dad's voice through a crack in the door, complaining about having to take time off work. As Mr Bingham began to apologise, a woman's voice cut in: "What we have here, I'm afraid, is most irregular." She sounded very proper, like Valerie Singleton from *Blue Peter*. "If I can speak frankly, Mr and Mrs Dodsworth, the situation is unprecedented in the whole of the district Social Services. We're at a loss as to how to proceed."

"Although the education department is adamant," said Mr Bingham, "that we do something. The situation has impacted on the entire school. No one wants to blame you …"

"Although I have to tell you," said the woman, "that I consulted with my senior as to whether we should notify the police."

"But I'm sure you felt you were acting for the best," Mr Bingham interjected. "Although a little notice wouldn't have gone amiss. I've got an excellent staff team here but, to tell you the truth, they're out of their depth."

Someone, presumably my mother, began to cry.

The woman from Social Services pressed on: "What we must keep in mind is what is in the best interests of the child. What's done is done, our job is to minimise any further damage."

"She'd be right as a cart if you lot would leave her to get on with it," said my mother.

I sprang back as the headmaster's face loomed in the doorway. Looking somewhat flustered, he asked me to give them a couple of minutes, and firmly closed the door.

The voices continued on the other side, muffled and indistinct. Dread stirred in my stomach. Why were my parents getting a ticking-off when I was the one in the wrong?

After what felt like forever, Mr Bingham ushered me inside. A slim woman with long blonde hair smiled pityingly as I entered. Wooden bangles clattered along her arm as she stretched out her hand: "Good to meet you, Diana. I'm Ms Thompson from Social Services. I understand you've been having a hard time."

She wore a flared embroidered skirt bordered with tiny mirrors. I knew my mother wouldn't like her: the strap of her brassiere was visible through the skimpy cotton of her blouse. "I'm okay," I said.

Ms Thompson flashed a smile around the room. "We've been talking about how best to help you."

I couldn't look at Mr Bingham or my parents, so I stared at the wall of floor-to-ceiling bookshelves instead. "I don't need no help."

"I'm sure you've been very brave," said Ms Thompson. "And how are you getting along with ... with being a girl?"

"It's all right."

"But maybe more difficult than you thought?"

I studied the grey spine of an Old Testament on the fourth shelf down.

"We were thinking it might be easier if you went away to boarding school."

There was a snapping sound as my mother closed her handbag, but she didn't speak.

"Borstal?" I knew that even girls could be sent there, if

they were bad enough.

Ms Thompson swivelled the ring on her middle finger. "Quite the opposite. Dorothea Beale is more of a finishing school for young ladies. The local authority has generously offered to finance your education there till you're eighteen."

"We thought you'd be more at ease in a single-sex school," said Mr Bingham. "A fresh start. New friends."

Cairo was supposed to be a fresh start. How would a new school be any better? You could never guarantee friends.

"They can't force you to go away if you don't want to," said my mother.

A strange look passed between my father and the headmaster. They were asking me to choose, but it felt as if it had already been decided. I glanced from the social worker to my mother. "What do *you* want me to do?"

"Your mother wants what's best for you," Ms Thompson interjected. "We all do."

Mr Bingham nodded vehemently. "And it would be good if we could get it tied up before the tabloids get wind of the story."

———

"DOES SIMON KNOW?" says Venus.

"Not yet."

She gets up from the table and grabs my phone from the worktop where I left it a couple of hours ago, after ringing The Taj Mahal to order a home delivery. "In fact, ring him now! While I'm here for moral support."

It's tempting, but two confessions in one evening might be overdoing it. I reach for the Beaujolais bottle, give it a shake, but there's not even a teaspoon of sediment in the bottom. "You're drunk and, besides, I need to do it face to face."

Venus tears off a scrap of naan bread and swirls it around in the slops of fluorescent sauce in a foil container: "Of course."

"Should I open another bottle?"

"In for a penny …"

I cull a random bottle of red from the cupboard under the sink. Turning back to the table, I almost trip over Marmaduke, sauntering towards the cat flap with her tail in the air. My eyes start to prickle: not long ago I thought she was the only friend I'd have left.

Venus retrieves the corkscrew from among the debris of our meal: "In fact I'll do it. I'm better at it and a tad less blotto."

She scrapes off the foil seal, a studious look on her face. Red circles grace her cheekbones and, just above, smears of black where her tears washed into her mascara. "It's a blasted screwtop."

I grab the bottle and pour the wine, not caring about the splashes on the tabletop. I raise my glass: "To us!"

"To Simon and Cairo!"

Only now do I truly believe I'm going. Only now, my senses dulled by alcohol, can I begin to contemplate the risk: "You know, I'm scared to go back there."

"Of course you are," says Venus. "It was a colossal thing you went through, and so young. But you're not alone now, obviously. You've got Simon to hold your hand."

"But I don't know how he'll be about it, do I? He might

never want to see me again."

Venus hiccups, presses her fingers to her lips, nails and flesh an identical florid burgundy. "We could do a role-play. Like at Fear of Flying."

"It isn't a game."

"I know." Her eyes moisten as she squeezes my hand: "But it isn't necessarily a doomsday scenario. He'll be shocked, obviously. Therefore you might need to give him time to take it in. But Di, if he loves you, he'll love you whatever you came from …"

A slap of sobriety takes me back to my GP surgery, to Libby Dean and her girlish plaits. I *want* to trust them, but I'm the one facing potential rejection.

Venus wipes her eyes, muddying her mascara still further: "In fact if *I* can forgive you when you've lied to me for nearly thirty years …"

"I didn't lie to you. I just didn't tell you the whole truth."

"*I never suspected my best friend was a transsexual.* In fact I wonder how much *Hello* magazine would pay me for a scoop like that."

She's taking a blade to my stomach and twisting it round. Is *this* what Venus means by support?

"It isn't funny," I say, and yet, all of a sudden, it is. She's stabbed me, not with a knife, but with a feather, tickling me until I can't help but laugh. Great belly-aching chuckles that, finally, bring tears to my eyes. It's as if we've recast *Romeo and Juliet*; rewritten it as a comedy and, what's more, it works.

We fall upon each other, hugging, laughing, squeezing,

crying. Her breath hot with spices, her hair caressing my face. The plump cushion of her torso, her breasts squashed against my chest. The sandalwood smell of a friendship that doesn't judge.

Eventually, we pull apart. After all, we have to breathe. I tell her *Hello* wouldn't take her story. They only want celebrities.

Grinning, she sips her wine: "In fact I always thought gender studies was a load of nothing, like doing research on *The Very Hungry Caterpillar* or *The Gruffalo.*"

Was *that* what my predicament was about? Gender wasn't a term I had much use for at fifteen. I wanted to go to the places where boys weren't welcome. I wanted to choose what I could wear. I wanted to avoid growing up cold and cruel. "Of course it's humongously complex," she continues. "In fact it's such a fuzzy concept, so hard to pin down, it ought not to matter a jot. But it does. Tremendously. Like God and the square root of minus one."

"I'm in good company then." I'm not sure about God, but I do remember Venus as an undergraduate getting terribly animated about the mathematical operations that were enabled by imaginary numbers.

"The power of the unreal. We should write a paper on it. We could win the Nobel Prize."

She's drunk, and she's hardly less bonkers when she's sober, but I've never been so grateful for her friendship. "Not if we publish it in *Hello* magazine," I say. "Now, before I get too pissed, let me remind you you're in no state to drive home. So should I order you a taxi or are you going to stay the night?"

"In fact, I'd like to stay." She sounds as surprised at her decision as I am. Venus has never stayed over since she had the kids.

"I think I've got a spare toothbrush somewhere."

"Pity you don't have a spare galabeyah," she says. "We could wrap ourselves in blankets like when we were students, sharing our dreams about our illustrious futures."

Chapter 30

TERMINAL THREE IS as frantic as Northumberland Street in the January Sales. I try to keep calm as I weave my trolley through the concourse, peering above people's heads for the Egypt Air desk. It's a while before the check-in closes, but I won't be able to relax till I'm safely on board.

For the third time since I got here, I unzip the pocket of my backpack to check my documents: my return ticket and the burgundy passport made out to DODSWORTH, DIANA, BRITISH CITIZEN, 18 AUG / AOUT 59, M, CHESTERFIELD, 11 NOV / NOV 04, UNITED KINGDOM PASSPORT AGENCY. Embedded in the list of printed letters and numbers, perhaps no-one will spot the M for male. As Venus says, *What's the worst they can do?* They can hardly arrest me.

As I tuck them away in the pocket, my phone shakes itself awake with another text from Venus: *Go 4 it, babe.* Babe? Her text-speak is even more eccentric than her vocals, but they can't fail to inspire me. Spotting the blue-and-white falcon-head logo, I push the trolley onwards.

I've been stunned by the support I've had from Venus over the last few weeks. Despite her disappointment I hadn't told her earlier, despite her inability to comprehend why I don't want to come out and declare it to the world, she's been cheering me all the way. It's taken some getting used to, another person knowing and looking out for me, having a place where I don't have to hide. I get the feeling Venus would fight my cause harder than I would myself.

She was indignant when I told her Garth Bradshaw was hesitating about funding my trip to the APA conference. She urged me to put in a grievance under the university Equality and Diversity policy. I laughed: "But I want to be treated like everyone else."

"That's the point of equality legislation, you goose," said Venus. "It's an opportunity to take that obnoxious little upstart down a peg or two."

Actually, I think it's right for me to hang back from the APA for another year. I'm onto something big in reviving my adolescent decision-making research, but there's a piece of the jigsaw I can't quite place. I'd like to mull it over, run a few experiments and see where I am in another twelve months. No more rushing into decisions before I'm ready.

I've almost reached the tail of the Egypt Air check-in queue when someone stumbles out from behind a giant Christmas tree straight into my path. My rucksack slides off the trolley as I swerve to avoid riding over her foot. "Sorry," I say, meaning *What the fuck!* As I stoop to grab my bag, I notice she's wearing flat suede ankle boots that shove her feet out of line with her legs. The girl crouches down and reaches for the rucksack a split-second after I do.

Her slight frame is dwarfed by an expedition-size backpack, so that once she's down on her haunches she can't get her balance to push herself up again. Lodging my own small rucksack securely under one arm, I offer her my other. "Dr Dodsworth." She tries to make it sound like she's pleased to see me, but her face gives her away. "Fancy seeing you here."

"I thought you'd left the country." I'm still a little hurt that Megan dropped out of her course without so much as an email to me, leaving it to Garth's secretary to tell me she'd gone. Perhaps I'm old-fashioned, but it does seem inconsiderate given the lengths I'd gone to, to give her a leg-up through to the final year.

"I'm just about to!" Neither her guilt nor the colossal weight dragging on her shoulders can crush the exuberance that brought her to the airport. "I'm off to India for six months. Flying out to Mumbai and travelling overland through Goa and Kerala and Tamil Nadu."

"Sounds lovely." Although she's older, I recognize my teenage self in her shiny open face, in the squeaky inflections of her voice. It's an age-old cliché for young people to inflict themselves on the Third World to find themselves, but that's what I did at fifteen, what Megan seems to be doing at twenty. I say it again, but this time I mean it: "Sounds lovely. Just what you need."

Megan looks aghast: "Dr Dodsworth, is something wrong?"

I shake my head, smudge the moisture from my cheek with the back of my hand. These last few weeks I've been bursting into tears at the flimsiest provocation. I don't even feel sad in the main; more making up for lost time. Atoning for thirty years of dry-eyed stoicism; like a frozen pipe that, now it's thawed, can't help but leak. "Getting sentimental in my old age."

Megan bites her lip: "I was, like, ohmygod, is she off to a funeral or something?"

I glance down at my slate-grey trousers and jacket, the outcome of a shopping trip with Venus: "My friend thought I might get an upgrade if I wore a suit." What I don't tell Megan is that she also thought the anomaly in my passport might be less striking if I presented myself as an androgynous business executive.

Megan giggles: "Well good luck with that!"

My eyes well up again. Poor kid, still feeling compelled to check that the older generation is all right. Her stepfather should never have saddled her with his shit. Now I'm glad that she *didn't* feel obliged to tell me she was leaving. Adolescents need their self-absorption to discover who they are. I might have lingered longer in that ambiguous space between childhood and adulthood too, if there'd been anyone to show me how useful that could be. I dare to let my hand graze her sleeve: "It's fantastic you've decided to go travelling, Megan."

"Really? Thing is, I thought you'd be cross. You know, giving up my degree."

"We'll still be there for you if you ever want to pick it up again." I sound like some wise woman from ancient times or, heaven forbid, Ms Thompson. But I like the feel of it. "Believe me, Megan, you've got much more important things to do with your life just now."

THE FIXED RANKS of chairs at the flight-gate brings to mind

a hospital waiting room: the infantile passivity, our real lives in abeyance until we're summoned through to the next stage.

Another text from Venus: *The worst that could happen is they put u straight back on the plane & I have to pick u up from Heathrow.* I wouldn't let her drive three hundred miles to get me, but I'm grateful she'd consider it. My thumb hovers over the keys as I ponder my reply. But it's time to let go of all that. I type *Thanx,* press *Send* and switch off the phone. Until I meet Simon, it's just me and my thoughts.

How did they take so long to twig you were so humongously unhappy? Venus had asked me. I hardly knew myself. That was half the problem; we didn't talk about feelings back then.

In fact if one of mine had to go through two bouts of self-harm and a couple of overdoses before I'd listen, obviously I'd expect my friends to report me to Social Services. Yet my parents were as confused as I was. They hadn't a clue what to do with a child who wasn't able to conform.

You were very young when they took you to Cairo. How did they know they were doing the right thing? I thought they were finally waking up to what I wanted, but now I'm not sure. I've no regrets about the outcome: I couldn't function as a man, or moving back and forth like Susan Marlow. But my tears in the clinic must've been more than crying because it's what girls do.

I wanted, as Juliet did, to awake from a drug-induced coma to find the world had rearranged itself to one where I would finally fit in. I thought I was old enough to make my own decisions, but I was only fifteen. I needed a mother to wrap me in her arms and let me down gently, a father wise enough to find a better solution than the one I dreamt up myself.

Yet my parents must have been as scared as I was: scared of the oddball they'd created, scared of not knowing what to do. Scared when the experts didn't know the answer either. You can't think properly when you're scared; panic makes you rush towards a resolution before you've considered all the options. I remember Megan after the exam, bubbling with inspiration sparked by the Necker cube. Now I see that I've been coming at my research from the wrong angle. It's parental intolerance of ambivalence I should be investigating. It's parents who struggle when their child demands incompatible things.

At fifteen, I deluded myself that I'd persuaded them, that I'd finally got them to attend to my point of view. In reality, we never even opened up the debate. They listened to my sister, they listened to the youths at the bus stop, they listened to their own shame and embarrassment, they listened to the ghost of Wilf Pettigrew, but they didn't listen to me. I can't say I'd have come to a different decision if we'd examined all the balls in the jar, but perhaps I chose impetuously. There was a certain triumph in disappointing my dad.

A small boy in a Spiderman outfit nudges his mother and points at me. I give him a smile and wipe the tears from my eyes.

My father's wartime friend bequeathed me something, and it wasn't the long-necked vase from the souk. Dad wanted to save me from a fate like Wilf Pettigrew's, from the abuse that cowards inflict upon men who are drawn to the feminine within themselves. That he wanted to protect me was obvious, but there was another side to his cautionary tale of life in the camp. He wanted me to see beyond the risks of not conforming to the equivalent horror of being one of the lads. It was a confession of his own weakness, of his guilt and shame that he wasn't man enough to protect either his friend or me.

I used to puzzle over that Bible story where Abraham leads Isaac up the mountain, not telling the boy he's the sacrificial lamb. The story glorifies Abraham's obedience to the Almighty; he's never berated for his disregard for his son. I used to ask myself what kind of father would sacrifice his son's life for a principle. Might it be a father somewhat like my own?

What was in my father's mind when he relinquished his parental responsibility to the God-like surgeon? Did he feel betrayed when Mr Abdullah agreed to wield the knife?

The story treats Isaac like he's his father's chattel, no feelings and motivations of his own. Yet Isaac, like me, was approaching the age when he'd have to choose his own route to salvation. Did both our fathers fear the power within their sons?

I keep going back to that taxi ride in Cairo, my father saying I could still change my mind. His was the signature on the consent form, yet it was as if only *I* could decide. Did he feel betrayed when I refused to release him from his promise?

———

"AFTER THE MEN had done with him," said my dad that day in the clinic, "Wilf Pettigrew lay curled up on his bunk, stone quiet. We all felt rotten, but I can't have been the only one relieved we'd put paid to his infernal snivelling.

"When he didn't report for roll call next morning, they moved him to the sick bay to lie among the cases of dysentery and TB. Nobody let on they'd noticed there was an empty bunk in the hut. I wasn't much more than a kid myself, remember, but I traded the last of my smokes with the guard outside the sick bay. When he saw me come in, Pettigrew turned to the wall. *Don't blame yourself,* I told him. *There was nowt you could've done to stop it.*

"He didn't stir himself, so I waited a while amid the groans and the stench of shit and musky formaldehyde, dreaming of the life I'd have when the war was finished. A job at the pit, a wife and kids — everything normal. I'd put this right out of my mind.

"Eventually Pettigrew rolled over. *You still here?*

"He looked all right, apart from a few bruises. Hard to credit anything so outlandish had gone off. *Don't be like that,* I said.

"He practically hissed at me. *Maguire and Porlock I might've expected. Teddy Simpson even. But you?*

"*Believe me, I would've stopped them if I could. But what can one man do on his own?*

"Pettigrew's face was a blotchy puce. *You would've stopped them, would you?* He reached out and tried to grab me by the throat. I sprang away and Pettigrew collapsed in a heap on the bed. *Go fuck yourself!* he said."

I INTENDED TO seek out the queue with the least stern immigration officer at the end of it but, from the back of the hall, each looks as scary as the rest. It doesn't help that there's a soldier parked in the corner, some kind of rifle slung bandolier-style across his chest.

I shuffle along behind a party of overweight retirees toting matching holdalls stamped in mock hieroglyphics with *Nefertiti's Nile Tours*. They exchange brash banalities with a couple called Chuck and Mary-Lou who've had the audacity to break ranks and join a different procession. I hope, after them, the immigration officer will find me refreshingly sober and demure.

I don't feel very fresh, however. The weather in Cairo should be pleasantly mild at this time of year, but the rush of passengers and the hyperactivity within my sympathetic nervous system has brought me out in a sweat. I'd be more comfortable if I were to remove my jacket, but that might make me appear even less composed, especially with two great damp patches under my arms.

A voice flares in my head: *Put it behind you, Diana sweetie!* What use is Ms Thompson to me here? What use was she at any time really, urging me to wipe out all trace of who I'd been? I check my phone, but there's nothing new from Venus, and I won't ring Simon until I'm officially on Egyptian soil.

"I'm *so* looking forward to seeing the sun rise behind the pyramids," says a woman up ahead. She's almost as broad as she's tall and I can't imagine the maroon tracksuit she's wearing has ever been used for sport.

"You can't do that, hon," says a man with a glut of photographic equipment strung round his neck. "They don't let you through the gates till eight."

"YOU ALL RIGHT, hon?"

"Here, take a Kleenex!"

I take the proffered tissue and dab my eyes. Up ahead, the first of the tourists steps up to the booth and slides her passport under the grille. "Gee," one of them whispers, "you forget not everyone's on holiday."

"Yeah," says her friend, insufficiently sotto voce, "I heard someone say she was here for a funeral."

I ball the tissue and stuff it in my pocket, giving the Yanks a thanks-but-I'm-all-right-smile. I have witnessed the sun's rebirth behind the pyramids and no one has died.

"Hank, where's my passport?"

Put it behind you! Was Ms Thompson out of her depth, or did I misinterpret what she meant?

"I thought *you* had them."

Even Susan Marlow, despite her difficulties, managed to be a parent and a musician. What have I got to show for the last thirty years?

"No, no, I gave them to you."

I could have been a dancer with my very own tutu. I could have scored goals in the women's football league. Instead, I hid in my house with a gin and tonic and a misnamed cat. I wanted to excise Andrew's awkward bits, but I didn't appreciate that I still had his blood running through my veins.

"Look in your darned purse for God's sake!"

I am the boy who prayed for a miracle. I am the woman daring to take a chance on love. Does gender really matter? As with the Necker cube, we can view it as figure or ground.

I hold my head high as I step up to the booth. My smile doesn't falter as I slip my passport across to the uniformed man. Grim faced, he riffles through the pages to scrutinise the visa. His gaze flits from my face to the photo at the back.

I am the boy who wanted it both ways. I am the woman who is no longer afraid to fly. The Americans are safely through the border to reclaim their baggage. Behind me, the lines of travellers snake back to the door.

The immigration officer closes my passport and pushes it towards me: "Welcome to Cairo, madam. Enjoy your stay."

Acknowledgements

A first novel is built on the foundations of previous projects that didn't make it, so thanks to everyone who fuelled my belief that trying to write for publication wasn't crazy long before the ideas behind *Sugar and Snails* took form. Foremost among them, my sister Clare Burgess, my first and most loyal reader, and Jane and Pete who bought me a chunky *Roget's Thesaurus* for my twenty-first birthday many moons ago. More recently, I owe a debt of gratitude to the editors of the various anthologies and literary magazines who have furnished my short fiction with a home.

Thanks to Lynne Patrick for recognising the potential in my tentative first draft of *Sugar and Snails*, and to Shelley Weiner for convincing me to silence the voices of the parents and rewrite the story solely from Di's point of view.

Thanks to the speakers, teachers, students and other brands of fellow writers at the various online and off-line courses, critique groups, blogs and fora whose wisdom I've drawn on over the years. The names of some of these fine people can be found on my website. Special mentions to Geoff LePard, Juliet O'Callaghan and Shelley Purchon for ploughing through earlier drafts in their entirety.

I couldn't have wished for a better reception for *Sugar and Snails* at Inspired Quill, exemplified by Sara Slack whose ruthless approach to the unnecessaries combined with exuberance about the better bits has rendered the editing process sheer joy. Thanks to Vince Haig for the cover design, a beautiful package for my words.

Although I've worked as a professional psychologist, I claim no expertise regarding adolescent development. Di's PhD research is a total fiction, albeit building on my limited reading around the subject. The ingenious two-jars methodology is borrowed from a genuine research paper:

Huq SF, Garety PA, Hemsley DR (1988) Probabilistic judgements in deluded and non-deluded subjects. *Quarterly Journal of Experimental Psychology*, <u>40</u>, 801-812.

A huge cheer for the two people who have kept me relatively sane through my writing journey, without (yet) reading a word of my novel: my husband, Terry Anderson, and That Woman, as he calls my therapist.

Finally, I thank you, the reader, the last but most important link in the chain. I hope you find my words worthy of your time.

About the Author

Anne Goodwin studied Mathematics and Psychology at Newcastle University around the same time as the narrator of *Sugar and Snails*. After twenty-five years as a clinical psychologist in Newcastle and North Nottinghamshire, she now focuses on writing and reviewing fiction. She has published over 60 short stories and blogs about reading and writing, with a smattering of psychology on her website, Annethology at annegoodwin.weebly.com.

Sugar and Snails is her first published novel.

Twitter: @Annecdotist

Inspired Quill is proud to support Gendered Intelligence.

Our mission at Gendered Intelligence is to increase understandings of gender diversity through creative ways. Working predominantly with the trans community and those who impact on trans lives; we particularly specialies in supporting young trans people aged 11-25.

gendered intelligence

understanding gender diversity in creative ways

Gendered Intelligence aims are:

1. to increase the quality of trans people's life experiences, in particularly young trans people

2. to increase the visibility of trans people's lives and to raise awareness of trans people's needs, especially young trans people

3. to contribute to the creation of community cohesion across the whole of the trans community and the wider Lesbian Gay Bisexual and Trans (LGBT) community throughout the UK

4. to engage the wider community in understanding the diversity and complexity of gender

We do this in a variety of ways including (but not limited to) carrying out creative workshops, support groups and other regular activities for young trans people; providing educational sessions for young people in schools, colleges and other settings; providing professional and policy development consultation for professionals, agencies and businesses, bringing trans people and professional services together to form partnerships.

We want the world to be more intelligent about gender. We believe that trans people (used to mean the broad spectrum of people who feel they are gender variant in some way, including but not limited to transsexual, transgender and non-binary people), and young trans people in particular, can play their part in achieving this.

Website: www.genderedintelligence.co.uk

By buying this book you help Gendered Intelligence offer truly amazing support to transgendered youth in the UK. Inspired Quill will donate 10% of all profits made from the sale of this title to this charity.

Lightning Source UK Ltd.
Milton Keynes UK
UKOW02f1912010416

271362UK00004B/68/P